S0-ACO-232

"All right, then.
Teach me how to play pool."

Noah shook his head as he began racking the scattered balls. "I'm not touching *that* with a twenty-foot pole."

"Why not?" Riley asked.

He stared at her, and saw with some surprise that her expression was perfectly innocent. "This whole setup. You asking me to teach you how to play pool. It...it..." Hadn't she read books or watched movies where the man teaching a woman how to play pool invariably wound up "teaching" her a hell of a lot more?

And that's when it came to him. The solution to his problem.

In order to get rid of Riley Kane once and for all, he had to do something horrible. Kissing her hadn't worked—though, admittedly, driving her away had been the *last* thing on his mind when he'd kissed her.

It was time to up the ante, raise the stakes so high she'd have no choice but to flee.

He had to seduce her.

Books by Maureen Smith

Kimani Romance

A Legal Affair
A Guilty Affair

Kimani Press Arabesque

With Every Breath
A Heartbeat Away

MAUREEN SMITH

has enjoyed writing for as long as she can remember, and secretly suspects she was born with a pen in her hand. She received a B.A. in English from the University of Maryland and worked as a freelance writer while she penned her first novel. To her delight, *Ghosts of Fire* was nominated for a *Romantic Times BOOKreviews* Reviewers' Choice Award and an Emma Award for Favorite New Author, and won the Romance in Color Reviewers' Choice Awards for New Author of the Year and Romantic Suspense of the Year. Her subsequent novel also garnered praise from critics and readers.

Maureen lives in San Antonio, Texas, with her husband, two children, a cat and a miniature schnauzer. She loves to hear from readers and can be reached at author@maureen-smith.com.

A GUILTY AFFAIR

Maureen Smith

KIMANI
ROMANCE

If you purchased this book without a cover you should be aware
that this book is stolen property. It was reported as "unsold and
destroyed" to the publisher, and neither the author nor the
publisher has received any payment for this "stripped book."

To my sister, Sylvia Hightower, who is always
the first person to read my novels and provide her
honest feedback. Thank you for helping me to believe
in myself and the power of dreams come true.

 KIMANI PRESS™

ISBN-13: 978-0-373-86017-3
ISBN-10: 0-373-86017-X

A GUILTY AFFAIR

Copyright © 2007 by Maureen Smith

All rights reserved. The reproduction, transmission or utilization
of this work in whole or in part in any form by any electronic, mechanical
or other means, now known or hereafter invented, including xerography,
photocopying and recording, or in any information storage or retrieval
system, is forbidden without written permission. For permission please
contact Kimani Press, Editorial Office, 233 Broadway, New York, NY
10279 U.S.A.

This is a work of fiction. Names, characters, places and incidents are
either the product of the author's imagination or are used fictitiously,
and any resemblance to actual persons, living or dead, business establishments,
events or locales is entirely coincidental.

® and TM are trademarks. Trademarks indicated with ® are registered in
the United States Patent and Trademark Office, the Canadian Trade Marks
Office and/or other countries.

www.kimanipress.com

Printed in U.S.A.

Dear Reader,

After I finished writing my previous Kimani Romance book, *A Legal Affair,* I knew that Daniela's fiercely overprotective brother had to have his own story—hence the sequel, *A Guilty Affair,* was born. I wanted to give Noah Roarke a strong, feisty heroine who could match him in passion and temperament, someone who was as loyal to others as Noah was to his family. And then I decided to torture him a bit by giving him the one woman he thought he could never have—Riley Kane, his best friend's fiancée.

I hope you have enjoyed following Noah and Riley on their journey to falling in love and finding peace with the past.

I love to hear from readers! Please e-mail me at author@maureen-smith.com, and visit my Web site at www.maureen-smith.com for news and updates on my upcoming releases.

Happy reading!

Maureen Smith

Chapter 1

When Riley Kane left San Antonio three years ago, she swore she'd never return.

In a moment of sheer desperation, she'd packed her bags and driven halfway across the country, hoping to give herself a chance at a new life—and the chance to make new memories.

Memories that didn't torment her with images of Trevor. Trevor, laughing and teasing her as they wrestled over the last slice of pizza. Trevor, broad shoulders swaying as he sauntered across a bustling police station to greet her with a kiss.

Trevor, gunned down in an alley forty-six days before their wedding.

Although time had softened the pain of his death,

the nightmares that plagued Riley were as sharp and vivid as ever. And the same memories that had driven her away from home were the same memories that ultimately lured her back.

She wanted answers. And this time, she would not leave without them.

Which was why she was parked outside a private detective agency at eight o'clock at night, trying to work up the courage to leave the safety of her car and face the man inside the nondescript building.

Noah Roarke. Trevor's best friend and former partner on the police force.

A man who'd made it perfectly clear to Riley that he wanted nothing to do with her.

She closed her eyes for a moment, her hands tightening reflexively on the steering wheel. Even after all these years, Noah Roarke's aversion to her remained a mystery. He and Trevor had been friends since childhood. They'd attended the same college, graduated from the police academy at the same time, and had been assigned partners. As Trevor's girlfriend—and then fiancée—Riley had always hoped, and expected, that she and Noah would become friends. After all, they had the most important thing in common: their love for Trevor. But despite her efforts to reach out to Noah, he'd always treated her with polite reserve, making it clear he didn't share her desire for a friendship.

At Trevor's funeral, Noah could barely look at her. It was she who'd approached him after the service to thank him for the beautiful eulogy, which she knew had been as heartrending for him to deliver as it had been for her to hear. She'd wanted to comfort him, and a part of her had wanted to be comforted in return, to be held and told that everything would be okay. Instead they'd stood at the graveside—not touching, not speaking, regarding each other with the awkwardness of strangers, instead of two people who'd lost a mutual friend.

The memory of that strained encounter had haunted Riley for the past three years, surfacing at the oddest moments, and lingering in her mind longer than it should have.

And speaking of lingering too long...

Riley heaved a deep sigh and frowned at the digital clock on the dashboard. She'd spent nearly half an hour inside her Toyota Avalon, her stomach tied up in knots, trying to convince herself she was doing the right thing by coming to Noah. He was the only one who could help her find the answers she sought. He was the only one who could help her find closure.

And the sooner she could put the past behind her, the sooner she could get on with her life.

Without giving herself another chance to reconsider, Riley cut off the ignition and opened the door. As she stepped from her car, a gentle breeze caressed her face, stirring tendrils of hair that had escaped from her ponytail. One thing she'd always appreciated about summers in San Antonio was that no matter how sweltering the days were, the cool, breezy nights always provided a welcome reprieve. It was one of many things she'd missed about home.

She walked up to an old single-story brick building that had once housed a print shop, a real estate office and a family-owned travel agency. The name of the current tenant was painted in white lettering on the plate-glass window—Roarke Investigations, Inc.

Riley could see through the miniblinds that the reception area was mostly dark, save for a solitary lamp perched atop the large reception desk. Knowing that the agency was closed for the day, she tried the glass door anyway and was surprised to find it unlocked. She stepped inside the building and took a quick glance around. The tastefully decorated room with its rustic pine furniture, lush potted plants and papaya-colored walls was not what she'd expected to find in a private detective agency.

Stepping further into the office, Riley called out, "Hello? Is anyone here?"

There was no answer. But from somewhere down the narrow corridor, she could hear the low whir of a machine. She hesitated, wondering if she should just wait until someone emerged to help her. She knew Noah, at least, was back there. Before heading out to Roarke Investigations that evening, she'd called Noah's direct line, remembering what a workaholic he'd always been. She was counting on him being at the office after hours, burning the midnight oil. When he answered the phone, she'd hung up without a word and hightailed it over there, praying he wouldn't leave before she arrived.

Afraid she might lose her nerve if she waited around a second longer, Riley started down the corridor, following the whirring noise to an office located near the end of the hallway, where light spilled from the half-open doorway. The brass nameplate on the wall read Noah Roarke, Licensed Private Investigator.

Drawing a deep, steadying breath, Riley pushed the door open all the way.

Noah Roarke sat behind a large oak desk littered with files. His back was to the door as he fed papers into an old shredder that had likely seen better days. The machine was so loud he didn't even hear Riley enter the room.

Not wanting to startle him while he was at the mercy of the paper shredder but seeing no other alternative, she said, "Noah."

He spun around, and those dark, deep-set eyes she remembered so well widened at the sight of her. "Riley?"

She mustered a half smile. "Hello, Noah. It's been a while, hasn't it?"

Paper shredder all but forgotten, Noah Roarke slowly rose to his feet, staring at her as if she were an apparition. Riley had almost forgotten how tall he was. Six-three, with a lean, muscular physique he'd honed while on the police force and maintained four years after leaving it. He wore charcoal-gray trousers, a white broadcloth shirt with the sleeves rolled to his elbows, and a silk tie that hung loose around his collar, as if he'd been meaning to remove it but hadn't gotten around to it yet. How had she forgotten how incredibly broad his shoulders were? Or how rich and smooth his chestnut-brown skin was?

As Riley gazed at him, she became aware of a slight tension building in her muscles, tiny hairs rising on the back of her neck. She quickly dismissed the odd sensation, attributing it to nerves and fatigue. After all, she was still recovering from her twenty-four-hour drive from Washington, D.C. She needed a whole lot more than the two hours of sleep she'd allowed herself that afternoon before taking a shower and heading out there.

Finally Noah seemed to find his voice, and the deep, husky timbre of it roused Riley from her silent musings. "How did you get in here?"

"The front doors were unlocked," she told him, somewhat apologetically. "I called out, but you didn't hear me." A smile tipped one corner of her mouth. "You must be losing your touch, Roarke. There was a time *no one* could sneak up on you, not even a cat tiptoeing on feathers."

He barely cracked a smile, his dark gaze intent upon her face. "What're you doing here, Riley?"

"In San Antonio, or in your office?"

"Both."

Though he hadn't offered, she walked over to one of the visitor chairs across from his desk and sat down, hoping Noah would follow her lead. For some reason, she thought he might be less…overpowering if he were seated.

He remained standing.

"I took a leave of absence from work," she explained, folding her hands in her lap. "I'll be home for two months. I'm staying at my parents' house."

Although Noah's expression didn't change, Riley had the vague impression he wasn't terribly thrilled about the news.

"Is everything okay?" he asked quietly.

"My family's fine, if that's what you're asking. In fact, my parents are vacationing in Hawaii, and my grandmother will be celebrating her seventy-fifth birthday in a few weeks. She sends her warm regards, by the way."

This, finally, brought a smile to his face. Noah and Florinda Kane had met at Trevor and Riley's engagement party four years ago. Riley's grandmother had taken an instant liking to Noah and had spent the entire time introducing him to every single woman at the picnic, then dismissing each prospect as "unsuitable" or "not good enough" for him. When she wasn't playing matchmaker, she'd flirted shamelessly with him—much to Riley's chagrin. But Noah had been a good sport about it, indulging the old woman's antics with a warmth and relaxed humor that Riley and her mother, watching from across the yard, had found endearing.

"Tell your grandmother I said hello," Noah said now.

"I will," Riley agreed, "if you'll do me a favor and sit down. I swear I'm getting a cramp in my neck from looking up at you, Noah Roarke."

His mouth twitched as he lowered himself into his chair. "How's that?" he murmured.

"Better," Riley said, wondering if it really was. Because now that they were almost at eye level, she couldn't help but notice just how handsome he was, with his granite-hard cheekbones, square jaw and slightly crooked nose—broken during a training exercise at the police academy. Before she could stop herself, her gaze dropped to his lips, and she realized that she had never really *looked* at them before, never noticed how beautifully sculpted they were, never noticed just how lush and sensuous his bottom lip—

Shocked by the direction of her thoughts, Riley forced herself to look away, anywhere but at Noah. What in the world was wrong with her?

"Riley?"

She schooled her features into an impassive mask before meeting his speculative gaze. She wondered if he'd caught her ogling his lips. God, she hoped not! "I'm sorry," she murmured. "I was just thinking that this is the first time I've ever been here, to your office. I remember how surprised I was when Trevor told me you were leaving the SAPD to start a private detective agency with your brother. How *is* Kenneth, by the way?"

"Fine, thanks."

"And Daniela? How's she doing?"

"Daniela's doing very well. She's actually in Italy right now. On her honeymoon."

Riley's eyes widened. "Your sister got *married?*"

Noah chuckled softly. "I know. I'm still getting used to the idea myself."

Riley grinned. "I thought you'd never let her out of your sight, much less get married. Who's the lucky man?"

Noah hesitated. "Caleb Thorne."

Riley's jaw dropped. "Wait a minute. *The* Caleb Thorne? Crandall Thorne's son?"

"One and the same."

"No kidding!"

Crandall Thorne was a prominent criminal defense attorney worth millions. His son, Caleb, was a law professor at a local university and had been one of the most sought after bachelors in the state of Texas.

"How'd they meet?" Riley asked curiously.

A grim look passed over Noah's face. "Long story. I'll tell you about it some other time." Before she could probe any further, he turned the tables on her. "What brings you here at this time of night, Riley?"

And Riley knew, then, that she'd finally run out of time. It was now or never.

She drew a deep breath and moistened her dry lips with the tip of her tongue, too nervous to think much of the way Noah's dark eyes followed the gesture. "I came to talk to you about Trevor," she began.

A veiled look passed over Noah's face, so fleeting she could have imagined it. "What about him?"

Riley could feel her heart hammering painfully against her rib cage. "I want to know why he died, Noah."

He frowned. "What are you talking about? You already know the reason."

"I want to know the *real* reason." She paused, looking him straight in the eye. "And I think you're the only one who can help me."

Chapter 2

Noah stared at Riley as if she'd just escaped from the local asylum. She supposed she couldn't blame him. She'd been questioning her own sanity for the past three years, ever since Trevor died and left her with more questions than answers.

"What are you talking about, Riley?" Noah asked warily. "What are you suggesting?"

"I think there was another explanation for Trevor's death. Something other than what we were told."

Noah's expression darkened. "What are you saying? That there was some sort of police *cover-up?*"

Riley tried not to flinch at his sharp tone. "I don't know. It's possible that *no one* really knows—"

Noah shook his head at her. "You're not making a whole lot of sense right now, Riley."

She swallowed hard, then blurted, "I think Conrad Weiss shot Trevor because he knew Trevor was going to kill him first."

Noah scowled. "*What?* That's ridiculous. Trevor wouldn't have killed him. He always played by the book, and you know it."

"I thought I did," Riley whispered.

A heavy silence descended upon the room, broken only by the low drone of the paper shredder. As if they were touching, Riley could feel every muscle tensing in Noah's body, causing his jaw to harden as he stared at her.

"Conrad Weiss was a convicted felon," he said in a low, quelling voice that made Riley shiver. "He was on the verge of robbing a convenience store when Trevor walked through the door and interrupted him. That's the reason Weiss ran, and *that's* why Trevor chased him down that alley."

Riley closed her eyes briefly against the painful memories. "I read the police report, Noah," she said huskily. "I know what happened."

"Then what's going on here, Riley?" Noah demanded. "Are you trying to tell me that Trevor did something wrong? Weiss shot *him,* not the other way around."

"I know that!" Riley lurched from the chair and paced to the only window in the room, which overlooked a stretch of highway flanked by dense green forest.

She didn't need to be reminded of the details surrounding Trevor's death. They were chiseled into her memory like carvings etched into a wooden talisman. She'd viewed the graphic crime-scene photos, listened to eyewitness testimonies and pored over the police report until she could recite it verbatim. And the fact that Conrad Weiss had been shot and killed that same day while fleeing from the arresting officers had done little to lessen the anguish of losing Trevor.

Behind her, Noah pushed out a long, deep breath. "Look, Riley, I know how difficult these past three years have been for—"

"I didn't come here to cry on your shoulder, Noah. The time for that has come and gone." She was surprised by the bitterness she heard in her own voice.

So was Noah, apparently. For several moments he didn't say a word. Then, softly, he asked, "Why did you come here, Riley?"

She turned slowly to face him. "I think it's possible Trevor already knew Conrad Weiss. I think he met him before that day in the convenience store."

Noah couldn't have looked more stunned if she'd announced she was giving birth to his baby by Immaculate Conception. "*What* did you say?" he whispered.

"I have reason to believe Trevor and Weiss might have already known each other."

"Based on what?"

Riley hesitated, biting her bottom lip. "Ever since Trevor died, I've been having these strange dreams—"

"You're basing your suspicions on *dreams?*"

"Wait, just hear me out! In the dreams, I see Trevor and Weiss talking to each other, but I can't hear what they're saying. In one dream, I'm standing at the door of Trevor's apartment trying to eavesdrop on their conversation. But when Trevor sees me, he walks over and slams the door in my face. But it's not just the dreams I've been having," she hastened to add, seeing Noah's skeptical expression. "Once when Trevor and I were visiting Fredericksburg, I was taking too long in an antiques shop, so Trevor went outside to wait for me. When I came out, he was talking to some man I'd never seen before, an older man with a heavy German accent. He left as soon as I appeared, and when I asked Trevor who the guy was, he said he was just some stranger making small talk while his wife finished shopping. I didn't think much of it at the time, until I saw the man again a few months later—at Trevor's funeral."

Noah was watching her carefully. "I don't remember seeing any strangers at the funeral," he said tightly. "Everyone there was accounted for. We made sure of that."

Riley shook her head. "He was there, Noah. I saw him. I meant to go to him, to find out who he was and what he was doing there. But people kept stopping me to talk, and by the time I looked up again, the man was gone. I'm telling you the truth, Noah," she added, because he still looked unconvinced.

"Even if you did see this man, what does that prove? Maybe he heard about Trevor's shooting on the news and came to pay his last respects to a man he'd once met. Why do you see a connection between this German guy and what happened to Trevor?"

"Conrad Weiss was German. What if this man was a friend of his, or a relative?" She hesitated. "Or a partner in crime?"

Noah's dark eyes narrowed and focused on her with dangerous intensity. "I'm not sure I like where you're going with this, Riley," he said, his voice a low, steely warning. "I hope you're not trying to suggest that Trevor was somehow responsible for his own death."

Riley swallowed with difficulty. "I don't know, Noah," she whispered.

"You don't know," he repeated flatly.

"No, I don't. I was hoping you could help me find out."

"Help you find out *what,* Riley?" Noah exploded, lunging to his feet with a fluidity that defied his powerful build. "You want me to help you find out whether your fiancé—and my best friend—was involved in some sort of criminal activity that got him *killed?*"

"Yes!" Riley cried hoarsely. "That's *exactly* what I want you to do!"

"Damn it, Riley! Do you know how many women have walked through that door and *begged* me to help exonerate their convicted husbands and boyfriends? Trevor died honorably in the line of duty while trying to apprehend a criminal. Everyone who spoke at his funeral called him a hero. A *hero,* Riley! And here you are, determined to prove the exact opposite. Why?"

"Because I need closure!" she cried. "Because ever since he died, I've been plagued by nightmares and questions that won't go away! Because I can't shake this horrible feeling that something's wrong, *terribly* wrong, and until I find out what it is, I won't be able to move on with my life." Hot, stinging tears blurred her vision. "Do you think I enjoy this, Noah? Do you think I *want* to have these ugly fears about a man I was going to spend the rest of my life with?"

Noah looked at her with an expression of fury mingled with grief. "I think you're angry with Trevor for dying and leaving you, and this is your way of punishing him."

She gave a harsh, mirthless laugh. "Don't try to psychoanalyze me, Noah. It doesn't become you."

A muscle worked in his tightly clenched jaw. "I think it's time for you to leave, Riley."

Something shriveled up inside her. She recognized it as hope. "Does this mean you're not going to help me?"

He said nothing, regarding her in stony silence.

Blinking back tears, Riley crossed to the door and walked out of the room.

Only when Noah heard the front door close behind her did he move. And then it was to clear the contents of his desk with a violent sweep of one arm.

Sheets of paper went sailing through the air like confetti at a ticker-tape parade before scattering across the floor.

Taking no satisfaction in the mess he'd made, Noah rounded the desk and began to pace the length of the room.

Damn her!

Damn her for waltzing back into his life after three years and making such an impossible demand of him.

Damn her for reopening the wound that had never quite healed in the aftermath of Trevor's death, for awakening old memories he'd sooner forget.

Damn her for being the only woman he'd ever loved but could never have.

With a savage oath, Noah sank into the chair behind his desk and dropped his head into his hands.

He'd been in love with Riley Kane for five years, an obsession that began almost from the moment he met her. As if it were yesterday, he still remembered the fateful encounter that had changed his life forever.

He'd been returning to the police station after an unproductive morning of interviewing witnesses for a homicide case he was working. He was hot, tired and in a foul enough mood to strangle the first person who crossed him.

As he was pulling into a parking space, he was rear-ended by another vehicle that had just sped into the lot. Cursing a blue streak, Noah killed the engine and jumped out of the car to see what kind of an idiot would speed in the parking lot of a *police* station.

A pair of long, shapely legs had emerged from the other car, and the next thing he knew, the most beautiful woman he'd ever seen was hurrying toward him, apologizing profusely for her clumsiness. Impressions bombarded him at once. Flawless, velvety brown skin. Shoulder-length black hair cut in long, stylish layers that accentuated a face dominated by large, thick-lashed eyes the color of Godiva chocolate, high cheekbones, and an exquisitely lush mouth that threatened to send his imagination into overdrive.

Before Noah could utter a single word—he'd been too tongue-tied, anyway—the woman hiked up her skirt and crouched down behind his Crown Victoria to investigate the damage she'd caused.

But the only damage Riley Kane caused that day was to Noah's heart.

Especially when he learned that she and his best friend, Trevor Simmons, had been dating for a month. *She* was the "incredible, amazing, smart, sexy, beautiful" woman Trevor had been raving about since meeting her at a law-enforcement convention in Houston. Riley, a police beat reporter for the *Houston Chronicle,* had been there to cover the story for the newspaper.

Ironically, it was Noah who was supposed to have attended the convention. But at the last minute he'd gotten a crucial break in one of his cases, and he'd asked Trevor to go in his place.

Fate had an unbelievably cruel sense of humor.

Even after all this time, the sight of Riley Kane

still unraveled him. One look from her, and he was that same tongue-tied sap in the parking lot, not knowing whether to write her a speeding ticket or ask her out on a date.

When she left San Antonio three years ago, he thought he'd never see her again. And though he'd secretly mourned her absence, he knew it was for the best. Riley was a constant reminder of Trevor, of the senseless shooting that had claimed his life. Noah couldn't look at her without remembering how much Trevor had loved and worshipped her, how ecstatic he'd been when she finally agreed to marry him.

And Noah couldn't look at Riley without being reminded of his own forbidden feelings for her.

From the very beginning she'd intrigued and fascinated him, tempting him as no other woman ever had. He'd quickly learned that being anywhere near her was the worst form of torture he could imagine, so he'd kept his distance. Having her in Washington, D.C., hundreds of miles away from him, had brought him a little peace of mind. He didn't have to worry about pulling up beside her at a gas station, or running into her at a restaurant they'd frequented with Trevor. He didn't have to be tormented by the constant knowledge that she was somewhere nearby. Within close proximity—yet hopelessly out of reach.

But now she was back.

Back to find closure, she'd said.

Noah's gut clenched at the memory of her outrageous proposition. He couldn't believe she would even

suspect Trevor of any sort of illegal activity. Trevor
Simmons had been one of the most trustworthy, up-
standing men Noah had ever known. For Riley to suggest otherwise was downright insane. He couldn't
begin to comprehend what had led her to such an unspeakable conclusion, but there was no way in hell he
would help her betray Trevor's memory by dragging
his name through the dirt.

As far as Noah was concerned, coveting his best
friend's fiancée was betrayal enough.

Chapter 3

If Noah thought he'd seen the last of Riley, he was sorely mistaken.

After tossing and turning all night, she rose at six in the morning, took a quick shower and dressed in a lightweight gypsy skirt, a white tank top and a pair of strappy sandals. In the kitchen a few minutes later, she downed a glass of cranberry juice, then packed up the lemon pound cake Florinda Kane had baked last night. She scribbled a note to her grandmother, who was still sleeping, then slipped quietly from the house.

Noah lived on the northeast side of town in an older subdivision that boasted lush, manicured lawns and brick ramblers shaded by giant oaks. Noah's one-story house was located on a cul-de-sac, and as

Riley pulled up to the curb, she was relieved to see his black GMC Yukon parked in the driveway. Although it was Saturday, she knew he wouldn't be sleeping in, just as she'd known he would be at the office late last night.

It was funny how she could know so much about a man who'd always made a point of keeping her at arm's length.

Just as she was about to climb out of her car, she glanced in the rearview mirror and saw the man in question jogging up the street toward the house. Riley waited until he'd nearly reached the Avalon before opening the door and stepping from the vehicle.

Noah stopped on the other side of the car, sweaty and undeniably sexy in black athletic shorts and a gray sweatshirt with the sleeves torn off. Muscles bunched and rippled everywhere she looked, so she forced herself to look elsewhere, and found herself staring at the hard angle of his stubble-darkened jaw.

"What're you doing here, Riley?" he asked in a low, guarded voice.

She lifted her eyes to his and saw that he didn't appear at all pleased to see her. "I came to talk to you," she said.

"I think we did enough talking last night," he said flatly.

"I did a poor job of explaining myself. If you'd just give me another chance—"

Noah shook his head. "Nothing you can say will change my mind about helping you. You wasted your time coming here. Now if you'll excuse me, I have things to do." With a curt nod, he turned and started up the driveway.

Riley panicked. "Maybe I should speak to Kenneth," she blurted out, surprising herself. It had never occurred to her to approach Noah's older brother about investigating the circumstances surrounding Trevor's death. But now that she'd proposed the idea, she knew it had been the right move.

Noah stopped and turned slowly to face her. His expression was inscrutable, but she could feel the coiled tension emanating from his body. A sane person might have backed off, but Riley had long since abandoned any pretense of sanity.

"Maybe you're right," she continued pragmatically. "Maybe you're *not* the right person to help me, Noah. You're too personally involved, and I should have realized that. But I'm sure your brother would have no problem remaining objective. After all, Kenneth once worked in Internal Affairs. He's used to investigating other cops, whether they were his friends or not."

"Kenneth won't take your case," Noah said tersely.

"I guess there's only one way to find out. I'm a paying customer—I'm sure I can persuade your brother to treat me as such." She glanced at her slim gold wristwatch. "Do you think I can catch him at the office this early?"

Noah gave her a long, measured look. Riley waited, chin tilted at an expectant angle, not backing down.

After another moment, Noah growled, "Come inside," and without waiting for her to follow, he turned and stalked off toward the house.

Riley ducked inside her car to retrieve the pound cake, then closed the door and hurried after him. "I brought something for you," she told him.

He glanced over his shoulder at her as he unlocked the front door. "What is it?"

"My grandmother's lemon pound cake. She remembered how much you enjoyed it at the picnic a few years ago, so she baked one just for you."

Noah's expression softened. "She didn't have to do that."

Riley shrugged. "What can I say? She's crazy about you."

Chuckling softly, Noah opened the door and stepped aside to let her enter. As she walked past him, her shoulder brushed against his chest, sending an unexpected tingle of awareness through her body. Her startled gaze flew to his face, but thankfully, Noah didn't seem to notice as he followed her inside the house and closed the door.

Golden pine floors gleamed under her feet as she stepped further into the foyer. Early-morning sunlight poured through wide glass windows on the facing wall. Riley glanced around the spacious living room with its dark, masculine furnishings and brick fireplace that stretched to the twenty-foot ceiling.

"Goodness, I haven't been here since…" She trailed off as a knot of sorrow wedged in her throat.

Behind her, Noah said quietly, "Since Trevor's surprise birthday party four years ago."

She turned around, and their eyes met and held in a moment of shared remembrance. "I miss him," Riley whispered before she could stop herself.

"I know," Noah said gently.

Mustering a feeble smile, she held out the cake to him. "Better take this before I change my mind about parting with it."

Noah's mouth curved ruefully as he accepted the offering. "You can't possibly expect me to eat this entire thing by myself."

"Why not? I used to do it all the time after I moved to the East Coast. Whenever I got homesick, Grandma would send me one of her cakes, and within a few days, it was all gone." She grinned sheepishly, patting her hip. "Which would probably explain the reason I gained fifteen pounds after my first year in D.C."

Noah's lazy gaze ran the length of her. "I can't tell," he murmured.

"It's the skirt," Riley explained, and wondered why her palms were suddenly damp. "It hides everything."

He nodded, his mouth twitching. "I'll take your word for it. Come on, I'll fix some coffee so we can have it with the cake."

Riley wiped her hands on her skirt and followed him down the hall.

The updated kitchen had been done in black and stainless steel, with a center island that gleamed like an iceberg at midnight. A pair of tall French doors looked out over a wooden deck, a sea of green lawn and blooming flower beds lovingly maintained by Noah's mother, Pamela Roarke. Plastic chew toys were strewn around the yard, but there was no sign of their owner.

"Wait a minute," Riley wondered aloud. "Where's—"

Before she could complete the question, a black-and-white Alaskan malamute came bounding up the steps and barreling across the deck toward the house, barking excitedly.

"Eskimo!" With a cry of delight, Riley opened the French doors and dropped to her knees to greet the large, furry dog who bathed her cheek with a wet, eager tongue. She laughed, looking up at Noah. "He remembers me!"

"Of course he remembers you," Noah said mildly. "Why wouldn't he?"

"Because it's been four years since I last saw him."

"You're unforgettable, Riley."

There was a strange, subdued note in Noah's voice, but when Riley glanced up again, he'd walked over to the center island and begun busying himself with making coffee.

She returned her attention to Eskimo, who had rolled onto his back and offered his belly for scratching. She obliged him, running her fingers through his thick, woolly coat and crooning, "What a *good* boy you are. Aren't you the most handsome boy I've ever seen?"

"Careful," came Noah's warning from across the

room. "He'll get an inflated ego, and then I'll be the one fetching *his* slippers."

Riley laughed, then leaned close to murmur to the dog, "That's okay. We both know who's the *real* king of this castle."

"I heard that," Noah muttered.

Chuckling, Riley rose from the floor, toed off her sandals and padded across the room, enjoying the warm glide of wood beneath her bare feet. Eskimo trailed after her as she walked over to the sink and washed her hands, then opened a drawer and retrieved a knife to cut the cake, silently marveling that she'd remembered where Noah kept his cutlery.

As she turned from the sink, Noah turned from the island at the same time, and they bumped into each other. The knife slipped from Riley's hand and clattered to the floor, but neither of them noticed, their gazes locked on each other for a long, charged moment.

It was Riley who stepped back first. Every nerve ending in her body felt as if it was on fire. "I—I'm sorry," she stammered. "I didn't know you were right there."

"It's all right," Noah said huskily. Without releasing her gaze, he knelt and picked up the knife from the floor. As he slowly rose, Riley moved aside so that he could rinse the knife at the sink. When he'd finished, he set it down carefully on the countertop.

She gave a shaky little laugh. "That was a close call."

Dark, hooded eyes met hers. "Yeah, it was," Noah

softly agreed, and Riley wondered if he was referring to the dropped knife—or something else entirely.

"I'm going to take a shower," he told her. "The coffee's ready. Help yourself."

She nodded wordlessly, not trusting her voice.

When he'd left the kitchen, she sank weakly onto one of the bar stools at the island and blew out a long, ragged breath.

Eskimo came over to where she sat, and looked up at her in curious inquiry.

"I don't know what just happened," Riley murmured, absently scratching behind the dog's ear. "And just between you and me, I don't *want* to know."

Noah stayed in the shower until the water turned cold. He needed time to get himself together, to calm his jittery nerves and bring his galloping pulse under control.

He took his time getting dressed, tugging on a pair of jeans and easing a black T-shirt over his chest as slowly and deliberately as if he were made of glass. He felt like that, as if he were teetering precariously on the edge of a cliff, and just one little push would send him over, shattering into a million pieces. It was downright maddening to know that one woman could hold this much power over him. In the space of one night, Riley Kane had turned his world upside down. Again.

Knowing he could no longer put it off, Noah went in search of his uninvited houseguest. When he reached the entry to the living room, he froze, riveted by the sight that greeted him. Riley was curled up on the leather sofa with her head propped on her arms and her legs tucked underneath her long skirt. She was fast asleep. Dozing soundly on the floor at her feet was Eskimo.

For several moments Noah just stood there, air stalled in his lungs, unable to look away. It was only when Eskimo quietly flicked his tail that Noah came out of his trance and remembered to breathe again.

Drawing several deep breaths, he started purposefully across the room, intending to wake Riley and tell her, as politely as possible, that it was time for her to go home.

But when he knelt in front of her and took in her sleeping face, the words dried up in his throat. She was beautiful, even with the faint, dark shadows beneath her eyes that told him she hadn't slept well in a long time. Her skin was flawless, the rich color of melted brown sugar. Her lips, as exquisitely lush as he remembered, were parted slightly as she slumbered. He imagined leaning down and brushing his mouth against hers, tasting her, kissing her as he'd dreamed of doing for years. And he imagined her moaning softly and opening for him, her breath mingling warmly with his, their tongues gliding sensually together.

Noah closed his eyes and bowed his head as the familiar want swept through him, dark and potent, heating his blood and throbbing heavily in his groin. He dragged air into his lungs and inhaled the scent of her perfume—a light, citrus fragrance he'd smelled in his dreams long after she was out of his life.

Opening his eyes, he slowly rose to his feet and stepped back, needing distance, though no amount of distance would ever help him.

Eskimo lifted his large head and stared at Noah, but made no move to get up and follow him. Noah glared balefully at the traitorous animal, then turned and stalked out of the room.

Even the damn dog knew how special Riley Kane was.

Riley awakened with a start.

Disoriented, she lifted her head from her arms and surveyed the large room, which was at once familiar and not. And then she remembered where she was, and the mission that had brought her there, and she sat up quickly. Too quickly—sending a rush of blood straight to her head. With a muffled groan, she leaned her head back against the sofa and waited for the dizziness to pass.

She couldn't believe she'd fallen asleep. She'd come here with her full armor on, prepared to do battle. But as soon as her opponent was out of sight, what had she done? She'd lain down and gone to sleep like a drowsy toddler at nap time.

Frowning, she checked her watch and was shocked to find that it was nearly one o'clock. She'd slept for six hours! Where was Noah? And why had he let her sleep for so long?

Riley scrambled to her feet and went in search of those answers.

She only needed to follow the deep, husky timbre of his voice around the corner and down the hall to the second bedroom, which had been converted into a home office. The room was small and functional, dominated by a sturdy bookcase, a pair of black metal filing cabinets, and a wide metal desk—the kind of furniture that could be purchased at government auctions.

Noah stood at the narrow window talking on the phone, one hand thrust carelessly into the pocket of dark jeans that clung to the corded muscles of his thighs and hugged a rear end you could bounce quarters off. Riley's mouth went dry as cotton.

At that moment, Noah turned and reached across the cluttered desk for a notepad. With the cordless phone pressed between his ear and shoulder blade, he leaned down to scribble instructions dictated to him by the person on the other end.

Without warning, Riley saw herself nestled between the desk and his hard, muscular body. She imagined his big hands at her waist, her head flung back against his chest as he kissed her throat and—

Shocked by the wicked turn of her thoughts, she coughed then choked. Noah lifted his head and looked over at her questioningly. *You okay?* he mouthed.

Her face burned, but not from the temporary lack of oxygen to the brain. Nodding jerkily, she backed out of the room and hurried to the kitchen, where she poured herself a tall glass of water.

Noah appeared a few moments later, frowning. "Are you all right?"

She waved off his concern, gulping down the water as if she'd just run the Boston Marathon. "I'm fine," she rasped when she'd finished her drink. "I was just thirsty. Must have been a little dehydrated."

He walked over, took the empty glass from her hand and refilled it, then passed it back to her.

"Thanks," she murmured gratefully. "I apologize for interrupting your phone call."

"Don't worry about it." Folding his arms across his broad chest, he leaned a hip against the center island. "Have a good nap?"

"Yes," she said, feeling suddenly shy. "Why'd you let me sleep so long?"

He shrugged. "You were tired. I figured you could use the rest, after driving all the way from Washington, D.C. Without stopping somewhere to get a good night's sleep," he added, giving her a censorious look.

Her eyes widened. "H-how do you know that?"

"Your grandmother called while you were sleeping. She was worried, wanted to make sure you hadn't driven your car off the road in your exhaustion. When you didn't answer your cell phone, she called the house."

"Oh." Embarrassed, Riley could only stare down into her glass.

"Why'd you do a stupid thing like that, Riley?"

Noah asked in a tone she imagined he'd use to interrogate suspects. "Drive almost twenty-four hours with no rest?"

"I was on a mission. I wanted to get here as soon as possible." She lifted her head and looked at him. "I'm sorry for holding you hostage at home half the day. I hope I didn't keep you from anything important."

"Just the office. But I was able to get some things done here, so it's no problem." He turned his head and glanced out the French doors. She smiled at the sight of Eskimo bounding back and forth across the lawn, chasing down a rubber ball.

"He must think I'm so lame," Riley said ruefully. "One minute we were playing together and eating pound cake, the next minute I was out like a light."

Noah arched a brow. "You fed my dog cake?"

"Just a little," she admitted sheepishly, holding her thumb and index finger two inches apart. When Noah scowled, she chuckled. "Oh, come on. Don't get mad. Everyone should experience Grandma's lemon pound cake at least once in their lives. Besides, I couldn't resist, not when he looked up at me with those big brown eyes."

Noah shook his head. "You just fell for one of the oldest cons in the world, woman."

"I know, I know. That's always been one of my weaknesses—puppy-dog eyes. I used to sneak so much food under the table to my grandmother's miniature schnauzer it's a miracle he didn't get fat." She sighed at the memory, then slanted Noah a sullen look. "We can't all be like you, Noah Roarke. Strong and resolute, impervious to temptation."

Something flickered in his dark eyes. "Yeah, that's me all right," he muttered under his breath, turning away and sauntering over to the refrigerator. "Impervious to temptation."

Riley laughed, but the moment Noah leaned over to peer inside the refrigerator, the sound died on her lips. Once again, she found herself checking out his firm, muscled butt.

How had she never noticed before what a magnificent tush Noah Roarke had?

Because you were engaged to his best friend, her conscience reminded her. *You weren't supposed to notice things like that.*

Noah glanced over his shoulder just then. "Are you hungry? I was going…" His voice trailed off. Mortified, Riley realized he'd caught her in the act of staring at his butt. No, not just staring. *Ogling.*

Her pulse hammered at the base of her throat.

"I should go," she blurted out. "I didn't mean to take up your whole day like this. And Grandma is probably worried sick about me, wondering when I'll be home. So I should go."

Noah said nothing, watching as she hurried across the room to where she'd left her sandals earlier and hastily slipped them on.

"My keys," she muttered, sweeping a wild look around the kitchen. "Where'd I leave my keys?"

Noah picked them up from the counter and calmly

held them out to her. She rushed over and practically snatched them from his hand, then raced from the room, as if by outrunning him, she could outrun the foreign sensations coursing through her body.

"Riley—"

"I really have to go, Noah," she tossed over her shoulder. "We still need to talk, but not now. I…I'll call you tomorrow."

"Drive carefully," he said softly.

She didn't.

She raced down the highway, and couldn't even get mad when she was pulled over. As it turned out, she recognized the young Hispanic officer who appeared at her window to request her license and registration. He'd just graduated from the academy three years ago—a few months before Trevor died.

A wide, dimpled grin spread across his face as he removed his mirrored sunglasses and stared down at her. "Well, I'll be damned. It's Riley Kane. You're back!"

"Sure am," she said, shielding her eyes from the sun to smile easily at him. "How's it going, Mario?"

"Can't complain, especially now. Everyone misses you. When'd you get back into town?"

"Yesterday afternoon."

His grin turned hopeful. "You coming back to us, Riley?"

"Afraid not, Mario. I'm only staying for two months, then it's back to the East Coast."

"Aw, man," he grumbled. "Why you wanna live all the way up there, anyway? What does D.C. have that we don't?"

"Nicer cops," she teased.

"No way. They don't get any nicer than us. And just to show you how nice I am, I'm not even gonna give you a ticket. But you'd better slow down. The next guy who pulls you over might not be as understanding as me. Unless it's Harward, Bosquez, Stinson, Vallejo, or—" He broke off and shook his head. "Damn, Riley, I guess you got us all wrapped around your pretty little finger."

She winked at him, turning the key in the ignition. "Thanks, Mario. You're a sweetheart."

He smiled. "Wait until Noah hears that you're back. He's gonna be so excited."

Riley didn't bother telling the young officer that she'd already seen Noah, which was the reason she'd been flying down the highway in the first place. She also didn't bother correcting him about Noah's anything-but-excited reaction to her return.

As Mario backed away from the car, he called out playfully, "Don't go rear-ending any cops!"

Riley couldn't help but laugh as she pulled off.

The tale of how she'd met Noah five years ago had become a long-standing joke at the downtown precinct where he and Trevor had worked, a story that had been shared over drinks at the local bar and passed down to new recruits like oral tradition. By all accounts, Riley shouldn't have been welcomed into the brotherhood of blue the way she had. Not only was she a member of the despised press—who'd always maintained a somewhat adversarial relationship with the police department—but then she'd had the audacity to rear-end a beloved detective. In the parking lot of the police station, at that.

But she'd been Trevor's girl, and by virtue of him being Noah's partner and best friend, she'd been given the benefit of the doubt. It wasn't long before she was receiving invitations to cookouts, departmental softball games, kids' birthday parties, weddings, retirement dinners—you name it. She'd been eagerly embraced by the men and women of the Central Substation on South Frio Street, and she, in turn, had regarded all of them as extended family members. When Trevor died, the outpouring of sympathy and support she'd received had been overwhelming. Which was what made Noah's strange, distant behavior during that time even more devastating.

But she was over that, she told herself firmly. It hadn't been easy, but she'd gotten over the feeling of betrayal, the sense of desertion and…loss. Yes, loss. She'd worked especially hard on that one. After all, she and Noah had never been very close. She couldn't lose something she'd never really had.

So, just as she'd worked through those painful issues, she would also get over her unwanted attraction to Noah. Attraction, that's all it was. Nothing deeper than that. And, as inconvenient and embarrassing as it was, what she felt was perfectly normal. She hadn't been with another man since losing Trevor. After enjoying a healthy physical relationship with her fiancé, three years was a long time to go without having sex. So, yeah, maybe she was a little horny. And it didn't help that the object of her attraction was even finer than she remembered, with those dark, piercing eyes and that sinfully sexy mouth. Not to mention a body to rival any classic Grecian statue. And that was based on the parts she *had* seen.

Riley groaned loudly and banged her fist against the steering wheel. She was behaving as if scales had just fallen from her eyes and she was seeing Noah for the first time. And that wasn't the case. She'd always been aware, on some unconscious level, that he was handsome. She'd have to be blind not to have noticed the way women stared at him wherever he went. Even some of the females he'd worked with at the police station had sat up like show dogs whenever he strolled past, and had flirted shamelessly with him every chance they got. At cookouts and fund-raiser dinners, they'd huddled in groups to gossip and speculate about his love life, and to place bets on the kind of woman who would be lucky enough to someday win his heart.

Riley frowned and shook her head, turning into the gated community where her parents lived. This couldn't be happening to her—not now, and not with Noah. Being attracted to him *wasn't* normal, and it *wasn't* acceptable. He'd been Trevor's best friend and partner on the police force, and if all had gone according to plan, Noah would have stood as Trevor's best man at the wedding. Just as it would have been inappropriate for her to—oh, God—check out his butt during the ceremony, so was it now.

When it came right down to it, she couldn't afford to be distracted by a taboo attraction to Noah. She'd come back home to seek his help, to find closure so that she could finally move on with her life. Once she received the answers to the terrible questions that had haunted her for the past three years, she would return to Washington, D.C., to her job at the *Post* and the new friendships she'd been too depressed to cultivate up to that point.

And once she was away from here and finally freed from the ghosts of the past, Noah Roarke would become nothing more than a distant memory.

As far as she was concerned, that day couldn't come fast enough.

Chapter 4

When Riley arrived home and found her grandmother sprawled across the family room floor, she panicked.

"Oh my God! Grandma!" she cried, rushing over and dropping to her knees beside the prone woman. "Grandma, are you okay?"

Florinda Kane's cinnamon-brown eyes blinked open. "Riley?"

"Yes, it's me, Grandma," Riley said soothingly, checking her grandmother's pulse, striving to calm her own. "I'm here now. You're going to be okay."

"Of course I am," Florinda said, gently swatting away Riley's hand and pulling herself to a sitting position. "Why wouldn't I be?"

Riley stared at her. "Because you fell down... didn't you?"

Florinda chortled. "No, baby. I was doing my deep-breathing exercises."

"Deep-breathing...?" For the first time, Riley noticed the tiny beads of perspiration on her grandmother's forehead, the damp towel draped around her slender neck, and the black leggings and oversize T-shirt she wore. "You were exercising?"

"Don't sound so shocked. How else do you think I maintain this girlish figure?"

Awash with relief, Riley laughed and gave her grandmother a quick, warm hug. "Thank God! I saw you lying on the floor and thought something terrible had happened."

Smiling, Florinda patted Riley's cheek. "You can just put your mind at ease," she cheerfully assured her. "It's not my time to go yet. There's still much work to be done. Hand me my water, will you, baby?"

As Riley crawled over to the cherry coffee table and retrieved the water bottle, she spied a Pilates DVD case on the floor nearby. Grinning to herself, she crawled back over to her grandmother and passed her the water.

"Thank you, baby," Florinda murmured, dabbing at her face and neck with the towel before taking a swig from the bottle.

Riley had always thought of her grandmother's face as handsome, etched with strength and character that deepened as she grew older. Her creamy skin glowed with health and vitality. Her eyes were bright and keenly intelligent, gleaming with a preternatural wisdom that never failed to astonish. When Florinda Kane predicted rain, it didn't matter that the forecast called for clear blue skies. It rained. When Florinda spoke of the addition of a family member, an aunt or cousin would call a few days later with exciting news of someone's pregnancy. Growing up, Riley would have challenged anyone who told her that her grandmother wasn't psychic. She'd bragged about it at school, until her second-grade teacher sent her home one day with a note about telling lies. After her parents scolded her, Florinda had taken Riley aside and wiped her tears, then, her eyes twinkling with mischief, she'd told her granddaughter that her "special gift" was something others would never understand, so it had to be their little secret. Riley had never breathed another word to anyone about Florinda's "clairvoyance," content to bask in the knowledge that while her classmates' grandmothers were only good for knitting sweaters and baking cookies, hers could predict the future.

At the age of seventy-four, Florinda showed no signs of slowing down, enrolling in computer classes at the local community college, signing up for salsa lessons and now, apparently, taking up pilates.

As Riley watched, her grandmother carefully folded her legs into a half-lotus sitting position and closed her eyes as if preparing to meditate.

"I'll just come back when you're finished," Riley whispered, starting to rise from the floor.

"No, don't go, baby. Stay here and keep me company. How was your visit with Noah?"

Scary. Nerve-racking. Aloud she said, "It was fine. He told me you'd called. I'm sorry I worried you. I didn't mean to stay over there so long."

"No apology necessary. I knew you were in good hands. And I'm glad you felt comfortable enough with Noah to get the rest you needed."

Riley blushed, and felt compelled to add, "He was in another room the whole time. It's not like we were sleeping together, er, I mean, at the same—"

A quiet smile curved Florinda's mouth. "I know what you meant, dear. I spoke to him myself. He told me you'd fallen asleep in the living room."

Riley bit her lip, comforted by the fact that as long as her grandmother's eyes remained closed, she wouldn't see Riley's apprehensive expression. "Did he sound irritated?"

"Not at all." The smile became soft, intuitive. "I don't think you'd ever have to worry about irritating Noah."

Riley was inclined to disagree but saw no reason to point that out. "He really appreciated the pound cake. By the time I left, it was half-gone."

"I know. He was eating a piece when I called. I told him I'd bake another one and give it to him when he came to my party."

Riley's mouth fell open. "You invited Noah to your birthday party?"

"Of course. I knew *you* wouldn't do it."

"Grandma—"

Florinda opened her eyes and gave her grand-daughter a reproving look. "Don't I have a right to invite whoever I want to my own birthday party?"

"Of course, Grandma. It's just that—"

"I like Noah Roarke," Florinda said emphatically. "I think he's a wonderful young man, and I know you'd think so too if you took the time to get to know him better."

Riley sputtered. "*Me?* With all due respect, Grandma, I think you've got it backward. Noah's the one who's been pushing me away for the last five years, *not* the other way around!"

Lips pursed, Florinda gave her a long, measuring look. "That really bothers you, doesn't it?" she murmured.

Riley forced a dismissive shrug. "Not anymore. Not like it used to."

"And you don't know why he's been pushing you away?"

Riley heaved a long, weary sigh. "I have no idea, Grandma. Maybe because I dented his car the very first day we met, and after that he decided I was an airhead. Or maybe he didn't approve of his best friend dating a reporter. He may have thought I was using Trevor to get the inside scoop on things happening within the police department." She frowned. "Or maybe he just thought Trevor was too good for me and could do better."

Florinda's mouth tightened, and a flash of indignation flared in her eyes. "Trevor Simmons was *not* too good for you. If anything—" She broke off abruptly, snapping her mouth shut and averting her gaze.

For several moments the two women were silent. From somewhere outside, the lazy drone of a lawn mower could be heard.

With her head bent low, Riley plucked a piece of lint from her skirt. "I know you were never crazy about Trevor," she said in a subdued voice. "But I loved him, Grandma."

Florinda reached over and gently squeezed her hand. "I know you did, baby. And he loved you, too. I never doubted that."

Riley lifted her grandmother's hand and held it to her heart, looking the other woman in the eye. "You're the only one I've told about my dreams, my fears. I hope you know…I hope you understand why I have to find out the truth."

"Oh, sweetheart." Florinda reached up and cupped Riley's face in both hands. "I understand so much more than you could ever imagine. And someday, dear granddaughter, the confusion you've been feeling—about everything in your life, not just Trevor's death—will all make sense. Do you believe me?"

Tears burned at the back of Riley's throat. She nodded, but deep down inside she wondered if, perhaps, this was one time her grandmother's prediction about the future wouldn't come to pass.

When Noah left the San Antonio Police Department four years ago to start a private detective agency with his older brother, many of his comrades had feared he wouldn't keep in touch, that he'd simply drop off the face of the earth, never to be seen or heard from again.

He'd proved them all wrong.

The first time he showed up for the Sunday-night game of pool at Fast Eddie's, the deafening cheers and applause that greeted him made him feel like a rock star. Four years later, not much had changed, other than a few expanding waistlines and hairlines that were beginning to recede—fodder for many of the jokes that were exchanged between the close-knit group of cops.

Thick smoke hung in the air over the bar and pool tables, and hard-edged hip-hop music blared from a jukebox in the corner. After winning his match, Noah sidled up to the bar and ordered a beer for himself and the detective who slid onto the stool beside him. The barmaid, an attractive young brunette wearing a tight T-shirt and cutoff jeans, offered Noah and his companion a sultry, inviting smile as she set the frothy beers on the counter before them.

"Enjoy your drinks, fellas," she purred.

Paulo Sanchez winked at her. "We'd enjoy them even more if you'd join us, beautiful."

She gave a demure little laugh. "Maybe next time."

"That's what you always say," Paulo protested, his dark gaze following the girl's shapely bottom as she moved off to tend to the next customer. "Damn. What a tease."

Shaking his head, Noah scooped his cold bottle off the counter and took a healthy swig of beer. "Look on the bright side," he said pragmatically.

"What's that?"

"She says the same thing to everyone. So she's an equal-opportunity tease."

Paulo laughed, choking on a swallow of beer. Wiping his mouth with the back of his hand, he gave Noah a sideways look. "I bet she'd go out with you if you asked her."

"Guess we'll never find out."

Paulo gave his head a mournful shake. "Damned shame, that."

At thirty-six, Detective Paulo Sanchez had been with the SAPD for fourteen years. In Noah's judgment, having worked with him in homicide and on patrol, Paulo Sanchez was one of the best of the best: aggressive, hard, intelligent. A cop's cop. Wearing a black T-shirt, faded jeans, scuffed leather boots, and sporting a perpetual five-o'clock shadow, Sanchez looked every bit the tough guy he was. But few people knew the depth of the emotional scars he bore, by-products of a failed marriage and the brutal murder of a woman he'd once had an affair with. The guilt he'd suffered in the aftermath of both had nearly destroyed him, sending him into a tailspin of self-destructive behavior until his cousin, an FBI agent at the local field office, had intervened. Sanchez had taken a six-month leave of absence to, as he put it, "get his scrambled marbles in order."

The self-imposed sabbatical seemed to have worked. He'd quit smoking and now adhered to a strict two-drink limit whenever he went out. Noah, like every other cop gathered at the pool hall that Sunday evening, had a tremendous amount of respect for the way Paulo had turned his life around. How could you not respect a guy who was willing to admit he needed help?

Noah wondered grimly if he could apply the same solution to his obsession with Riley Kane. But it wasn't as if a sabbatical would cure him. The woman already lived halfway across the country—how much more distance could he ask for?

"So what's going on with you, *mi amigo?*" Paulo asked conversationally. "How's life as a P.I.?"

"Business is good," Noah said, shoving thoughts of Riley aside. "So good, in fact, that we're seriously considering hiring another investigator."

"No kidding? Even with your sister as the third partner, you still need help with the caseload?"

Noah nodded. "Especially now that Daniela's thinking about going to law school." *For real this time,* he mused, inwardly grimacing at the memory of his younger sister going undercover as a law student in order to get the goods on her husband's father, a prominent defense attorney suspected of criminal negligence. The undercover assignment had ended disastrously, and Daniela's role in it had nearly cost her the love of her life. Noah had been racked with guilt for months afterward, even after the couple reconciled.

He, like Paulo, definitely knew a thing or two about guilt.

"Daniela wants to become a lawyer?"

"She's considering it. She and her husband have talked about opening their own law firm someday."

Paulo snorted. "Why doesn't Thorne just run his old man's firm? Hell, it's already well established and successful."

"Caleb's not interested in practicing criminal law anymore. I respect that about him—the man knows what he wants and doesn't give a damn what anyone else thinks."

"You're like that, too, Roarke. Remember how much flak you caught when you announced you were leaving the force to start a business with your brother?"

Noah chuckled grimly. "Yeah. I think there were bets going around about how soon I'd be back in the chief's office, begging for my old job."

"I know." Paulo grinned. "I started one of 'em."

"Bastard," Noah grumbled without rancor.

"Well, you proved us all wrong, so it's water under the bridge." After a moment, Paulo's expression turned thoughtful. "So you're thinking you need another investigator, huh?"

"Yep. Know anyone who might be interested?"

"I might be."

"Yeah?" Noah paused, beer bottle halfway to his mouth as he studied his companion. "I think you'd make one helluva P.I., Sanchez. Give it some thought."

Paulo nodded slowly. "Maybe I will."

A round of raucous male laughter drew their attention toward the pool table in the corner, where several of their comrades were teasing Mario Cruz, a young officer who'd recently been invited to join the Sunday Night Pool Sharks, as the group had dubbed themselves several years ago. The coveted invitation hadn't come without a price. As the youngest cop present, Mario couldn't take a shot without someone whispering taunts in his ear or "accidentally" bumping into his cue stick, throwing off his concentration.

Noah was lazily contemplating when to bail the poor kid out when Paulo said, "I heard the damnedest thing yesterday. About Riley Kane. Turns out she's back in town."

Noah grew very still, his fingers tightening around the neck of his beer bottle, wishing it were Mario Cruz's neck instead. Since yesterday, the kid had been blabbering to everyone about pulling Riley over for speeding.

Paulo looked at him. "You already knew, didn't you?"

Noah hesitated, then reluctantly nodded. "I saw her."

"Really? How's she doing?"

"She seems all right," Noah lied. No way was he telling anyone—especially another cop—that the fiancée of their fallen comrade was on a mission to prove Trevor had been responsible for his own death.

"Did she say how she's enjoying life up North? Her job at the *Washington Post?*"

Noah shook his head, sipping his beer. "We didn't really talk about it."

"What *did* you talk about?" Paulo prodded.

"Not much. It was a short visit."

As Paulo regarded him in shrewd silence, Noah braced himself for the question he knew was coming. But even when it did, he felt as if he'd taken a hard blow to the chest.

"When are you finally going to tell her how you feel?"

Noah closed his eyes for a moment. "I'm not."

"So you'd rather keep torturing yourself."

"I'm not tortured."

Paulo said nothing. The lie hung between them, as thick and palpable as the cloud of cigarette smoke that hung over their heads. Paulo was the only one who knew about Noah's feelings for Riley. Not even his brother knew. If he'd been in his right mind, the secret would've followed him to the grave.

On the night of Trevor's funeral, Noah had wanted nothing more than to obliterate his grief and pain by drowning himself in a bottle of whiskey. When he arrived at the bar that fateful night, he'd found Paulo already hunched over the counter, nursing a drink. The two men started talking, and by Noah's third glass of whiskey, he was spilling his guts to Paulo about his feelings for Riley. Paulo had listened to his slurred ramblings in silence, so silent that Noah figured Paulo was probably drunk himself and wouldn't remember a word of Noah's confession once they left the bar.

He was wrong.

The next day, Paulo called him up and asked one simple question. "What're you going to do about Riley?"

It was the last time Noah had allowed himself to drink following an emotional crisis.

"Why are you punishing yourself for being in love with Trevor's fiancée?" Paulo asked now, keeping his voice low enough not to be overheard by others.

"Think about what you just said," Noah bit off tersely. "She was my best friend's fiancée."

"Yeah, I get that. But Trevor's not here anymore, man. And, as hard as it is for you to accept, he's not coming back."

"So does that mean I should just move in on his girl?" Noah growled.

Paulo frowned. "It's been three years. You wouldn't exactly be 'moving in' on her, *mi amigo*. And I don't think anyone else would see it that way, either."

Noah scowled. "This isn't about what other people think. It's about what *I* think is right and wrong. What I feel here," he said, stabbing a finger at his heart, "is wrong."

"Why the hell is it? I mean, why *can't* it be you, Roarke? Because Trevor met her first?" When Noah said nothing, Paulo shook his head in exasperation. "Riley Kane is a damned beautiful woman. You and I both know she's not gonna be single forever. Eventually, when she comes out of mourning, she's going to be ready for another relationship, and when she is, do you want her to end up with you—or some other lucky bastard? Think about that, my friend. Think real hard."

Noah already had. It was all he'd thought about for the past three years. The idea of Riley with another man made him fiercely jealous—and profoundly miserable. He couldn't stomach the thought of her being held, kissed, made love to by someone else. And the day she fell in love again…God help him. He hoped he'd never have to endure that agony. If it happened, he hoped he never had to hear about it.

"For all we know," he brooded, hunched over his beer, "she might already have a boyfriend. She's been gone for three years. We don't know what kind of life she's been leading in D.C."

Paulo made a face. "Not much of one, according to what I've heard. Her friend Lety at the *Express-News* has kept in touch with Riley. And she says Riley pretty much threw herself into work after she got hired at the *Post*. She puts in long hours at the office and hasn't made much time for socializing—or dating."

Noah's relief upon hearing this news was tempered by a sharp pang of guilt. It shouldn't please him to know that Riley was leading such a solitary life, closing herself off from the rest of the world. The last thing she needed, in the aftermath of losing Trevor, was to be alone.

His mouth twisted cynically. As if *he* was an expert on what Riley Kane needed.

As Paulo studied Noah's brooding profile, he cocked his head slightly to the side, as if he were angling for a better look into his soul. "Let me ask you something," he said thoughtfully. "What do you think Trevor would say if he knew how you felt about Riley?"

Noah frowned darkly. "I try not to think about that too much," he muttered.

"Well, I'll tell you what *I* think, man. I think he'd tell you to go for it."

Noah shot him a look. "You obviously didn't know Trevor Simmons very well."

"I knew him well enough. And I think he'd rather have *you,* his best friend that he trusted with his life, to take care of his woman, than some prick who might not treat her right."

Noah wasn't so sure about that. As close as he and Trevor had been, there'd always been a slight undercurrent of tension between them where Riley was concerned. He still remembered the look on Trevor's face when he'd stepped outside the police station that fateful day and found Riley, her skirt hiked up to her thighs, huddled beside Noah as they examined the fender of his car. Noah hadn't missed the way Trevor had pulled her gently to her feet, curved an arm around her waist and held her possessively at his side while he performed the introductions.

There had been other things, as well, such as the fact that Trevor seldom let Riley out of his sight whenever Noah was around. Once, during a cookout at a fellow officer's house, Noah had escaped to the privacy of the kitchen to take an important call when Riley appeared in the doorway.

Seeing him on the phone, she'd motioned to a tray of uncooked hot dogs on the counter behind him. "I need to take those outside," she'd whispered.

Noah had stepped out of her way at the same time she moved, bumping into him. They'd laughed and mumbled sheepish apologies to each other. Noah had reached behind him, picked up the tray and passed it to her. As she murmured her thanks, their eyes met and held for a moment, then slid away as Trevor walked into the room. He'd remained by Riley's side for the rest of the day.

If Trevor had ever asked Noah outright how he felt about Riley, Noah honestly didn't know how he would've responded. But as it turned out, the topic never came up between the two men. In the back of his mind, though, Noah had always wondered if Trevor suspected the truth—which only compounded his guilt in the aftermath of his friend's death.

Shoving aside the painful reverie, Noah tossed down the rest of his beer, then stood and fished two twenties out of his wallet. "I'm gonna go rescue the kid," he said, hitching his chin toward the pool table where Mario Cruz was trying to figure out which one of the poker-faced cops surrounding him had stolen his cue stick.

Paulo nodded, a knowing look on his face. As Noah walked away, he heard the detective say, just loud enough for him to hear, "Why don't you rescue yourself while you're at it?"

If I could, Noah thought grimly, *I would've done
it a long time ago.*

Chapter 5

Riley waited until Monday morning before attempting to approach Noah again.

She hadn't trusted herself to go to his house on Sunday. After what had happened—or *not* happened—between them on Saturday, she'd decided it was best that she avoid being alone with him for any prolonged period of time.

Besides, she reasoned as she stepped through the doors of Roarke Investigations bearing three steaming espressos, Noah would be less likely to toss her out on her ear if she threatened to make a scene in front of his clients. And if that didn't work, she'd simply march down the hall to Kenneth Roarke's office and ask for his help. Of course, she was counting on not making it past the threshold of Noah's office before he capitulated to her demands.

"Oh my goodness!" A woman's surprised voice broke into her musings. "Is that *you*, Riley?"

Riley smiled, recognizing the pretty Hispanic woman seated behind the large oak reception desk. "Hey Janie. It's so good to see you."

The words were barely out of her mouth before Sanjuanita Roarke was on her feet and rounding the desk to wrap her in a warm, tight hug. "I can't believe you're back," she exclaimed, drawing away to give Riley a quick once-over and fluff her hair, which was cut in short, breezy layers that skimmed her cheeks. "You look great. I *love* the new hairdo. Very haute couture."

Riley grinned. "Thanks, Janie. You look pretty amazing yourself." And she did, with her glowing dark eyes, glossy black hair that rippled past her shoulders, and smooth, olive-toned skin that had been kissed by the summer sun. Everything about Janie Roarke radiated happiness. "Married life really agrees with you," Riley observed.

A soft, poignant smile curved Janie's mouth. "You could say that. Oh, hey, are these for us?" she asked, noticing the espressos for the first time.

"Yep. If I'd known you worked here, I would have brought a double mocha latte. Hope you don't mind settling for an espresso instead?"

"Not at all," said Janie, divesting Riley of the drinks and setting them down on the desk counter before helping herself to a cup. "I could definitely use a jolt of caffeine. Don't be fooled by the empty reception area—it's been a madhouse around here. This is the first time the phone has stopped ringing all morning." The last was said with a pointed glare at the silent phone, as if daring it to contradict her.

Riley laughed. "How long have you been working here?" she asked curiously.

"A year in September. I know," Janie said, seeing Riley's surprised expression. "The last time you saw me, I was toting the twins around and vowing never to return to work. But when this opportunity came up, I just couldn't resist." Her dark eyes twinkled with mischief as she added, sotto voce, "I can't begin to tell you how much fun it can be when your boss is the man you sleep with every night. Suffice it to say, lunch breaks have taken on a *whole* new meaning."

Riley chuckled. "That good, huh?"

"And then some." She took a sip of coffee and closed her eyes with a long, luxuriant sigh. "Oh, that hits the spot."

Riley grinned. "Don't say that too loud, or Kenneth will think you're out here cheating on him."

Janie laughed, rounding the desk to reclaim her chair as the phone trilled. "Roarke Investigations," she answered in a brisk, professional tone. "How may I help you this morning?"

Riley's heart sank when she heard Janie inform the caller that Noah was out of the office. "How long?" she blurted without thinking the moment Janie hung up the phone.

Janie arched a thick brow at her. "How long what?"

"How long will Noah be gone?" Riley asked, then, in a calmer voice, "I need to speak to him."

But it was too late. The other woman's curiosity had already been aroused. "Sounds urgent."

Riley hesitated. "It's pretty important," she murmured.

"Is it something Kenneth can help you with? He'll be finished with his conference call any minute now."

Riley shook her head. "I'll wait for Noah." She wouldn't play her big-brother card until it was absolutely necessary. "Do you expect him back anytime soon?"

"He's down at the courthouse, providing expert testimony in one of his cases." She glanced at her diamond-encrusted wristwatch and frowned. "He should be back by now. Want me to give him a call on his cell?"

"No, that's okay. I'll wait a little longer."

As Janie took the next call, Riley wandered over to the windows and glanced outside, half-wondering if Noah had returned, spied her car, and decided to hide out in the parking lot until she gave up and left. She scanned the lot but didn't see his Yukon.

Didn't matter. She wasn't leaving until she got what she came there for.

She turned at the sound of a door opening down the corridor. A moment later, a tall, dark-skinned man who bore a striking resemblance to Noah appeared in the reception area. Without glancing in Riley's direction, he made his way over to the desk, stopped behind Janie's chair and leaned down to nuzzle the nape of her neck.

With a soft murmur of pleasure, Janie turned her head to offer her mouth for a kiss, before belatedly remembering that they weren't alone. Catching Riley's amused eyes, she cleared her throat briskly. "Uh, honey, we have a visitor."

Kenneth Roarke's head lifted. When he saw Riley standing there, his dark eyes widened in shock. *"Riley?"*

"Hello, Kenneth," Riley said, starting forward with a warm smile. "How've you been?"

"Damn, girl. It *is* you." He crossed the room in three powerful strides and, ignoring her outstretched hand, drew her into his arms for a big bear hug.

Riley laughed, and couldn't help noting the difference between Kenneth's warm reception and his brother's decidedly cool one. Come to think of it, she couldn't remember the last time, if ever, Noah had given her a hug.

"When'd you get back in town?" Kenneth asked, drawing her down onto an upholstered sofa beside him.

"Late Friday afternoon," Riley answered.

"Does Noah know you're here?"

She nodded. "I saw him that night."

"Really?" Kenneth looked across the room to exchange surprised glances with Janie, who shook her head in disbelief.

"He didn't say a word to us," she complained. "Not even when he came to church on Sunday for Lourdes's choir solo. Oh, he's in big trouble."

Riley wasn't at all surprised to learn that Noah hadn't told his family about her return. He'd been less than thrilled to see her and probably wished she'd catch the first thing smoking back to D.C.

Well, he was in for a rude awakening.

"How long are you staying?" Kenneth asked, as if he'd read her mind.

"Two months. I took a leave of absence from work." She smiled at Kenneth. "How's your mother doing? My grandmother told me she remarried."

"That's right. She married a deacon from her church." Kenneth grinned proudly. "So I've walked *two* special ladies down the aisle within the last year. I'm sure Noah told you about Daniela getting hitched?"

Riley nodded, smiling warmly. "Two weddings in one year. Wow, that's something else."

"Daniela had the big, beautiful wedding," Janie chimed in. "Mama Hubbard didn't want to take away the spotlight from her daughter, so she and Deacon Hubbard had a nice, quiet ceremony several months before. Both were incredibly romantic in their own ways."

"That's wonderful," Riley murmured.

An awkward silence fell over the room, as if Janie

and Kenneth had suddenly remembered that Riley had lost her fiancé shortly before her own wedding.

"How've you been?" Kenneth asked quietly.

She forced a smile. "I'm doing fine. I really like Washington, D.C. The museums are incredible, and it's gorgeous in the fall when the leaves change color on the trees. You guys should visit sometime."

"Definitely," said Kenneth.

"We'd love to," Janie echoed.

At that moment, the front door opened and Noah strode purposefully into the building.

Riley's breath caught in her throat at the sight of him in a double-breasted navy-blue suit worn with a crisp ivory shirt and a charcoal-and-blue-striped silk tie. The last time she'd seen him dressed up had been at Trevor's funeral—which would explain why she hadn't noticed before how magnificent, how powerfully male, Noah looked in a suit.

Halfway to the reception desk, he paused and slowly removed his mirrored aviator sunglasses. If he was surprised to see Riley seated in the waiting area, he didn't show it. Those dark, fathomless eyes touched hers for the briefest moment, then slid away to meet Kenneth's speculative gaze.

"Why didn't you tell us Riley was back in town?" his brother demanded.

One corner of Noah's mouth lifted wryly. "I figured you'd find out soon enough."

"You still should have told us," Janie chided. "We could have invited Riley over for dinner yesterday."

"She'll be here for the rest of the summer," Noah drawled, and this time when his eyes met hers, Riley felt a tingle of awareness that she dismissed as nerves. "Isn't that right, Riley?"

She nodded. "I need to talk to you."

His expression remained impassive. "Of course you do." As Riley got up, he turned his back on her and walked to the desk to retrieve his phone messages from Janie.

"How'd it go this morning?" Kenneth asked, rising to his feet and starting across the room.

"Good. If you've got some time, I'd like to run a few things past you."

"I don't have any more appointments until later this afternoon. We can talk after you and Riley are finished."

Before Noah could protest, Janie cheerfully interjected, "Look, fellas. Riley brought us all coffee. Wasn't that sweet of her?"

"Sure was," Kenneth agreed, grabbing a cup from the desk and taking a grateful sip. He winked at Riley over the rim. "Good stuff. You'll have to come around more often, Miss Kane."

Riley smiled, but she couldn't help but notice that Noah, sifting through his phone messages, completely ignored the coffee on his way out of the room.

Kenneth and Janie exchanged quizzical glances before turning to look at Riley, as if expecting her to provide an explanation for Noah's strange behavior.

"It's a long story," Riley muttered, then started down the corridor after Noah.

He was already waiting by the door when she reached his office, his head averted. After she brushed past him to enter the room, he closed the door and waved her into the visitor chair then rounded the large desk, which was as cluttered with paperwork as the one at his house.

He sat, propped his elbow on the desk, rested his fingertips against the side of his temple and gave her his undivided attention.

Resisting the urge to squirm, Riley crossed her denim-clad legs and folded her hands neatly in her lap, as if by perfecting her posture, she could maintain her composure.

"I was wondering if you've given any more thought to what we spoke about on Friday," she began.

"I have," Noah said evenly, "and my answer is still the same."

Though she'd been prepared for such a response, Riley felt a sharp stab of disappointment. "Let me ask you this, Noah. What if you didn't know me? What if I'd just walked in off the street and shared the same story with you. Would you still refuse to take my case?"

"We turn people away all the time, Riley. That's the nature of the business."

"That's not what I asked you."

"No, I wouldn't take your case."

"I don't believe you. I know the only reason you won't even consider helping me is that Trevor was your best friend."

"And your fiancé," Noah reminded her coldly.

"Yes, my fiancé," she said with a brittle half smile. "The man I gave up a good job for to move back to San Antonio just to be near him. The man I loved enough to want to marry and have children with. The man I shared my—"

Noah's jaw hardened. "Enough, Riley. You made your point."

"Don't ever question my love for Trevor," she said in a voice that trembled with suppressed fury. "This has *nothing* whatsoever to do with that."

"I disagree," Noah bit off tersely. "I think if you love someone as much as you claim to have loved Trevor, you wouldn't be entertaining these outrageous suspicions about him. Suspicions, by the way, that are based solely on dreams. *Dreams,* Riley."

Her nostrils flared with anger. "It's not just the dreams. I told you, there was a man at the funeral—"

"Which proves absolutely nothing."

"Maybe if you put me in front of a police sketch artist, we could come up with a composite of this man, then run it through the system to find out if there's a match."

Bemused, Noah shook his head at her. "If you've got it all figured out, what do you need me for?"

Riley frowned, biting her lower lip for a moment. "Because no one will talk to me."

"What do you mean?"

"I mean, when I went to see Chief Pittman a few weeks after the funeral, he treated me as if I were a hysterical woman who couldn't cope with the death of my fiancé. When I told him about the German man at the funeral, he dismissed it as coincidence." Her mouth twisted cynically at the memory. "He pretty much patted me on my head, offered his condolences, and sent me home with the promise that he wouldn't mention a word of our conversation to anyone else, because he knew how much it would hurt Trevor's comrades to know what my concerns were."

"He's right," Noah said grimly. "Every one of those cops worships the ground you walk on, Riley. If they find out what you're doing, what you're *trying* to do, they'd never forgive you."

Riley looked him square in the eye. "That's a chance I'm willing to take." She paused. "But I guess you're not."

His expression darkened. "My decision not to help you has nothing to do with what other people will think."

"Are you sure about that?" she challenged.

"Damn it, Riley," he growled, leaning forward in his chair. "I don't have to sit here and defend myself to you. Nothing you can say or do would convince me to launch an investigation into Trevor's death. I spoke extensively to every last member of the Officer Involved Shooting Team responsible for investigating Trevor's murder. You don't have enough evidence to suggest there was anything more to the shooting than what the OIST determined. And if you were a complete stranger waltzing into my office, I'd tell you the same damn thing!"

"All right then," Riley said with measured calm. It was time to play her ace in the hole. "Maybe you're not the person I should be speaking to."

Noah just watched her, saying nothing.

With as much dignity as she could muster, Riley stood and walked to the door, expecting Noah to call out to her. He didn't, even as she put her hand on the doorknob and slowly turned. She silently counted to ten, then opened the door and stepped out into the hallway.

She got as far as the supply closet before she spun on her heel and marched back to Noah's office, stepping inside and closing the door.

To his credit, he didn't greet her with a triumphant grin. He said quietly, "You don't want to involve Kenneth in this matter, because deep down inside, you know if you're wrong about Trevor, you'll never forgive yourself for calling his character into question, and causing anyone else to do the same."

Riley swallowed with difficulty, her back pressed to the door. He was right. God help her, he was right. And even if her suspicions about Trevor were correct, she knew she would keep the truth to herself. It would be her own terrible secret to bear. Hers—and Noah's.

Closing her eyes, she tried one final appeal. "You have inside connections, Noah. People who would give you information, no questions asked. Believe me, if I could do this on my own, I would have a long time ago."

"I'm sorry, Riley." For the first time, she heard a trace of genuine regret in his voice. "I can't help you."

She opened her eyes and looked at him. "Can't or won't?"

"Both." His expression softened. "I think you should see someone, Riley. About the dreams—"

Anger swelled in her chest. "And here that's what I thought I was doing," she said bitterly. "So much for *that* idea."

Without another word, she yanked the door open and started down the corridor, nearly colliding with Janie, who was emerging from the supply closet with an armful of Xerox paper.

She took one look at Riley's face and frowned. "Are you all right?"

Riley blinked back the sting of tears. She would *not* cry. One way or another, she'd walk out of there with her pride intact.

"I'm fine," she told Janie, her words belied by the tremor in her voice.

Janie pursed her lips, glancing in the direction Riley had just come from. "Listen, do you have a minute?"

Riley glanced at her watch. "I really should be going. I have an appointment with the caterers for my grandmother's party in a few weeks."

"Oh, yeah, that's right. Her seventy-fifth birthday bash. Mama Hubbard mentioned something about it a few days ago. She and your grandmother were talking about the party when they saw each other at the senior center. She told us we were all invited."

"Of course," Riley said, managing a wan smile as she followed Janie down the hallway to the reception area. "The formal invitations will be mailed out this week. In fact, that's one of the projects my grandmother and I will be working on this afternoon."

"I won't keep you much longer then," Janie said, loading the package of paper into the printer. "I wanted to run an idea past you. You can take your time and think about it, then get back to me at your earliest convenience."

"Um, okay," Riley said slowly, her curiosity piqued. "What is it?"

"Well, I don't know whether Noah mentioned it or not," Janie said, frowning as the printer paper got jammed, "but we're thinking about hiring another private investigator to help with the caseload. We've got clients coming out of our ears, and with Daniela being on her honeymoon for a month, we're really feeling the pinch."

Riley frowned. "I don't understand. Are you asking me to fill in for Daniela?"

"Not exactly. You have to be licensed to work as a private investigator in the state of Texas, and that process takes months. However," she said, pulling out the printer tray, "there are things you can do while working under a licensed investigator."

"Such as?"

"Well, you can help with online research, background checks, asset and court searches, missing person searches, serving legal papers. You could even help Noah and Kenneth conduct surveillances and install hidden videos to protect children from abusive babysitters. You could be, like, their apprentice."

Riley was intrigued, even as a germ of an idea began to take root in her mind. "You mean I can do all those things without a license?"

Janie nodded, giving the printer one good whack with the flat of her palm. "You'd be really good at it, too. Being an investigative journalist who also specializes in law enforcement, you're already familiar with a lot of laws and criminal codes. Plus you can probably do research in your sleep."

Riley grinned. "That's definitely true."

"You'd be perfect." Janie gave a satisfied nod when the printer jam finally cleared. "I've got my hands full with the phones, scheduling appointments, doing the bookkeeping and payroll, maintaining the case-management system—not to mention a gazillion other administrative tasks that fall squarely on my shoulders. The fellas have divided Daniela's caseload pretty evenly between themselves, but there's only so much they can do, given the long hours they already work. They'd really benefit from having someone step in to help with a lot of the legwork, even if only on a part-time basis."

"What do Kenneth and Noah think about all this?" Riley asked carefully.

"I think it's the best idea I've heard all morning," Kenneth said, emerging from his office.

Riley turned to see him smiling easily at her, hands tucked into his pockets as he propped a shoulder against the wall. "Janie's right—although my brother and I have been too stubborn to admit it. We could really use some help."

"So, would you be interested, Riley?" Janie asked hopefully.

Before Riley could answer, Noah's deep voice interrupted. "Interested in what?"

Janie glanced over her shoulder as Noah appeared in the entryway beside his brother. "We may have found the solution to our staffing shortage," she told him.

"What?"

"You're looking at her," Janie said with a nod toward Riley.

Noah frowned, his dark eyes meeting hers. "Riley's not a licensed P.I."

"She doesn't have to be for what we need her for," Kenneth pointed out.

"So are you interested, Riley?" Janie asked again. "I mean, I know you didn't take a leave of absence to come home and work, but if you've got any free time to spare—"

"She doesn't," Noah said through gritted teeth.

"Actually," Riley said lightly, holding his steely gaze, "I do have time. As it turns out, I'm going to have *plenty* of time to spare. So, yes, I think I will take you up on your offer, Janie."

"Great," Janie said, grinning from ear to ear.

For the first time since arriving in San Antonio, Riley felt a glimmer of hope that all was not lost. After the showdown in his office, Noah may have thought he'd seen the last of her. But as any savvy reporter knew, the key to landing a good scoop was persistence.

Persistence was Riley's middle name.

The moment Riley left the building, Noah ground out tersely, "I'm calling a staff meeting. *Now*."

Janie glanced at the ringing telephone. "But what about—"

"Let voice mail pick it up," Noah growled over his shoulder, jerking his tie loose as he strode down the hallway toward the conference room that would eventually be converted into a fourth office. Kenneth and Janie followed more slowly.

"What the hell was that all about?" Noah demanded once they were seated at the large conference table that dominated the long, narrow room. "Since when do we make decisions about hiring personnel without everyone's input?"

Kenneth and Janie traded amused glances. "If memory serves me correctly," his brother drawled, "we started that practice last year, when you and Daniela ganged up on me and offered Janie a job against my wishes."

Noah scowled. "That was different."

"How's that? I had objections to my wife working here, just as you obviously have very strong objections to Riley working here. The only difference I see is that my reasons—though they've since been proved wrong—at least made sense at the time."

Noah's scowl deepened. "I have perfectly legitimate reasons for not wanting Riley to work here."

Kenneth and Janie looked at him expectantly.

"Well?" Janie prompted after a prolonged moment of silence. "Let's hear your reasons for not wanting her here."

Because I'm in love with her, and the idea of working beside her every damned day and not being able to touch her, and tell her how I feel, is the worst form of torture imaginable.

Aloud he said, "For starters, I thought we'd already decided to hire another private investigator, *not* an assistant."

"We did," Kenneth agreed. "But getting the right person on board may take a couple of months. And we also decided we didn't want to hire another P.I. without Daniela's input. So either way we have to wait for her to get back from Italy."

"Then why don't we just hold off on hiring anyone—period?"

"Because we need help now. We all know that."

"And before you say Riley's not qualified," Janie chimed in, "I think we can all agree she's *more* than capable of doing the job. She's an award-winning investigative journalist, for crying out loud. If she wasn't returning to D.C. in two months, I'd offer her the P.I. position in a heartbeat."

Noah countered, "She's not licensed."

"So she'd get licensed," Janie said with a shrug. "No big deal."

"It *is* a big deal," Noah snapped.

His brother and Janie stared at him, their eyes alight with avid curiosity.

"Why is it a big deal, Noah?" Kenneth asked quietly. "The way Janie and I see it, it's a win-win situation for everyone. I don't know Riley's reasons for taking a sabbatical from work, but she's obviously not opposed to pinch-hitting for us here at the office. She'll probably welcome the opportunity to get out of the house for a while and do something productive with her time."

Janie chuckled. "It's not as if she's gonna sit around babysitting her grandmother. Florinda Kane has more of an active social life than all three of us combined."

Noah couldn't argue with that, much as he would've liked to. So he raised another issue. "Who's going to train Riley? I sure as hell don't have time, nor does Kenneth."

"I'll work with her," Janie blithely volunteered. "I can already tell she's going to be a quick learner."

That's an understatement, Noah thought darkly, remembering the veiled look of triumph in Riley's eyes as she'd accepted the job offer. He knew there was only one reason she wanted to work at Roarke Investigations, and it had nothing whatsoever to do with her interest in becoming a private detective. She planned to work him, wear down his defenses until he finally agreed to help her with her mission.

But she was soon to discover just how difficult it would be to penetrate Noah's ironclad will. Five long, torturous years of hiding and suppressing his feelings for her had been his proving ground.

No matter what tactics she resorted to, he wouldn't give an inch.

Because he knew that once he surrendered his will to Riley Kane, it was only a matter of time before his heart followed.

Chapter 6

When Riley reported to Roarke Investigations the next morning, she was more nervous than she'd been on her first day at the *Washington Post*, although there'd been far more pressure to perform well at that job than the one she was now embarking upon.

She'd dressed with extra care that morning, donning a simple white shirt with flared cuffs over a pencil-slim khaki skirt and wedge sandals—an outfit she'd settled on after changing three times. As she left the house and climbed into her car, she tried not to examine too closely the reasons—or *reason*—behind the vicious tangle of nerves knotting her stomach.

When she arrived at the office at eight o'clock sharp and learned that Noah was out on a surveillance assignment, she didn't know whether to be relieved or disappointed.

Fortunately, she didn't have much time to dwell on it as Janie got right down to business, giving her a quick tour of the facilities before ushering her into a small, windowless room that served as Daniela Thorne's office.

As Janie explained to her over coffee and a mountain of paperwork, Roarke Investigations was a full-service detective agency that specialized in missing person searches, civil and criminal investigations, child custody and abuse cases, spousal surveillance, and background checks for business and individual clients, to name just a few. Although their hourly rates were comparable to many of their local counterparts, what gave the Roarke brothers an edge over the competition was their reputation in the community and their combined law enforcement experience. Prior to launching the detective agency, both had worked for the San Antonio Police Department—Kenneth in Internal Affairs, Noah in Homicide.

Riley spent the morning reviewing open case files to bring herself up to speed and to identify areas where additional research would be needed.

By the time she looked up again, three hours had flown by.

"Hey, do you want to break for lunch?" Janie asked, appearing in the doorway.

Riley paused in the middle of scribbling notes onto a legal pad. "Lunch?"

"Yeah, that thing you do around noontime. Involves putting food into your mouth and swallowing?" Janie chuckled. "We're not slave drivers, you know." She paused. "Well, maybe just a teensy-weensy bit."

Riley smiled, setting down her pen. "Food sounds good."

"Cool. I ordered some pasta salad and sandwiches from Jason's Deli," Janie said as they left the office. "I was going to take you out to lunch to celebrate your first day with us, but I got really swamped."

"Oh, don't worry about it."

"Maybe we can go on Friday, when things are a little slower. Let's eat in here," she said, leading Riley into a small, windowless room dominated by a large conference table, where she'd already set up the food. "Kenneth left for an appointment, but Noah should be on his way back to the office. Do you want chicken, turkey or roast beef?"

"Chicken's fine."

As the two women settled at the table to eat, Janie asked, "How's it going so far? Are you already regretting your decision to come work with us?"

Riley laughed. "Not at all. The cases you guys handle are pretty interesting. I'm learning a lot."

"Glad to hear it. We're very happy to have you on board, Riley."

"Thanks." A wry smile tipped the corner of Riley's mouth. "I guess two out of three ain't bad."

Janie grimaced. "I'm really sorry about Noah. I don't know why he behaved like that yesterday."

"That's all right," Riley murmured, spearing a black olive from her pasta salad. "I'm used to it by now."

"Really? From Noah?"

Riley nodded, then, seeking to change the subject, said, "I hope Daniela won't mind that I'm using her office."

"Of course not. Even if she were that territorial—which she's not—it wouldn't matter in this case. Daniela's always been very fond of you."

A warm smile curved Riley's mouth. "I've always liked her, too. I can't wait to see her again and offer my congratulations on her marriage."

"Just wait until you meet Caleb. Hot—that's all I'm going to say."

Riley grinned. "But not as hot as your husband, of course."

Janie's dark eyes twinkled with mischief. "Of course." Sobering after a moment, she bit into her sandwich and slowly chewed.

Riley could see the wheels spinning in her mind, and wasn't surprised when Janie returned to the topic of her brother-in-law. "Noah's always been pretty easygoing. In fact, I used to tease Kenneth all the time by telling him I'd married the wrong brother, the uptight one. In contrast to Noah, Kenny can come across so serious at times—too serious."

"I've never really seen the easygoing side of Noah," Riley admitted, nibbling on her sandwich. "He's always seemed so intense to me." .

"Oh, he is, believe me. Especially when he's focused on a big case or something he's really passionate about. But he definitely knows how to relax and have a good time. And you should see how good he is with his niece and nephew. They adore him."

Riley could believe it. She'd seen Noah work his magic on others, from the cops he'd once worked with to a waitress serving him at a restaurant. She knew he could be charming, compassionate, and generous to a fault—even if she'd never been on the receiving end of those traits.

"Give him time," Janie said gently. "He'll come around."

Riley had her doubts, but she wasn't going to let those doubts discourage her. Thanks to Janie, she'd been given the perfect excuse to see and interact with Noah five days a week for the next two months. She was convinced that if he only got to know her better, he'd realize she wasn't crazy or malicious for wanting to investigate Trevor's death. If she couldn't persuade him to help her...well, she refused to consider that possibility. Failure, as far as she was concerned, wasn't an option.

As she and Janie finished their meals and cleared the table, Noah returned to the office. Today, instead of a double-breasted suit, he wore a black T-shirt, black jeans, and black boots that made him look decidedly menacing as he sauntered down the hallway toward them, his eyes concealed behind mirrored sunglasses.

"Hey, sunshine," Janie greeted him cheerfully. "I left your sandwich and drink on your desk."

"Thanks." He inclined his head briefly toward Riley. "Afternoon."

"Hey Noah," she chirped, striving to sound normal when butterflies were fluttering wildly in her stomach. Those damned nerves again. "How's it going?"

"It's going," he murmured, disappearing into his office.

Riley followed Janie to the reception desk to pick up a form she'd requested earlier. "By the way, I have some follow-up questions about one of the cases I was reading about this morning—the Gallagher case. I looked through the file, but didn't see who it had been assigned to."

"Talk to Noah," Janie answered. "That's his client."

Nodding, Riley went back to her office to retrieve the case file before going in search of Noah. He'd just hung up the phone when she appeared in the doorway of his office.

"Sorry to interrupt," she said, motioning toward the untouched sandwich on his desk, "but do you have a minute? I wanted to ask you a few questions about the Gallagher case. Janie gave me the file to review—"

He sent her a bemused look. "You're not seriously planning to go through with this, are you?"

Riley pretended not to understand. "Go through with what?"

"Don't insult my intelligence, Riley," he drawled. "You know very well what I'm talking about. This whole charade. You, working here at the agency just to get what you want out of me. It's not going to work."

"I'm here to do a job. I should think you'd welcome the extra help."

He studied her for a long moment, those dark, fathomless eyes narrowed on her face. "So that's how it's going to be," he said softly, a hint of challenge in his voice. "That's how you want to play this."

Her pulse thudded, but she didn't back down. "What can I say, Noah? If you have a problem with me being here, take it up with your partners."

The gauntlet had been thrown. Their eyes locked in a moment of shared understanding, two adversaries squaring off on the dueling field.

Without releasing her gaze, Noah reached for his roast beef sandwich and took a bite, chewing slowly and thoughtfully. "Forget the Gallagher case. I want you to work on background checks."

"But Janie said—"

"Forget what Janie said. She reports to me, not the other way around. In fact, from now on, you'll receive your assignments from me. Do you have a problem with that?"

Riley mustered a smile etched in steel. "Not at all."

"Good. When you're finished with those background checks, I have a stack of public documents I want you to read through. Nothing exciting, but then, you're not here for the thrill of it," he said mockingly. "You're here to help."

"Of course," Riley said easily. "Do you have the files for me?"

"Get them from Janie." He reached for his phone, dismissing her.

As Riley left the office and headed toward the reception area, she had flashbacks of being a recent college graduate reporting to her first day of work at the *Houston Chronicle*. Her managing editor had been a chain-smoking, cantankerous old relic who believed women didn't belong in the newsroom, and from the very beginning he'd set out to make her life a living hell, much as Noah had decided to do. But Riley wouldn't be deterred. Just as she'd stood up to her tyrannical editor and proved him wrong about her competency as a journalist, she would also stand up to Noah.

The way she saw it, there was nothing Noah or anyone else could do to make her life any more miserable than the past three years had already been.

By Friday, Riley was having serious doubts about the truth of that assessment.

Noah was doing everything in his power to make her life miserable at Roarke Investigations, and unfortunately for her, as a senior partner and co-founder of the agency, he had a *lot* of power.

Every time she completed an assignment, he handed her another, larger pile of work. And she wasn't just confined to the office. Noah also sent her on a number of errands that included delivering documents to the courthouse and serving papers to defendants. Once he'd even asked her to drive a client to and from a doctor's appointment. Though she hadn't minded helping out the elderly gentleman, she couldn't understand how such a task fell under her job description.

"Maybe it doesn't," Noah had agreed when she approached him about it. "But then again, seeing that we never got around to creating a job description for you, we really don't have anything to go by, do we?"

What could she say? He was right, of course. And judging by the satisfied gleam in his eyes, he knew it, too.

On Friday morning, Riley was in the supply closet stocking up on manila folders when she overheard a conversation between Kenneth and Noah out in the hallway.

"...told me she's doing a great job," Kenneth was saying. "She said she's picked up things really fast and gotten a lot of stuff done."

"She has," Noah said, and Riley couldn't help feeling a twinge of pleasure at the admission. It was the closest she'd ever come to receiving a compliment from Noah, secondhand or otherwise.

"Why don't you let her sit in on one of your appointments, to get a better feel for how we investigate our cases?" Kenneth suggested.

"She's been here less than a week. What's the rush?"

"She's leaving at the end of August."

"I know that," Noah said impatiently. "Which is why I don't think it's necessary to invest so much time in training her."

"I disagree," Kenneth countered. "I think she'd

really benefit from seeing firsthand how we interact with our clients."

As their voices drew nearer, Riley realized they were heading into the supply closet, where she stood near the entrance with an armful of file folders, shamelessly eavesdropping on their conversation.

Thinking fast, she dropped the stack of folders on the floor and bent to pick them up just as Noah stepped into the room.

"I'm so clumsy," she muttered, feigning embarrassment as he crouched down to help her. "They slipped right out of my hands."

Noah slid her a look that told her he knew better but was too polite to call her out in front of his brother.

As he passed her the folders he'd retrieved, their fingers brushed, sending frissons of heat through her body. Her lips parted in surprise, and for one charged moment they gazed at each other.

It was Noah who glanced away first.

In unison they rose to their feet and quickly stepped apart, while Kenneth looked on with undisguised interest.

"So, Riley," he said casually, "I was just telling my brother that he should let you sit in on one of his appointments."

"Really?" Riley exclaimed, ignoring the sardonic look Noah gave her. "That'd be great. I haven't had a chance to work on any cases yet."

"I know," Kenneth drawled, with a sideways glance at his younger brother. "Actually, Noah has a meeting later this afternoon. You could probably attend and take notes."

"I'd love to. Thanks, Kenneth." She turned to Noah, who was frowning. "I'll be in my office whenever you're ready."

He nodded curtly.

As Riley excused herself and left the supply room, she could feel the two men watching her. She smiled to herself, thinking of the way Noah had been maneuvered into working with her—for the second time that week.

Watch out, Noah, she mused. *At the rate I'm going, you don't stand a chance of winning this duel.*

Chapter 7

"**I**'m here to see Noah Roarke."

Riley, who stood behind the reception desk using the printer later that afternoon, turned to identify the owner of the smooth, cultured voice. A tall, stunning woman with skin the color of café au lait and wearing an expensively tailored red skirt suit with designer stiletto pumps stood there, drumming long, manicured fingernails on the desk counter.

Janie offered a polite smile. "And your name is?" she inquired.

"Delilah Stanton," the woman replied with a hint of arrogance. "I have a three-o'clock appointment with him. I'm running a little late."

A little? thought Riley, aiming a discreet glance at her wristwatch. *Try thirty minutes late.*

"I'll tell Mr. Roarke you're here. Would you care for some coffee while you wait?"

"No, thank you. Do you know how long the wait will be? I'm on a tight schedule."

"I'm not sure," Janie answered evenly. "Mr. Roarke is on a very tight schedule himself. We usually ask people to reschedule if they're going to be more than fifteen minutes late to an appointment."

"It was unavoidable," the woman clipped.

"I understand." Janie dialed Noah's extension. "He's not answering his phone," she said after a few moments. She rose from her chair. "Let me go see if he's available."

Delilah Stanton huffed out an impatient sigh and continued tapping her fingertips on the desk. As Riley retrieved her print job and started from the reception area, the woman's cold, imperious voice stopped her in her tracks. "On second thought, a cup of coffee would be nice."

Riley turned, pasting a saccharine smile onto her face. "Certainly. How do you take yours?"

"With a drop of cream and two sugars," the woman replied.

"Janie can get that," Noah said, walking into the reception area. He extended a hand to Delilah Stanton. "Noah Roarke. Pleased to meet you, Mrs. Stanton."

Riley watched, with a mixture of disbelief and amusement, as Delilah Stanton literally became putty in Noah's hand. Her light brown eyes grew warm and inviting, her coral-painted lips softened into a smile, and all the starch seemed to melt from her spine. The transformation was like night and day.

"I can assure you, Mr. Roarke," she purred, giving Noah a slow, appreciative once-over, "the pleasure's *all* mine."

Noah's relaxed smile told Riley he was used to getting hit on by his female clients, which, she supposed, couldn't be bad for business.

"Let's step into my office," he told the woman, guiding her away with a light touch to the small of her back. When Riley hung back, unsure whether or not to follow, he sent her a lazy glance over his shoulder. "Are you coming?"

Riley grabbed a legal pad from Janie's desk and hurried after him.

Inside Noah's office, he led Delilah Stanton over to a small round conference table in the corner and pulled out a chair for her, then Riley, before seating himself next to the woman.

Janie entered with a steaming cup of coffee, which she handed to Delilah Stanton before slipping quietly out of the room.

"Now then," Noah began, folding his hands on the table, "how may we help you, Mrs. Stanton?"

Lips pursed, Delilah cast a dubious look at Riley seated across from her. "This is a rather personal matter," she said, making it clear she expected—and wanted—Riley to leave the room.

When Riley looked askance at Noah, his mouth twitched. "My apologies, Mrs. Stanton," he drawled smoothly. "I forgot to introduce my assistant, Riley Kane. She'll be taking notes during our meeting, just to make sure I don't miss anything. Whatever you share with us will be kept strictly confidential."

"All right," the woman reluctantly acquiesced. Turning slightly in her chair, she focused all of her attention on Noah. "I want you to help me leave my husband."

Noah didn't so much as blink. "Go on," he murmured. "I'm listening."

"We've been married for five years," Delilah began. "Four of those five years have been the worst of my life. Joseph isn't the man I thought he was. For starters, he hasn't been able to hold down a steady job since we got married. He's bounced around from one blue-collar job to the next. Whenever I try to talk to him about it, he gets mad and storms out of the house to go drinking with his low-life friends, who are as useless as he is. *They* tell him it's perfectly all right for him to sponge off his wife, because as long as I have the earning potential, why not take advantage of it?"

"Has he ever said this to you, Mrs. Stanton?" Noah asked.

"Not outright, no. But it comes across loud and clear in his attitude. I'm a vice president at a Fortune 500 health-care company, so I earn a lot of money. Wouldn't you think that would motivate Joseph to do better for himself? Well, it doesn't. If anything, my six-figure salary makes him lazier. He knows that as long as we're married, he doesn't have to worry about working, because I make more than enough for both of us. And now, to add insult to injury, that leech has the nerve to be cheating on me!"

"How do you know this?" Noah asked.

She frowned. "I don't have any proof, if that's what you mean. But there have been signs."

"Such as?"

"Well, he's lied a few times about his whereabouts, telling me he's at one place when he's actually somewhere else. And he's been coming home late with no explanations and getting off the phone quickly whenever I enter a room. Very suspicious behavior."

Riley glanced up from scribbling notes. "Do you have any reason to believe your husband is unhappy in the marriage?"

Delilah looked at her as if one of the potted plants on the windowsill had started talking. "Have you ever been married, Miss Kane?" she coolly inquired.

"No, I haven't," Riley murmured, acutely aware of Noah's dark, watchful regard. She didn't know how to interpret his expression. Sympathy? Concern? Irritation with her for butting into the conversation?

Delilah gave a curt nod. "I figured as much. If you'd ever been married, Miss Kane, you would know that men don't have to be unhappy in order to stray. They're men—that's what they do. No offense to you, of course," she added, laying a conciliatory hand upon

Noah's arm. "Somehow I know *you'd* never cheat on the woman you love, Mr. Roarke."

Noah smiled. "Thanks for the vote of confidence."

Delilah laughed, temporarily forgetting her ne'er-do-well husband as she stared into Noah's eyes.

Riley gave a mental eye roll. Maybe Joseph Stanton was the one who should be worried about a cheating spouse.

She pointedly cleared her throat. "Has anything else happened that would make you suspicious of your husband, Mrs. Stanton?"

Reluctantly tearing her gaze away from Noah, Delilah skewered Riley with a look. "Haven't I given you enough to go on? I mean, if I'd caught him in the act myself, I wouldn't be trying to hire a private investigator, now would I?"

Before Riley could open her mouth to respond, Noah smoothly intervened. "We'll take your case, Mrs. Stanton. But before we get started, I have to let you know up front that if you're trying to prove your husband's infidelity in order to gain an advantage in a divorce settlement, more time, documentation and investigative work will be required on our end. This means preparing a very detailed report, properly identifying the other woman—if there is one—and conducting multiple days of surveillance to show a pattern and provide conclusive evidence that your husband *is* cheating on you, and not just hanging out with a 'friend.' Do you understand that?"

"Perfectly. You have to catch him with his pants

down in order for me to get out of paying alimony to the freeloading bastard."

Noah grimaced. "Something like that. But even then, there's no guarantee of anything. Because infidelity is so common these days, some judges are reluctant to move away from a fifty-fifty split in a divorce settlement, even when there's proof of fault. Did your husband sign a prenuptial agreement?"

"You bet he did," Delilah said with a satisfied nod. "And according to the terms of the prenup, he gets absolutely nothing if I can prove he cheated on me. I'm counting on you to help me get that proof, Mr. Roarke."

"I'll do my best," Noah said, "but as I tell all of my clients, I can't promise anything. But the more information you give me about your husband, his friends, his favorite pastimes, and where he likes to hang out, the easier it'll be for me to conduct a thorough investigation."

"All right. I'm willing to do whatever it takes." Leaning back in the chair, she crossed one long, shapely leg over the over and smiled demurely at Noah. "So what're we talking about here? Following him around in a car to see where he goes and who he sees?"

Noah nodded. "That's part of it, yes. And we don't limit our surveillance to what can be seen from the window of a car. We have state-of-the-art long-range and hidden video cameras that'll give us the ability to observe your husband's activity inside his place of work, in rural areas, at the mall, and nearly everywhere else he might go. We also utilize vehicle-tracking devices and can provide you with software to monitor your husband's e-mail, chat room discussions, and Internet activity, which you can install yourself."

He pushed back his chair, stood and walked over to a metal file cabinet near his desk. Opening the top drawer, he said, "I have a comprehensive checklist of items you can use to better determine if your husband *is* actually cheating—signs to look for."

"Wow," Delilah murmured, suitably impressed as he returned to the table and passed her the checklist. "You're *very* thorough, Mr. Roarke. There are things on here that I never even thought of. No wonder your agency came so highly recommended."

Even Riley was impressed, pausing in her note taking to stare at Noah. While Delilah was preoccupied with the checklist, he winked playfully at Riley. Her heart gave an irrational little leap, and the smile she sent him was that of a shy teenager trying to flirt with the gorgeous captain of the high school football team.

"Where do we start?" Delilah asked, looking up at Noah. "What do you need to know?"

If Riley wasn't mistaken, she would have sworn Noah had difficulty pulling his eyes away from hers as he turned back to Delilah. "Start by telling me where your husband currently works, and we'll go from there."

Forty minutes later, Noah emerged from the office with a large retainer and a smiling woman on his arm.

Delilah, who'd claimed to be on a "tight schedule" when she first arrived, seemed in no hurry to leave as he walked her to the front door.

"How long have you been in business, Noah?" she asked.

Behind the reception desk, Janie arched a brow at Riley, who was also wondering when Noah and the woman had gotten on a first-name basis.

"My brother and I opened the agency four years ago," Noah answered. "He's out of the office this afternoon, or I would have introduced you to him."

"Hmm. Four years, huh? It takes the average small business at least five years to get off the ground. And look how successful you've already become." Delilah paused, pursing her lips thoughtfully. "When Joseph and I got married, he had all these wonderful plans to launch his own plumbing business. He did some research, looked into applying for a small business loan, made a few contacts, and then…nothing. He never followed through with the plan. He was all talk and no action." She shook her head in disgust. "That was the beginning of the end for me."

"I'm sorry to hear that," Noah murmured.

"Don't be. I truly believe everything happens for a reason." She leaned closer to him, smiling coquettishly. "Perhaps when this is all over, and I'm a happily divorced woman, you can take me out to dinner to celebrate. We can celebrate all…night…long," she said, drawing out the last three words in a sultry purr.

"Let's play it by ear," Noah drawled softly. "You never know—you and your husband might reconcile when it's all said and done."

"Not a chance in hell. Even if he's not cheating on me, I still want a divorce. As I'm discovering," she said silkily, running a finger up and down Noah's muscled forearm, "there are a *lot* better fish in the sea. Take you and me, for example. I can already think of one thing we have in common."

"What's that?" Noah said, smiling down at her.

"You're named after someone in the Bible, and so am I."

"Who? Jezebel?" Janie muttered under her breath, and Riley had to bite the inside of her cheek to keep from laughing out loud.

"I'll be in touch, Mrs. Stanton," Noah said, holding open the door for her. As she edged past him, she deliberately brushed her breasts against his chest. The laughter died in Riley's throat as the couple's eyes met and held for a brief moment.

Noah stood at the window watching as Delilah sashayed to a shiny white Mercedes parked outside the building. When she reached the car, she smiled and fluttered her fingers at him. Chuckling softly, Noah lifted his hand and waved back.

As he turned and sauntered toward the reception desk, Riley assiduously avoided eye contact with him. She was afraid of what he'd glimpse in her eyes if he looked into them.

Hell, *she* was afraid.

"Please don't tell me you're taking that woman's case, Noah," Janie said in exasperation.

"Okay, I won't tell you," Noah said simply, passing Delilah Stanton's check across the desk. "But feel free to deposit this into our account whenever you get a chance."

Janie's eyes widened in shock as she beheld the amount made payable to the detective agency. "Oh my God. That's one of the biggest retainers we've ever received. Did you *see* this, Riley?"

Riley managed to smile. "I was there when she wrote it."

"Oh, yeah, you were." Janie shook her head slowly. "I still think the woman's trouble. Trouble with a big fat capital *T*."

Noah grinned. "Which is why you can't take your eyes off that check, right?"

Janie shot him a dirty look. "The way that woman was throwing herself at you, I'd say *she's* the one who needs to be under surveillance, not her husband. Poor man, having to put up with a diva like that."

"I'm sure he doesn't mind," Riley murmured. "Delilah Stanton is a very beautiful woman. I'm willing to bet most men have a hard time resisting her. Wouldn't you agree, Noah?"

His lips curved in a lazy half smile. "I think that's probably a safe assumption."

For some reason, that wasn't the answer she'd been looking for. "Well," she said, forcing a light tone to soften her censorious words, "to avoid a conflict of interest, you might want to refrain from going out on any dates with the lovely Mrs. Stanton until her divorce is final. After all, you wouldn't want her husband contesting the settlement because the private investigator who busted him for cheating was messing around with his wife at the same time."

The moment the words left her mouth, she wished she could take them back. *What* in the world had gotten into her?

Noah's eyes narrowed on hers, a muscle clenching in his jaw. "Not that I don't appreciate your concern," he said in deceptively soft tones, "but I think I know better than to get involved with a client. I've been doing this for four years, while you've been here all of, what, four days?"

Heat stung Riley's cheeks. Checking her watch, she saw that it was just after five o'clock. "I have a few things to finish up before I leave," she mumbled, before turning and beating a hasty retreat down the hallway toward her office.

"Have a great weekend, Riley," Janie called after her.

"Thanks. You, too."

Inside her office, Riley shoved files into her leather attaché case, intending to do some reading over the weekend. Why not? It's not like she had any exciting plans—unlike her grandmother, who would be attending a formal ball on Saturday night at the senior center where she volunteered.

Noah appeared in the doorway just as Riley was logging off the computer. He wore a thunderous scowl.

"You mind telling me what the hell that was all about?" he demanded.

Riley drew her bag slowly onto her shoulder. "I was out of line," she admitted, not looking at him.

"Damn straight you were," he growled.

Her eyes snapped to his face. "If you hadn't been flirting shamelessly with that woman in the first place, I wouldn't have felt it necessary to say anything."

His expression turned incredulous. "How was *I* flirting shamelessly with *her?*"

"Oh, give me a break, Noah! 'Let's play it by ear'? How about this for a response— 'No, thank you, Mrs. Stanton. You're a married woman who also happens to be my client, so a date with you would be out of the question.' Oh, and let's not forget the way you stood at the window ogling her while she walked to her car."

"Ogling?"

"Yes, ogling," she snapped.

Noah fell silent for a moment, his dark eyes narrowed on hers in silent appraisal. "If I didn't know better," he said mildly, "I would think you were jealous, Riley."

She gave a mirthless laugh. "Yeah, right, Noah. I'd have to actually *like* you to be jealous, now wouldn't I?"

He stepped into the office, causing it to shrink even more by the sheer breadth of his wide shoulders. His expression was unreadable. "You don't like me, Riley?"

"No, that would be *you* who doesn't like *me!*"

Something dark and dangerous flashed in his eyes. "I don't like you?" he echoed flatly.

"That's what I said."

He came forward, a slow and predatory advance. "You think I don't like you, Riley?"

Her breath snagged in her throat. The air between them was charged with a tension that was almost suffocating in its intensity. Suddenly Riley wanted to run, get away from him as fast as possible. Instead she lifted her chin and defiantly stood her ground, even as Noah stopped directly in front of her, standing so close she could practically count each of his thick, spiky eyelashes.

Her heart beat a wild tattoo in her chest. Her attaché case fell, unnoticed, to the floor. "Noah—"

Before she knew what was happening, he cupped her face in his big hands and slanted his mouth over hers. The first touch of his lips to hers was electrifying, scorching through her body like a live wire. She gasped, and he took her breath and gave it back to her in a searing, possessive kiss that demanded her surrender. And she gave it, wreathing her arms around his neck, helpless to do anything but surrender as every part of her body sizzled with awareness and ached with desire.

"Does this feel like I don't like you?" he whispered huskily, drawing a hard shiver from her as he kissed the sensitive skin behind her ear.

"How about this?" he murmured, feathering kisses over her cheeks, her eyelids, her nose, her chin. And returned to her mouth, brushing his lips softly over hers, coaxing them to part for the silken heat of his tongue, which he touched to the tip of hers before sliding deep into the cavity of her mouth.

It was sheer madness, and yet Riley knew exactly what she was doing. It was impossible not to be aware of what was happening and with whom, just as it would be impossible to tell herself afterward that she'd been swept away on a tide of mindless passion.

This was beyond mindless passion.

This was pure, driving need, the depths of which rocked her to the very core of her being. She'd been kissed before, had tasted a man's desire many times in her life. But it had never been like this before. Not with any man.

Not even with Trevor.

Noah's arms banded around her waist as he half lifted her against the taut, muscled strength of his chest. They shared a hard, deep, openmouthed kiss and an embrace that had her moaning and clinging and yearning for more.

All too soon he set her back down on her feet and stepped away from her. Feeling instantly bereft, Riley searched his eyes with her own.

He looked back at her with heavy-lidded eyes, a mocking half smile on his lips. In a low, husky voice layered with suggestion, he said, "I like you, Riley. Can't you tell just how much?"

Her face flamed at the insinuation. Not trusting her

voice, she bent and picked up her attaché case, then hurried from the room without a backward glance.

In the wake of her departure, it took Noah several minutes to get his ragged breathing under control.

What the hell had he just done?

He'd kissed Riley Kane, the one woman who'd been off-limits to him almost from the moment he met her. The one woman who'd dominated his thoughts and innermost desires for the past five years and effectively ruined him for all other women.

As he stood there, his body vibrating from the aftershocks of that explosive kiss, Riley's sweet scent lingered in his nostrils, and the exquisite taste of her filled his mouth. He'd dreamed about holding and kissing her for so long, he'd convinced himself it would never happen, and if by some miracle it did, the reality could never compare to his fantasies.

He couldn't have been more wrong.

How was it possible that a kiss could exceed his every fantasy? And with five years to fantasize, he'd imagined some pretty hot and heavy stuff, the kind that made a man wake up in a cold sweat in the middle of the night, hard as a lump of granite.

His body stirred, his blood heating up again. He'd not only kissed Riley, but she'd kissed him back, responding with a hunger that took his breath away.

Now that it had finally happened, now that he'd finally had a taste of her, he was in more agony than he'd ever been before. He wanted her, wanted her so bad he ached, wanted her more than his next breath. If she hadn't bolted when she did, there's no telling what he might have done to her.

As he stood in the middle of the tiny office, hands braced on his hips, too stunned to move, Kenneth appeared in the doorway. "I just saw Riley tear out of here like she was running from Satan," his brother said. "Is there something going on between you two I should know about?"

Noah scowled. "You should have asked that damn question *before* you hired her."

Without another word, he stalked past his frowning brother, strode down the hallway past his own office, and continued without stopping all the way out of the building.

Chapter 8

The next morning, Riley lay sprawled upon her bed, arms flung outward as she stared up at the ceiling, seeing nothing but Noah's darkly handsome face slanted over hers, his eyes smoldering with passion.

Several hours later, she still couldn't wrap her mind around what had happened.

Noah had kissed her.

He'd kissed her, and God help her, she'd kissed him back, moaning and clinging to him as if her very life depended on it. And since then, all she could do was imagine those soft, sensuous lips on hers, then imagine them everywhere else. She'd dreamed about him all night—vivid, erotic dreams that had her hand creeping down her feverish body until she stopped herself.

Now, in the light of day, a fresh wave of shame and guilt swept through her. She couldn't fantasize about Noah. It was wrong on so many levels. He'd been Trevor's best friend. And, for all intents and purposes, he'd been practically a stranger to Riley. Never mind that he was sexy as hell, and when he looked at her with those dark, penetrating eyes, she had trouble keeping her train of thought.

She shouldn't have allowed him to kiss her. He'd been merely taunting her, trying to get the upper hand in their argument. She shouldn't have let things go so far. She should have put him in his place and left while she still could.

Shoulda, woulda, coulda.

There was a gentle knock at her door. Without lifting her head from the pillow, Riley called out, "Come in, Grandma."

Florinda opened the door and stepped into the room carrying a wicker breakfast tray laden with food.

Riley turned her head as her grandmother walked over to the bed and set the tray down on the nightstand, then made her way to the window to pull back the heavy curtains.

Riley groaned and flung one arm over her eyes as warm, bright sunlight poured into the bedroom.

Florinda chuckled softly as she sat on the edge of the bed. She was already dressed, looking cool and summery in pale linen slacks and a silk turquoise blouse she'd bought during a shopping excursion to Santa Fe earlier that year.

"How long are you going to lie there staring at the ceiling?"

"For as long as—" Breaking off, Riley lifted her arm and peered out at her grandmother. "How'd you know that's what I've been doing?"

"I checked in on you half an hour ago, and you were lying in the same position. You didn't even hear me knock on the door and peek inside." She patted her granddaughter's arm. "Come on. Sit up and eat your breakfast. You skipped dinner last night. Don't think I didn't notice."

As Riley pulled herself into a sitting position and propped a pile of pillows behind her back, Florinda settled the tray across her lap. Riley's stomach growled eagerly at the sight of her grandmother's sourdough French toast sprinkled with powder sugar and dripping with maple syrup.

"Oh, Grandma, you didn't have to fix me breakfast," she murmured, reaching for a crisp slice of bacon.

"Of course I did," Florinda retorted, picking up a fork and knife to cut the French toast for her granddaughter, just as she'd done when Riley was a child. "I can't control how you eat, or *don't* eat, when you're away from home. But as long as you and I are under the same roof, I'm going to take good care of you. God knows *someone* has to."

Riley dutifully opened her mouth and accepted the forkful of French toast Florinda held out to her. Closing her eyes, she chewed slowly in appreciation. "Mmm, still as good as ever, Grandma."

Florinda patted her hand. "Someday I'll give you the recipe and you can make it for your husband."

Riley choked on her food. Sputtering, she reached for a glass of orange juice and took a long sip.

"Was it something I said?"

Riley shook her head quickly, setting the glass aside. "No, I just…It went down the wrong way, that's all."

Florinda looked unconvinced, eyeing her critically. "Are you all right, baby? You seemed out of it when you came home yesterday."

"I'm just a little tired," Riley lied. "Guess I'm still recovering from my long drive home last week."

Florinda fed her another bite of French toast. "Are you sure it's a good idea for you to be working at the detective agency? You took a leave of absence to get some rest and replenish your spirit. Yes, I realize you had other reasons as well, but you shouldn't neglect your health in the process of pursuing your mission."

"I won't, Grandma. Don't worry."

"I fail to see how working there five days a week is considered part-time," Florinda pointed out.

"My schedule is flexible," Riley explained. "As long as I put in twenty hours a week, I can pretty much come and go as I please. Janie set it up that way so I wouldn't feel chained to a desk all day and could still run my errands and help prepare for your party."

Her grandmother gave her a dubious look. "Twenty hours, huh? Seems more like forty to me. You've been there from eight to five every day. Hope they're paying you overtime."

"Of course," Riley murmured. "But you know it's not about the money, Grandma. Besides, I thought you were all in favor of me working at the agency in order to become better acquainted with Noah."

"I know." Florinda offered her another forkful of food. "How are things going between you two, anyway? Making any progress?"

Depends on your definition of progress, Riley thought grimly. *If the goal is to betray Trevor's memory by making a fool of myself over his best friend, then mission accomplished.*

Aloud she said, "He still refuses to help me, but then, I haven't asked him again since I started working there. I've been too busy, which, I suppose, is what he intended."

Florinda shook her head, smiling. "Young people nowadays. You complicate everything. Matters of the heart should never be so difficult."

Riley paused, a slice of bacon halfway to her mouth. "Matters of whose heart, Grandma?" she asked carefully. "Mine or Noah's?"

Florinda shrugged, rising from the bed. "I was speaking in general terms," she said, but there was something in her cinnamon-colored eyes, a glimmer of intuition—barely discernible, but there just the same.

Riley nibbled on her bacon, her expression thoughtful as she watched her grandmother pick up the folded jeans Riley had left on the bench at the foot of the bed last night. "Grams?"

"Yes, baby?"

Riley hesitated, waiting until Florinda emerged from the walk-in closet after hanging up the jeans. "Did you mean what you said earlier? When you said you'd give me your French toast recipe someday so I could make it for my husband?"

Florinda smiled at her. "Of course I meant it. It's an old family recipe, meant to be passed down from generation to generation. I would have given it to your mother, but she never showed any interest in having it. 'Course, that might have something to do with the fact that your mother hates cooking. Thank God you didn't take after her in *that* regard."

It was the most uncharitable thing Riley had ever heard her grandmother say about the woman her son had married thirty-three years ago, and Riley couldn't help but laugh. It was true. Barbara Kane, a busy obstetrician, detested cooking, and Riley's college professor father wasn't too prolific in the kitchen either. If it weren't for the fact that her grandmother had always lived with them and taken care of all the meals, Riley knew she would have grown up on a steady diet of takeout Chinese and Mexican.

"Not that I don't want the recipe," she said, smiling at her grandmother. "But that's not what I was talking about when I referred to the comment you made earlier. What I meant is…do you really think I'm ever going to get married?"

Florinda's expression softened. "Oh, sweetheart, of course I do."

Riley smiled a little. "Are you just saying that because you're my favorite grandmother and you have to say incredibly nice things to me?"

Florinda chuckled, returning to her spot on the edge of the bed. "You're a strong, beautiful, courageous young woman who has so much to offer. Why *wouldn't* I expect you to get married?"

Riley shrugged, toying with her food. "Maybe I missed my window of opportunity when Trevor died."

"You don't really believe that," Florinda countered quietly. "You're thirty-two years old, baby. You have plenty of time to meet someone special and fall in love again."

"Maybe, but Mr. Right only comes around once in a lifetime."

Her grandmother gazed at her for a long moment. "You're right," she said softly, "he does. Don't ever forget that."

Before Riley could respond, the phone rang.

Florinda stood. "That's probably someone from the senior center calling about tonight's event," she said. "I'll take it out there so you can finish eating in peace."

She returned ten minutes later as Riley was setting aside the empty tray and climbing out of bed. "You have a call," Florinda told her.

Riley's heart thudded. For one panicked moment she wondered if it was Noah, and she stared at the cordless phone in her grandmother's hand as if it were a coiled rattlesnake poised to strike.

But then Florinda announced, "It's Noah's mother."

Riley's eyes widened. "Noah's mother?"

Florinda nodded, the ghost of a smile on her lips as she held out the phone to her granddaughter.

Riley slowly took the phone and watched as her grandmother left the room before answering tentatively, "Hello, Mrs. Roarke."

"Why, hello, Riley," Pamela Roarke's warm, familiar voice greeted her. "I hope I didn't disturb you?"

"Not at all. I've been up for hours." *Fantasizing about your son.* "I'm sorry. You're Mrs. Hubbard now, aren't you? I heard about your beautiful wedding. Congratulations."

"Thank you, Riley. I appreciate that. When I saw your grandmother at the senior center yesterday, she told me you were back in town and working at the detective agency. Now I'm going to strangle those sons of mine for not telling me last week."

Riley chuckled. "It's all right."

"No, it is *not* all right. I would have called you sooner to welcome you back and invite you over for Sunday brunch. Are you free tomorrow afternoon?"

Riley hesitated. "Tomorrow?"

"Yes. Are you free?"

Sunday brunch at the Roarke household had been a longstanding tradition when Noah and his siblings were growing up. Trevor, who'd lived on the same block, had often spoken fondly of his memories of attending church with Noah's family and joining them for a lavish meal afterward.

"Mama Roarke could throw down," he'd laughed, playfully smacking his lips. "Ham, barbecue ribs, fried chicken, corn bread, collard greens, honey rolls—you name it, Mama Roarke made it. Why do you think I've stayed friends with Noah all these years?" he'd teased, light green eyes twinkling with mischief because he knew Noah, somewhere across the room, could hear him.

Although Trevor and Noah had both been raised by single parents, the similarities ended there. For while Pamela Roarke, widowed early in her marriage, had done everything in her power to provide for her three children and create a warm, loving environment, Trevor's mother had been young and irresponsible, changing jobs as frequently as she changed boyfriends. Trevor had never known his real father, and not one of the men his mother brought home could ever be considered father figures. The Roarkes had adopted the lonely, neglected ten-year-old into their own family, and he'd never forgotten that. Noah had been the brother he never had, and Pamela Roarke his surrogate mother.

"Riley? Are you there?"

Riley blinked, snapping out of her reverie. "I'm sorry, Mrs. Roar—I mean, Hubbard." She grinned sheepishly. "I'm going to have to get used to your new last name."

Pamela chuckled softly. "That's all right. I understand. Tell you what. Why don't you just call me Mama Pam? You've always been like a daughter to me, anyway."

Riley smiled, touched by the warm, heartfelt sentiment. "Thank you, Mama Pam. I really appreciate that."

"So you'll come to brunch tomorrow?"

"Yes, I'd like that very much." She couldn't very well refuse, could she?

"Wonderful. You and Noah can meet us at the house after church, or you're more than welcome to join us for the eight-o'clock service, if you're not already going to church with your grandmother."

Riley heard nothing else after the mention of Noah. "Did you say Noah and I can meet you…?"

"Yes. I thought he could pick you up since he knows where the new house is." Pamela paused for a moment. "Or I could give you directions, if you'd prefer to drive yourself."

"That'd be better," Riley said quickly, pulling out a notepad from the top nightstand drawer.

As she jotted down the directions, images of kissing Noah rewound in her mind, bringing heat to her face. She hurried off the phone with Pamela Hubbard, half-afraid the woman would somehow discern Riley's lustful thoughts about her son.

That's when it occurred to her what a quandary she faced. The less time she spent alone with Noah, the less likely she'd be to cross the line. On the other hand, in order to get what she needed from him, she had to spend time with him—and the more, the better.

She tapped the pen against her lips. Somehow she'd have to ignore the fact that she was wildly attracted to him, that he was without question one of the sexiest men she'd ever known. She'd have to get over that bone-melting sensation she experienced every time their fingers brushed or he looked at her a certain way. And God help her, she'd have to stop thinking about that scorching, forbidden kiss they'd shared.

There wasn't going to be an encore performance. She wouldn't allow it. What was the phrase she'd used on Noah? Impervious to temptation? That was it. No matter how attractive she found him, she would have to become impervious to temptation. She'd returned home for one purpose and one purpose only. Nothing and no one could interfere with that.

It had to be this way.

The alternative was too unsettling. For more reasons than one.

In San Antonio, whenever a police officer was killed in the line of duty or caused death or injury to someone else, an Officer Involved Shooting Team was assembled to investigate the incident. The team usually consisted of the Homicide Unit lieutenant, three sergeants, and at least six detectives.

On a Saturday afternoon when he should have been catching up on paperwork, mowing his lawn, or tending to any number of other tasks, Noah found himself seated in the living room of retired sergeant Jerry Burns, who'd served on the OIST that handled Trevor's shooting.

Burns, a fifty-two-year-old man with thinning gray hair, pale blue eyes, and the telltale beginnings of a paunch, had been forced into early retirement after injuring his back on the job last year. But anyone who knew Jerry Burns knew he wasn't enjoying the life of a retired cop. Instead of collecting disability checks, he'd much rather be supervising a team of overworked, underpaid homicide detectives, a responsibility he'd enjoyed for fifteen years with the SAPD. Although Noah had been assigned to a different detail within the Homicide Unit, he'd always had a tremendous amount of respect for Jerry Burns. Unlike the authoritarian sergeant Noah had once reported to, Burns gave his detectives room to breathe, providing a buffer against the captain and those above Burns in the chain of command. Time and again, he'd proven to be trustworthy and discreet. For that reason, Noah knew he'd never have to worry about Burns telling anyone about his inquiries into Trevor's death.

When Noah called him that afternoon, Burns had been so eager for contact with someone from his former life that he'd agreed to Noah's visit without asking too many questions.

Now, however, after they'd exhausted talk of the weather, the NBA playoffs, and updates on members of the Sunday Night Pool Sharks, Burns chuckled dryly. "Not that I'm complaining, Roarke, but I know you didn't drive all the way out here to drink my good beer and shoot the breeze. What's on your mind—or do I even need to ask?"

Noah managed a wry smile. "Guess it's that obvious, huh?"

Burns nodded. "You're here to ask more questions about the shooting," he said resignedly.

Noah inclined his head. *This has nothing to do with what happened yesterday,* he told himself firmly. *Just because you kissed Riley doesn't mean you now share her belief that Trevor may have caused his own death.*

Burns sighed. "I don't know what else I can tell you, Roarke. Because you were Trevor's best friend and former partner on the force, we gave you unrestricted access to all our files—the crime scene report, the autopsy results, the findings from the OIST investigation. You went through everything with a fine-tooth comb and interviewed everyone from witnesses at the scene to convicts Trevor had sent to jail within the past year. When it was all said and done, you learned nothing more than what you'd already been told. That Trevor was shot and killed by a robbery suspect fleeing arrest."

"I know." Noah pushed out a long, deep breath. "I just can't help but wonder if we missed something."

"Like what?"

"I don't know," Noah said honestly.

In the aftermath of Trevor's senseless death, Noah had investigated the shooting as thoroughly as the officers assigned to the case. It had never once occurred to him that Trevor may have been involved in something shady that got him killed. He'd had no reason to suspect such a thing—until Riley returned with her awful suspicions. Suddenly he'd found himself poring through the old case files again, dredging up painful memories he'd sooner forget.

Burns was watching him sympathetically. "You'd been off the force for over a year when Trevor was killed. I know you felt out of the loop, which was why I made every effort to keep you informed and involved in the investigation—without Chief Pittman's knowledge, of course. You know he would've nailed our hides to the wall if he ever found out we'd given you unlimited access to our files, former cop or not."

Noah nodded. "I know, and I appreciate what you did for me."

"But you still have questions." Burns paused. "Or does someone else?"

Noah tensed. "What do you mean?"

Those pale blue eyes narrowed thoughtfully on his face. "I heard through the grapevine that Riley Kane is back in town."

"She is. And before you ask, she didn't put me up to this, Jerry. I'm here on my own." Which was true. Riley didn't know he'd decided to pay a visit to the retired sergeant. As far as Noah was concerned, she would never find out, because he didn't expect to learn anything new that would substantiate her fears and suspicions.

"Well, what do you want to know, Roarke? If I remember correctly, you had the crime scene report memorized by the time we were finished with our investigation. At 9:35 a.m. on January 16, Trevor responded to a radio call about a robbery in progress at the E-Z Mart convenience store on the south side. When he entered the store, the suspect was wearing a stocking mask and wielding a .38. There were only three other occupants inside the building, including the cashier. When Trevor ordered the suspect to drop his weapon, the perp escaped through a rear exit leading into an alley. Trevor pursued him. Witnesses in the store reported hearing the exchange of gunfire for at least thirty seconds. By the time other responding officers arrived on the scene, Trevor was down, and the suspect had fled. Ballistics matched the slug found in Trevor's body to the .38 belonging to Conrad Weiss." Burns paused, his mouth thinned to a grim line. "Did I miss anything?"

Noah shook his head, frowning. "Something that's always bothered me…Trevor never radioed for backup."

"No, he didn't." Burns scowled. "His failure to follow protocol probably cost him his damn life. But you know as well as I do that Simmons was hotheaded that way. If there was a chance for him to play the hero, he jumped at it."

It was true. For as long as Noah could remember, Trevor had always possessed a misguided belief in his own immortality. In school he'd picked fights with bullies and kids that were much bigger than he was, just for the hell of it. And no matter how many times he got the crap beat out of him, nothing had deterred him. Growing up, the majority of the fights Noah had gotten into came as a result of Trevor's antics.

Yeah, he knew better than anyone what a hothead Trevor Simmons had been.

They couldn't have known that it would someday cost him his life.

"In the days and weeks leading up to the shooting," Noah asked, "did you notice any changes in Trevor's behavior?"

"No." Burns frowned. "We went over all this during the investigation, Roarke. Nothing's changed, as far as I know. There've been no new developments that would warrant reopening a closed case. What happened to Trevor was an unfortunate tragedy. But we have no reason to believe there was anything more to it than an armed robber shooting an officer in the course of resisting arrest. My advice to you—and to Miss Kane—is to move on with your lives, and let Trevor rest in peace."

Noah scrubbed a hand over his face and pushed out a deep breath. Burns was right, of course. He'd pretty much told Riley the same thing. It was time for them—for *her*—to move on with her life, as he'd already done. Hadn't he?

He gave Burns a rueful smile. "I don't suppose you could spare a little more of your time to walk me through all the files and reports again? They're in a box in my truck outside."

Burns stared at him for a prolonged moment, then huffed out a resigned sigh. "What the hell? My wife won't be back from her sister's until this evening anyway. But you owe me big time, Roarke. And if I ever need the services of a private investigator, I expect some sort of discount from you."

Noah grinned, rising from the sofa. "Anything for you, sergeant."

Hell, if Jerry Burns could help Noah put to rest any lingering questions about Trevor's death, Noah would be indebted to him for life.

Chapter 9

"You must be Riley Kane."

Riley smiled at the tall, handsome, gray-haired gentleman who greeted her at the front door of Pamela Hubbard's home the following afternoon. "Yes, I am. It's a pleasure to meet you, Mr. Hubbard."

Warm brown eyes crinkled at the corners in a welcoming smile. "The pleasure's mine, young lady. I've heard so much about you."

"Good things, I hope?"

Lionel Hubbard laughed, a quiet, gravelly sound that rumbled up from his chest. "Of course, of course. Come on in. Everyone's been waiting for you."

Everyone? Riley thought nervously as she stepped into the cool interior of the large single-story house. She had only a glimpse of a spacious, elegantly furnished living room off to her left before the rapid approach of footsteps on ceramic tile drew her attention.

"I'm so glad you could make it," Pamela Hubbard greeted her, beaming a smile of such genuine warmth that Riley wondered what she'd ever done to deserve this woman's incredible generosity.

She smiled as Pamela wrapped her in a tight, fragrant embrace. "Thank you for inviting me."

"You don't have to thank me," Pamela said, drawing away to grasp both of Riley's hands. "Like I told you on the phone, I would have called you last week if I'd known you were back home. Don't think I didn't give those boys an earful the first chance I got."

At sixty-two years old and standing at five-two, Pamela Hubbard was a petite woman with smooth, firm skin the color of mocha and gentle hazel eyes. Her silver hair was styled the same way Riley remembered, in short, sophisticated layers that accentuated her fine-boned features. She wore a pleated navy-blue skirt and cream silk blouse beneath a red apron with World's Greatest, Bestest Grandma stenciled in white letters across the front.

"You're looking very well," Pamela said, holding Riley at arm's length for a moment as she gave her a once-over. She nodded in approval at the pale yellow skirt and jacket Riley wore with a pair of strappy high-heeled sandals. "Just as pretty as a picture, isn't she, Lion?"

Her husband smiled at Riley. "You betcha."

"Did you go to church with your grandmother this morning?" Pamela inquired.

Riley nodded and smiled. "She wanted to show me off to all her friends."

Pamela laughed. "Of course. She couldn't stop bragging about you last night at the fund-raiser dance. She's going to have everyone at the senior center trying to marry you off to their eligible grandsons. Oh, has she shown you the pictures yet? Florinda was the belle of the ball. She said you helped her pick out that beautiful gown she was wearing. I told her you have excellent taste."

"Speaking of taste," Lionel Hubbard interjected good-naturedly, rubbing his stomach, "when are we going to eat, woman? My mouth has been watering ever since you took that glazed ham out of the oven."

"Oh, go on with you," Pamela laughingly chided.

Riley couldn't help but smile, seeing the tender look that passed between them.

"We can eat as soon as the rolls are ready," Pamela said briskly. "I was waiting for Riley to arrive before I stuck 'em in the oven. Riley, won't you be a dear and go fetch the others from outside? They need to get washed up before they step anywhere near my dinner table. Go right through those French doors to reach the backyard," she instructed, pointing down a wide expanse of corridor that led to what appeared to be a family room.

Riley obeyed without question, though her palms had grown moist at the prospect of seeing Noah again.

She wondered how he felt about his mother inviting her over for Sunday brunch. Would he resent her for showing up? Would he treat her like an intruder, an unwelcome guest at a sacred family gathering?

When he looked at her, would his gaze reflect the memory of their kiss?

As she stepped through the French doors onto the wide wooden deck, the first thing she noticed was an enormous yard framed by ancient cypress trees, manicured shrubs, and lush garden beds teeming with a colorful mélange of flowers that perfumed the air.

The sounds of male laughter, mingled with the slap of a basketball against pavement, reached her ears. Curious, she walked across the deck, sidestepping a set of wrought-iron patio furniture, and peered around the side of the house into a small courtyard. There, engaged in a rough game of thirty-three, were Noah, Kenneth and a young caramel-skinned boy who could only be Kenneth Junior—or KJ, as his family called him. All three of them were shirtless under the hot summer sun, but there was only one bare chest that made Riley's mouth run dry. Noah's impossibly broad shoulders and wide chest planed with hard, sinewy muscle evoked images of a Greco-Roman bronze statue. A light sheen of sweat clung to his glorious brown skin and made Riley wonder what it would be like to touch him, to press her hand against the solid warmth of his bicep and feel the steady beat of his heart beneath her palm.

Unable to look away, she watched as he lowered

one shoulder, drove past Kenneth and slammed the basketball through the hoop. The metal rim vibrated with the force of the dunk, drawing loud, protesting groans from his brother and nephew. Noah grinned cockily, his teeth flashing strong and white in his handsome face as he reached out to ruffle KJ's curly hair.

"Still think you and your old man can beat me?" he teased, his voice deeper and huskier from physical exertion. Knees weakening, Riley found herself leaning a little too heavily against the deck railing.

Noah glanced up then, meeting her eyes, and Riley's breath caught sharply in her throat. How had she missed the power of those deep, mesmerizing eyes five years ago she wondered, not for the first time.

"Hey Riley!" a voice called out cheerfully.

Riley straightened from the railing and turned around to watch Janie emerge from a gazebo across the yard with a miniature version of herself in tow, both dressed in their Sunday best. Eight-year-old Lourdes Roarke's dark, glossy hair was parted down the center and hung to her tiny waist.

Riley waved at the pair as they approached.

"When'd you get here?" Janie asked, leaning down to press a kiss to Riley's cheek.

"A few minutes ago." Riley smiled at the young, pretty girl standing beside her mother. "Hi, Lourdes. Do you remember me?"

"Of course," Lourdes responded with an air of child-like impatience. "You're Uncle Trevor's girlfriend."

Riley's smile softened. "That's right. You've gotten so tall—you and your brother."

The girl rolled her dark eyes heavenward. "That's what every grown-up says."

Janie pinched her daughter on the arm. "Don't be rude, *mija.*"

"Sorry," Lourdes mumbled sulkily, rubbing her sore arm.

Riley grinned ruefully. "You were right. I used to think the same thing at your age."

The girl eyed her suspiciously. "Are you here to see my uncle Noah?"

"Lourdes!"

"Does someone need a nap already?" came Noah's amused drawl.

Riley turned as he, Kenneth, and KJ stepped onto the deck, tugging on white shirts over their suit pants. She watched as Noah sauntered over to his niece and tweaked her pert nose. She beamed with pleasure, rewarding him with an adoring smile.

Janie wrinkled her nose at the newcomers. "You guys are all sweaty. Mama's gonna kill you—you know she told you not to play basketball before lunch."

Kenneth laughed. "She says that every week, baby. When do we ever listen? Hey girl," he said warmly to Riley. "Glad you could make it."

"Thanks, Kenneth. You know I couldn't say no to your mother. How's it going, KJ?"

Kenneth's son, who had a head full of curly, light brown hair and thick-lashed amber eyes, looked nothing like his fraternal twin sister. Their personalities were also as different as night and day.

KJ gave Riley a bright, eager smile. "Hi, Miss Riley. You gonna play basketball with us later, like you used to?"

Riley chuckled. "I don't think so, handsome. I'm not exactly dressed for it."

He looked her over and groaned with disappointment. "Aw, man, why do girls always have to wear skirts to church?"

Winking at Riley, Kenneth clapped a hand to his son's shoulder. "Because God knew we'd need more than a good sermon to be lured to the house of worship. Some of us, anyway," he hastened to add at Janie's narrow-eyed look.

Riley grinned at him. "Well, your mother sent me out here to tell you fellas to wash up before you're allowed anywhere near her dinner table. So, unless you want me to finish all that wonderful food by myself…"

She trailed off, her grin widening as Kenneth and KJ exchanged quick glances, then made a beeline for the French doors.

Noah followed more slowly, pausing for a moment to look back at her. Once again she was snared by his piercing ebony eyes. Air stalled in her lungs as he gazed at her for what seemed an eternity but was probably no longer than a few seconds.

Only when he turned and continued into the house did she let out a slow, shaky breath.

It was going to be a long afternoon.

Hell, it was going to be a long *summer*.

As she did every week, Pamela Hubbard had pulled out all the stops for Sunday brunch. A honey-glazed ham fit to feed a small army was served with baked chicken, sweet-and-sour meatballs, candied yams, green beans and cabbage, potato salad, deviled eggs, and flaky honey rolls that melted in Riley's mouth after the first bite.

By accident or design, she wound up seated next to Noah at the long mahogany table, while Kenneth and Janie sat across from them, and Pamela and her husband claimed opposite ends of the table. Lourdes insisted on sitting on the other side of Noah, determined to ensure that her beloved uncle's attention would not be divided between her and Riley.

"This is an extra special occasion for our family today," Pamela intoned with a glance around the table that settled warmly on Riley. "We're so glad to have you back home. I, for one, am very anxious to hear what you've been doing with yourself for the past three years."

"Working hard," Riley answered with a smile. "The paper keeps me pretty busy."

"Are you still covering the crime beat?"

Riley shook her head. "Education." After Trevor's death, she'd needed a long break from stories about fires, drug arrests, beatings and homicides. Attending reading fairs at local elementary schools and re-

porting on vouchers and national literacy standards
had provided a welcome, if sometimes frustrating,
change of pace.

Pamela offered an understanding smile. "I think
Noah's read some of your articles. He has a subscrip-
tion to the *Washington Post,* isn't that right, baby?"

Riley looked at him in surprise. "You do?"

Noah lifted one shoulder in an impassive shrug.
"I also subscribe to the *New York Times,*" he said
pointedly.

"Oh." Riley tried her best not to sound deflated.

"That said," he added after another moment, "I
have read some of your articles. You're a great writer,
Riley. You've always been. But I don't need to tell
you that."

She warmed with pleasure at his words. "No," she
agreed, striving for nonchalance, "but it's always
nice to hear."

"I'm sure you hear it all the time," he said sardonically.

"First I've ever heard it from you, though."

"Are you saying I've never complimented your
writing?"

Their gazes locked for several moments. Gradually
Riley became aware of six pairs of eyes focused on
them. A slow flush crawled up her neck and spread
across her cheeks.

Clearing her throat self-consciously, she reached
for her glass of chilled wine as Noah glanced away,
becoming absorbed in his food.

Silence descended upon the table for a moment, and then Janie began conversationally, "So, Mama, you never did tell us how the ball went last night?"

"It was wonderful," Pamela said with feeling. "Aside from the fact that Lion and I had the time of our lives dancing the night away, we also raised a substantial amount of money for the senior center. Thanks to everyone at this table for your generous donations. And speaking of that," she added, her hazel eyes twinkling with excitement, "Caleb's father also gave out of the abundance of his heart—*and* wallet—by writing us a check for one hundred thousand dollars."

There were surprised exclamations around the table. KJ stared up at his grandmother in wide-eyed fascination. "That's a lot of money, isn't it, Grandma?"

She smiled indulgently, reaching over to squeeze his hand. "You bet it is, sweetheart. More than enough to buy brand-new computers and educational supplies for the senior center."

Kenneth grinned, shaking his head from side to side. "Can't say I'm surprised, not after seeing how much Crandall spent on Caleb and Daniela's wedding. *Cha-ching.*"

"That reminds me," Pamela said. "When we've finished eating, Riley can look at the wedding photos. And don't let me forget to send you home with a plate for your grandmother. She told me she couldn't make it this afternoon because she had rehearsal for an upcoming salsa tournament she's competing in."

Janie stared across the table at Riley, her mouth agape. "Your grandmother's going to be competing in a *salsa* tournament?"

Riley nodded with a wry grin. "I know. I could hardly believe it myself when she told me."

Janie gave a whoop of unabashed delight. "Way to go, Grandma! Be sure to let me know when the competition will be held. I'd love to be there."

"She'd like that very much," Riley said.

"*I'm* going to be performing in a ballet recital," Lourdes announced, not to be outdone by a seventy-four-year-old woman who wasn't even present to bask in the others' admiration.

Everyone at the table offered their hearty congratulations—except for KJ, who merely rolled his eyes at his preening sister.

With the meal under way, the conversation segued from Lourdes's ballet recital and KJ's adventures at space camp—because it was only fair to let him share in the spotlight—to talk of politics. When Lionel Hubbard asked Riley, as an education reporter, to share her opinion of the No Child Left Behind initiative, she found herself launching into a passionate explanation of why she felt the federal program didn't benefit disadvantaged schoolchildren, as it purported. Her views resonated with everyone around the table and fueled a spirited discussion that lasted nearly an hour.

More than once throughout the meal, she'd glanced up to find Noah's subtly searching gaze on her. She didn't know how to interpret the expression on his face, other than to say he seemed mildly…fascinated. But she knew better. Despite the kiss they had shared, Noah Roarke was no more interested in her than she was in him. She'd consider it a feat if, by the end of the summer, they at least parted on speaking terms.

After devouring Pamela's scrumptious, award-winning peach cobbler for dessert, the group adjourned to the cozily furnished family room to pore over wedding albums. While Pamela had been understated elegance in a wine-colored sheath dress, Daniela Roarke had been a breathtakingly beautiful bride in a strapless mermaid gown of pure ivory silk that accentuated her lush curves. Her groom was equally arresting in a black Christian Dior tuxedo that made him look like he'd stepped off the cover of *GQ*. In every photo, the love and adulation each couple felt for their partner shone in their eyes and in the tender smiles they shared as they fed cake to each other or came together for the first dance.

As Riley sat and listened to the family's recollections of the two joyous occasions, she couldn't help but think of the ceremony she'd been deprived of.

She had never been the type of woman who'd dreamed of being swept off her feet by Prince Charming and whisked away to an ivory castle tucked deep in the forest. Because her parents had modeled a healthy, happy marriage, it was only natural that she'd grown up with the expectation of one day finding and settling down with her own soul mate. When she met Trevor at a law enforcement convention in Houston, it wasn't love at first sight. In fact, she'd been convinced that the cocky, good-looking cop who'd sauntered up to her during a session break wasn't her type. At six-two, light skinned with pale green eyes, dark wavy hair, and a square-jawed face made for police recruitment posters, Trevor Simmons was fine, and he knew it. But he'd also been sweet and charming, and persistent as hell. Before Riley knew it, she was having dinner with him at a local jazz club. When the conference ended a few days later and Trevor returned to San Antonio, he called her up and asked her out on another date—this time over the phone. It had been fun and surprisingly romantic to sit at a linen-covered table on the rooftop terrace of her downtown loft and sip imported wine while Trevor did the same miles away. By the time the call ended, they'd practically advanced to phone sex; when Trevor drove up to Houston the following weekend, they did the real thing. One year later, they were engaged.

Although Trevor could be moody and a little too possessive at times, she'd loved him unconditionally. She'd wanted to marry him, bear his children and give them the warm, nurturing home their father had never experienced in his own childhood.

But it wasn't meant to be.

And now, three years after the tragedy that had snatched Trevor from her life, she wondered if she'd ever allow herself to be that vulnerable again.

Could she let down her guard and give herself permission to fall in love again?

An hour later, she was still preoccupied with these questions as she left the Hubbard house and started home.

Deep in thought, it was several moments before she registered the telltale thumping noise of a flat tire. Swearing under her breath, she glanced in the rearview mirror to make sure no other motorists were behind her before she pulled off to the shoulder of the two-lane country road.

Of all the rotten luck, she mentally groused, peeling off her suit jacket and tossing it across the passenger seat in disgust.

Since arriving in town last week, she'd been meaning to take her car in for servicing, which she should have done before leaving D.C. But, as had been the case when she fled San Antonio three years ago, she'd been too impatient to start on her journey to worry about anything else.

As she stepped from the Avalon to inspect the flat tire, a shiny black Yukon came barreling down the road. Riley felt a combination of relief and embarrassment when she recognized the driver.

Noah slowed the truck and pulled in behind her car, then climbed out.

"Hi," Riley said, feeling awkward as he started toward her, slowly removing his mirrored sunglasses and tucking them into the front pocket of his shirt.

"Bet you didn't expect to run into me again until tomorrow morning," she said inanely, then pointed to the rear left tire. "I've got a flat."

"So I see," Noah murmured, dropping to his haunches to examine the tire. After a moment, he said, "Looks like you had a slow leak. There's a nail embedded inside."

"Really?"

"Yeah, really." He ran his hand up and down the smooth surface of the tire. "The tread's worn to nil. When was the last time you had your tires rotated?"

"Uh, it's been a while," Riley evaded.

"How long is 'a while'?"

She bit her lip. "A couple of years."

He scowled. "You're supposed to rotate your tires every six-thousand to eight-thousand miles."

She bristled. "I've been busy. Vehicle maintenance hasn't exactly been at the top of my list of priorities."

"Obviously," he growled. "You drove all the way from Washington, D.C. on bald tires. So not only were you sleep deprived, you could have gotten stranded out in the middle of nowhere. Do you have a spare?"

"In the trunk," she snapped, incensed by his lecturing. "Look, I'm not some dumb, helpless female, Noah. I know how to change a tire, and I'm perfectly capable of doing so."

Abruptly she knelt beside him, and had an instant flashback to the first time they'd met, when they'd found themselves huddled beside each other as they inspected the fender of his vehicle. At the time, she'd been too worried about the fact that she'd just rear-ended a cop to notice anything else...such as the heat from his body, or the clean, subtle scent of his cologne, or the pull of his black pants over his hard, muscular thighs...things she noticed now with intoxicating clarity.

When their eyes met, she realized Noah was remembering that long-ago encounter as well.

She swallowed with difficulty. "If you'd kindly step aside," she said, her voice husky with awareness, "I can change the tire myself and be on my way."

"Damn it, Riley," Noah murmured without any real rancor. "I'll change the tire. Pop the trunk so I can get the spare."

"I said I can do it myself."

He eyed her formfitting skirt and heels. "You're not dressed for it."

"Neither are you," she shot back.

He arched a brow. "I played basketball in this, remember? Pop the trunk."

"No, I'll—"

A warm, callused hand was clamped gently over her mouth. Noah leaned close, those magnificent onyx eyes boring into hers. "Pop the damn trunk," he said, a low, silky command.

Nodding wordlessly, Riley stood on legs that trembled, opened the car door and pulled the lever to release the trunk hood.

Noah got to his feet, rolled up his shirtsleeves and

lifted out the spare tire, jack and tire iron from the trunk of the car.

In no time at all he'd jacked up the Avalon, removed the flat tire, and gone to work installing the spare.

Riley propped a hip against the side of the car and forced herself to watch other passing vehicles instead of Noah. Because up until that moment, she'd never known just how incredibly sexy a man could look changing a tire. She'd seen it done on commercials and in movies, of course, but nothing compared to the reality. Or maybe what got her juices flowing was the sight of *this* particular man on his knees, his tie tugged loose, a smudge of grease on his rugged jaw, his powerful forearms flexing as he tightened the wheel lugs.

Either way, by the time he finished and was back on his feet, Riley was as hot and bothered as if *she* had done all the hard work.

"Thanks," she murmured, passing him a small clean towel from the trunk. "I couldn't have done it that fast or easily. I appreciate your help."

Noah inclined his head, wiping his soiled hands. "The pressure in the spare is low," he told her, "which means you can't ride on it very long. I'm going to follow you to the nearest auto center to get new tires."

Riley panicked. "Oh, that won't be necessary," she said quickly. Another minute around him and she'd be jumping his damn bones. "I'll take care of it sometime this week."

He scowled darkly. "Did you hear what I just said?

You can't ride on the doughnut for very long—the air pressure's too low."

"I heard you. I just—I can't—" Flustered, she blurted out, "I can't do this today."

"Yes, you can," Noah said in a low voice that brooked no argument. "And you will."

Without another word, he turned on his heel, strode back to his truck and climbed inside, leaving Riley no choice but to follow suit.

She cursed his high-handedness all the way to the Sears automotive center. Pulling into an empty parking space beside him, she buzzed down the automatic window and called out, "For all you know, Noah Roarke, I might be on a very tight budget right now. Maybe I can't afford to buy *four* new tires at this time!"

He was already climbing out of his truck and striding purposefully toward the building. By the time Riley realized what he was doing and had struggled out of her seat belt and hurried after him, he'd already paid for the tires and arranged for them to be installed.

She glared at him as he walked away from the service counter. "I *had* money," she said through gritted teeth, not caring that she sounded like an ingrate or that other customers were staring at her. "I don't need your charity, and I *don't* appreciate being man-handled."

"You can thank me later," Noah drawled, holding the door open for her as they stepped back outside. "In the meantime, let's pull your car around so they can get started on it."

Chapter 10

Noah liked it when Riley was angry.

He hadn't realized it until that very moment, as she sat ramrod straight in the passenger seat of his Yukon, her arms folded tightly across her chest and her long legs crossed, and stared straight ahead. If it were biologically possible, he would have sworn he saw steam pouring from her pretty little ears.

Oh, yeah, he definitely liked it when she was angry.

He could deal with her anger, however volatile it might be. What he *couldn't* deal with was Riley's sorrow, the tears she'd bravely tried to hold back at Trevor's funeral because she'd wanted to be strong for his mother. And for Noah.

On that awful January day, as he stood before a

chapel filled to overflowing with Trevor's friends, re-
latives and comrades who'd come to pay their last
respects, Noah was immobile with grief. He couldn't
think, couldn't drag enough air into his lungs. Everything was a blur, and he'd watched himself deliver
the eulogy as if he were having an out-of-body experience. In the middle of speaking, he'd looked out
into the sea of mourners and seen Riley. She'd been
staring at him with rapt absorption, hanging on to his
every word as if each utterance about Trevor was a
lifeline. When their eyes met, her chin went up a
proud notch, but there was a faint tremble to her lips
that betrayed her effort to hold it all together. And
then, a single tear had escaped and rolled down her
face. The sight of that one teardrop had cut through
him like shards of jagged glass. He felt as if his soul
had been ripped from his body. Trevor was gone,
and there was nothing he could do about it, nothing
he could do to ease Riley's pain or lessen the crush-
ing despair she felt.

It had taken a monumental act of willpower to remain standing at the podium, to continue addressing
the mourners when all he wanted to do was go to
Riley, hold her in his arms and tell her everything
would be all right, even if he didn't really believe it.
He'd wanted to comfort her, protect her, be her Rock
of Gibraltar.

But when the moment of truth arrived, he'd
failed her.

At a time when she needed him most, he'd failed

her. Because he was weak, and selfish. Because even in those dark days leading up to the funeral, he'd realized he still wanted her. His grief had done nothing to diminish his feelings for her. His breath still caught in his throat whenever she walked into a room, his body still tightened when she brushed past him, and his heart still ached from the pain of unrequited love.

He despised himself for coveting his best friend's fiancée, even as Trevor's cold, lifeless body lay on a steel gurney in the morgue. What kind of person was he he'd wondered in self-loathing, calling himself everything but a child of God.

Not only could he *not* handle a friendship with Riley, he didn't *deserve* one. So his punishment had been to stay away from her—even more than he already did.

But she'd needed his friendship and support, and he'd let her down. For weeks after the funeral, he could see the confusion in her eyes, the disappointment, the sense of betrayal.

No doubt about it. He definitely preferred Riley's anger over her sorrow.

So he couldn't understand or explain, for the life of him, what came out of his mouth next.

"You would have been a beautiful bride," he said softly, the words escaping before he knew they'd even formed.

Riley turned her head slowly to look at him. For several long moments she just stared at him in stunned silence. And then, to his horror, tears welled up in those deep, chocolate eyes.

Damn! Now why had he gone and said something like that?

Noah opened his mouth, only to be silenced when she lifted a trembling hand. "That was so unfair," she whispered huskily.

"I'm sorry," he said. "I didn't mean to upset you."

"I'm already upset," she grumbled.

"I know. I didn't mean to upset you more. I was just thinking about my mother and sister's weddings, and how that must have been difficult for you to look at all those pictures. But you were genuinely happy for them, I could see it in your eyes." He paused, his throat constricting as he glanced out the window for a moment. "I just wanted you to know that I think you would've made a beautiful bride, Riley," he finished gruffly. "A damned beautiful bride."

When he ventured another glance at her, her face was averted to the passenger window. Her eyes were closed, but he could see silent, mournful tears slipping down her face.

His heart wrenched in half, and he immediately felt like an ogre. The one thing he'd been trying to avoid for years—watching her cry—he'd made happen with one careless slip of the tongue.

That's why you should always think before you speak, Roarke.

And therein lies the problem, he mused grimly. He *had* been having those thoughts about Riley ever since leaving his mother's house, which was why the remark had tumbled so freely from his mouth in an unguarded moment.

"I'm sorry," he murmured a second time.

"Don't be," Riley surprised him by saying. She turned her head to look at him, a soft, winsome smile trembling on her full lips. "I think that's the nicest thing you've ever said to me, Noah."

The combination of her words, the shining gratitude in her eyes, and that bewitching smile hit him squarely in the chest. In that moment, he would have done anything she asked him to. *Anything.*

He reached behind him and fumbled for a clean handkerchief from the breast pocket of his suit jacket, which was draped across the back of his seat. Wordlessly, he passed the handkerchief to her.

"Thank you," she murmured, dabbing at her eyes and cheeks.

He didn't say anything else, just stared out the window at the steady flow of customers coming to and leaving the automotive center. The late-afternoon sunlight slanted through the windshield, heating the leather interior of the truck. He reached over and adjusted the air conditioner to make it a little cooler.

After a few more moments, Riley drew in a deep, shuddering breath and quietly exhaled, stirring the silky fringe of her bangs. "I'm sorry I was so peevish about the whole tire thing," she said sheepishly. "If you hadn't come along when you did, I probably would've been stranded there for a long time, either waiting for roadside assistance or trying to fix the flat myself. I appreciate all of your help, even if I didn't act like it."

"You're welcome," Noah said simply.

She focused thoughtfully on his face. "I don't think I ever realized what a bully you can be," she said with a trace of lingering reproach. "You *did* manhandle me, Noah."

He chuckled ruefully. "Sorry. Force of habit. Just ask my sister, Daniela."

Riley's lips curved in a sardonic grin. "Well, then, I guess it's lucky for her that she's finally out from under your thumb."

"Maybe, but Caleb's just as bad."

Riley gave a mock shudder. "God save us all from chivalrous, overprotective men."

As they exchanged teasing smiles, it occurred to Noah that this was probably the first pleasant conversation they'd had in years. It felt good. Too good.

"I had a really wonderful time this afternoon," Riley said softly. "Your family is so warm and accepting. Trevor always spoke of that, of how comfortable and at home they made him feel. That's how I felt today."

"I'm glad to hear that." Noah allowed his eyes to roam across her features, lingering on classically thick eyebrows, dark, almond-shaped eyes that tilted exotically at the corners, high cheekbones, and an exquisitely lush mouth. It was a face that had haunted his dreams and too many waking thoughts for the past five years. A face he'd never forget for as long as he lived.

"My family really likes you," he heard himself telling her. "Especially my mother." It was true. Almost from the moment Trevor had introduced the two women to each other, his mother had taken an instant liking to Riley, responding to her in a way she'd never done with any girlfriend Noah had ever brought home. Even Janie had had to work hard to earn a place in Pamela's heart. But with Riley it was different. It was like she'd been given free admission.

Riley smiled warmly. "Your mother is an absolute angel. And I really like Mr. Hubbard. I can tell how much they love each other."

"Yeah, it's pretty special," Noah agreed. "They'd attended the same church for several years, but didn't really become friends until sometime last year." He chuckled. "Daniela thinks Mom always had a secret crush on Deacon Hubbard but was too shy to do anything about it. And then one day he offered to drive her to Houston to visit her sister, and she found out *he'd* been interested in her for years."

Riley sighed, laying one hand over her heart. "How incredibly romantic."

Noah slanted her a look. "You think so?"

She nodded vigorously. "Are you kidding? I love hearing stories like that. Secret longing, unrequited love. Gets me every time." She issued another long, deep sigh, then grinned playfully at him. "It's a woman thing. You wouldn't understand."

Noah swallowed hard, his heart knocking against his rib cage. *If only she knew.*

Riley leaned her head back on the headrest, a gentle, reminiscent smile on her face. "Trevor understood that about me, the fact that beneath my tough-girl, hard-nosed-reporter facade, I'm a sucker for romance. He may have understood a little too well. Whenever we got into an argument, he'd let me cool off for a day or two, and then he'd call me. There was this little thing we used to do over the phone— we called it our 'virtual date.' Anyway," she said with a soft laugh, "it always worked like a charm for him. Smart man, silly me."

Noah forced himself to concentrate on the Herculean task of breathing, not on what Riley was telling him. He already knew all about the so-called virtual dates she and Trevor had shared. Trevor had bragged about them on several occasions, going into vivid detail about the naughty things Riley would whisper in his ear, until Noah couldn't take it anymore and abruptly changed the subject. Just like then, he didn't want to imagine Riley in the arms of another man, being held, caressed and made love to. He was tortured by the thought of her giving herself to anyone, even Trevor, with the same passion and abandon she gave to him almost every night in his dreams. He knew it was crazy to feel so possessive over a woman he would never have, but he couldn't help himself.

Riley turned her head slightly, studying him with a sidelong look. He kept his expression carefully neutral. "Noah?"

"Yeah?"

"If I ask you a personal question, would you give me an honest answer?"

His gut clenched, and his mouth went dry. "Depends," he said evenly.

"On what?"

"On what the question is."

"So your honesty is conditional?"

He shot her a look. "What do you want to know, Riley?"

She hesitated, searching his impassive face. "How much did Trevor tell you…about our relationship?"

"What do you mean?" he asked warily.

"I mean," she said, lifting her head from the back of the seat, "did he tell you the things we argued about? Did he ever ask you to take sides?"

Choosing his words carefully, Noah replied, "I'm not sure I understand how having that kind of information would be of any use to you at this point. But I will tell you that Trevor loved you and worshipped the ground you walked on. After you turned down his first marriage proposal, he started worrying that you were having second thoughts about him, and it made him miserable. For a while he was impossible to be around, because all he wanted to talk about was you, and his fear that you were falling out of love with him. On the day you finally said yes, he was dancing on cloud nine. I'd known Trevor twenty-three years, Riley, and I can honestly tell you I'd never seen him happier than when you agreed to marry him." He paused, then added somberly, "I hope that answers your question."

"It does," Riley whispered as she blinked back a fresh sheen of tears. They sat in silence for a few minutes, both lost in their memories, not all of them painful.

After a while, Riley glanced out the window in time to see the Avalon emerge from the service center garage. "My car's ready," she murmured. "That was fast."

Noah wondered if he'd only imagined the hint of regret in her voice, then decided it was just another example of wishful thinking on his part.

He started the truck and pulled around to let her out by her car, where the auto technician was patiently waiting with her receipt.

"Thanks again for everything, Noah," Riley said, as she reached for the door handle. "I'll pay you back for the new tires."

He shook his head. "I'm not taking your money."

"Noah—"

"No, Riley. Not a chance."

She pursed her lips, even as her dark eyes glittered with mirth at his stubbornness. And then, without warning, she leaned across the seat and planted a warm, gentle kiss on his cheek. His heart lurched and his blood heated. He was tempted, so damned tempted, to turn his face into hers and seize her mouth in a hard, deep kiss that would leave them both panting.

But, of course, he didn't. "Have a good evening, Riley," he murmured.

"You, too, Noah." She hesitated for a fraction of

a second, looking as if she wanted to say more before she changed her mind.

He watched as she hopped down from the truck, thanked the waiting technician and took her receipt. Noah waited until she'd climbed into her car and pulled off with a tiny wave.

And then he drove home in a daze, his cheek still burning where her soft, sweet lips had been.

Chapter 11

Noah wasn't in the office when Riley arrived the next morning, and as the day wore on without his return, she told herself the dull ache of disappointment she felt had nothing to do with the fact that she'd spent another restless night thinking about him, reliving not only their kiss, but the time they'd spent alone in his truck yesterday while waiting for her tires to be replaced.

She'd thought of little else since then, and it was Janie who finally noticed how distracted she was.

"Why don't you go home?" Janie suggested, appearing in the doorway and catching Riley staring at the spot where Noah had kissed her on Friday.

She started guiltily, her eyes snapping to Janie's face. "What did you say?"

Janie smiled. "I said," she enunciated, stepping into the office, "why don't you go home? It's already after three o'clock—you've put in your hours for the day. Besides, how productive can you really be when you're daydreaming?"

Heat flooded Riley's cheeks. "I wasn't daydreaming," she muttered, briskly shuffling a stack of papers on her desk. "I was doing research."

Janie arched a dubious brow. "Sure could've fooled me." She perched a hip against the corner of the desk and idly swung her foot, which was encased in a pair of stiletto Jimmy Choo pumps. She watched Riley for a few moments, a speculative gleam in her dark eyes.

"What?" Riley asked warily.

Janie's mouth curved in a coy smile. "Kenneth seems to think there's something going on between you and Noah. He told me when he arrived at the office on Friday evening after I'd left, you nearly ran him over in your haste to flee the premises. When he went to investigate the source of your, uh, agitation, he found Noah standing right here in this office, looking as hot and bothered as you're looking right now."

Riley flushed. "I'm not hot and bothered." Then, opting for honesty—since there seemed no way of getting around it—she looked the other woman squarely in the eye. "Noah and I had a big argument on Friday. That's what Kenneth caught the tail end of."

"Is that all?"

"Yes." A half-truth was better than nothing at all.

"You know," Janie said, striking a thoughtful pose as she tapped a fingertip to her dimpled chin, "I would have accepted that explanation before yesterday. But yesterday I saw with my own two eyes why Kenneth suspects something's up between you and his brother. And he's not the only one. His mother commented on it as well, almost as soon as you and Noah left. Within minutes of each other, I might add."

Riley frowned. "That was pure coincidence."

"Maybe, but it's no coincidence that three different family members—people who know Noah very well—saw the same thing yesterday during lunch."

"Which is?"

"The fact that Noah couldn't keep his eyes off you." Mischief glimmered in Janie's dark eyes. "And, unless we're all mistaken, you had the same problem."

"You're all mistaken." Riley stood abruptly and began packing up her belongings. Maybe it *was* past time for her to leave for the day.

"Are you sure we're all mistaken?" Janie challenged, a knowing grin tugging at her full lips. "I mean, first there was the fact that you didn't speak a single word to each other when you came outside to call us for lunch. You spoke to everyone but Noah, like you two were purposefully avoiding each other. And then there was that whole little exchange at the dinner table about him not complimenting your writing enough. Call me crazy, but that sounded an awful lot like a lover's quarrel to me."

Riley forced a laugh that sounded strangled to her

own ears. "Well, it wasn't. Believe me, Janie, there's absolutely nothing going on between me and Noah. Not now, not ever."

"Because of Trevor?"

Riley froze in the middle of stuffing files into her attaché case. Slowly she lifted her eyes to Janie's face.

"I'm sorry if that was out of line," the other woman said quietly. "I'm not trying to offend you or stick my nose where it doesn't belong. But when you say you and Noah could never be together, I can't help but wonder if it's because you both feel you'd be betraying Trevor."

Riley's fingers tightened on the soft leather of her briefcase. "I understand how you might think that," she said slowly, "but the reason I made that comment is a lot simpler than that. Noah and I aren't interested in each other. We never have been, and we never will be. The reason I made such a big deal about his compliment at the dinner table is that it was the first time he'd ever said anything like that to me. For whatever reason, we've just never clicked. There's no animosity between us," she added at Janie's concerned expression. "It was never like those situations where the best friend hates the girlfriend or boyfriend and constantly tries to sabotage the couple's relationship. Noah and I have always been cordial, sometimes even friendly to each other. But that's about the extent of it." She offered Janie a rueful smile. "Sorry to disappoint you, if you were hoping to play matchmaker."

Janie shrugged. "You don't have to apologize. I

had to throw the question out there." She paused, then couldn't resist adding, "You and Noah might not be bosom buddies, but there's definitely an attraction there. I can sense it every time you're around each other, and so can Kenneth."

Riley hesitated, then gave a slow nod of assent. "You're both right. I won't deny it. I am attracted to Noah."

Janie grinned. "And he's definitely attracted to you, girl."

"Maybe," Riley murmured, afraid to even consider the possibility. She was still convinced the kiss she had shared with Noah meant nothing. She could handle the attraction if it was one-sided, because she could control her own thoughts and actions. But if Noah began fantasizing about *her*...God help them both.

Janie tilted her head ever so slightly to the side, her eyes narrowed shrewdly on Riley's face. Riley could see the wheels spinning in her mind, but after several prolonged moments, Janie remained silent.

Finally, when Riley couldn't take the suspense anymore, she blurted out, "What? Why are you looking at me like that?"

"I was just thinking about something," Janie murmured. "But maybe I shouldn't tell you. I don't want to offend you."

"I won't get offended," Riley said, albeit warily. "What were you thinking?"

"Well, I know how much you loved Trevor. I would never question that. But have you ever wondered..."

Trailing off, she shook her head. "Forget it. It's probably an inappropriate question."

But it was too late. The air had stalled in Riley's lungs. She licked her dry lips and stared at Janie, wondering why she felt a sense of dread, as if whatever Janie said was going to tilt her world on its axis, never to be righted again.

"Have I ever wondered what?" she asked faintly.

Janie pinned her with a direct look. "Have you ever wondered what would have happened if you'd met Noah and Trevor at the same time? If they'd both attended that conference in Houston?" She paused, her tone softening. "Do you think you would have made the same choice?"

Do you think you would have made the same choice?

The question echoed in Riley's mind as she left the office a few minutes later and headed home. Thankfully, right after dropping her loaded bomb, Janie had been called away by the ringing telephone, and Riley had been spared from answering her.

Not that she'd needed the reprieve. She already knew that her response would have been a categorical, resounding *yes*. She would have made the same choice if she'd met Noah and Trevor at the same time. She didn't even have to think twice about it.

Hopeless romantic that she was, Riley had always believed in serendipity, the guiding hand of fate. She believed everything in the universe happened for a reason. If she and Noah had been meant for each other, *he* would have shown up at that convention five years ago, not Trevor. *He* would have been the one who charmed his way into her life and eventually into her heart. And then again, maybe not. If she and Noah had found themselves at that conference together, would their paths have even crossed? There'd been over five hundred people in attendance, representatives from nearly every law enforcement agency across the state of Texas. If their eyes had met across a crowded room, would Noah have approached her afterward, as Trevor had done? Given Noah's aloofness toward her over the past five years, she seriously doubted he would have put himself out there by asking her out on a date. For all she knew, she probably wasn't even his type. He hadn't stood at the window and ogled *her* the way he'd done with Delilah Stanton.

Riley scowled at the foolish turn of her thoughts. What did it matter whether or not she was Noah Roarke's type? He wasn't the man she was destined for. She knew that as surely as she knew her own name.

And yet, Janie's provoking question nagged at her conscience, taunting her, tormenting her.

Because she'd never even considered it before. And because, damn it, she *had* stopped to ponder her answer.

Two miles from home, Riley pulled into a tiny strip mall to pick up her grandmother's dry cleaning. As she climbed from her car and headed toward the storefront business, the familiar rasp of a woman's voice stopped her cold in her tracks.

"As I live and breathe, it *is* Riley Kane."

Riley turned to watch the approach of a tall, thin white woman with red hair worn in a bouffant and pale green eyes that were so piercingly familiar Riley's breath caught. Dressed in a pair of tight blue jeans, a satin emerald blouse with a plunging neckline, and high-heeled leather boots, the woman could easily have passed for forty. Until one got closer and saw the deep lines carved into her face, a result of grief and years of hard living.

Riley blinked in shock. "H-how are you doing, Ms. Simmons?" she managed weakly.

Lips painted a bright shade of scarlet pursed in disapproval. "Now, is that any way to greet the woman who almost became your mother-in-law?" Before Riley could react, Trevor's mother rushed forward and enveloped her in a hard, quick embrace. Ignoring the heavy odor of cigarette smoke that assailed her nostrils and stung her eyes, Riley returned the woman's hug with equal fervor.

Drawing back, Leona Simmons took careful measure of her. "You look wonderful. But then, you always were one of the prettiest girls my Trevor ever brought home. How long have you been back in town?"

"Just over a week." Riley hesitated. "You probably didn't get my voice mail message."

"No, hon, I'm sorry. I've been in Dallas visiting family. Just got in last night." But there was something in those pale green eyes that made Riley question the story.

As if sensing her skepticism, Leona pasted on a too-bright smile. "How're your parents doing? And your grandma—is she still as colorful as ever?"

Riley grinned. "You know it. Matter of fact, we're having a party in a few weeks to celebrate her seventy-fifth birthday. You're more than welcome to come."

"I'd like that very much. Let me check my calendar and get back to you, hon."

Riley's grin wavered. "Sure. No problem."

After an awkward moment of silence, Leona clasped her hand and gave it a warm squeeze. "So how've *you* been? I heard you're a big-time reporter for the *Washington Post.*"

"I don't know about the 'big-time' part," Riley said sardonically. "I'm surrounded by Pulitzer Prize–winning journalists with decades of experience in the business. I'm not being modest when I tell you that I'm a very small fish in a very big pond."

"Oh, that's all right, hon," Leona said, giving her hand a reassuring pat. "Everybody's got to start somewhere. But, gosh, now I'm wondering if it was such a good idea for you to take so much time off from work. Not that I'm not thrilled to see you, but two months is an awfully long time for a sabbatical from the *Washington Post,* don't you think?"

Riley opened her mouth, then snapped it shut, confused. If Trevor's mother hadn't received her voice mail message, how had she known that Riley would be in San Antonio for two months?

At the same time the thought occurred to her, she

could tell by Leona's stricken expression that she knew she'd been caught in a lie. Closing her eyes for a moment, she heaved a deep, nicotine-scented breath.

"Oh, Riley, I'm so sorry," she said resignedly. "I can't lie to you anymore. I did get your message, as well as all the nice letters you've sent me over the years. The reason I haven't responded is not because the letters got lost in the mail between my changing addresses, as I told your friend Lety. The reason I never responded is because I didn't *want* to."

Riley stiffened. "I see." She couldn't keep the hurt from her voice.

Leona's expression softened with regret. "No, hon, you *don't* see. I couldn't call or write you back because it was too painful for me. You were—*are*— a constant reminder of my son and everything I lost when he died. You were such a big part of his life, Riley. I couldn't think of you without thinking of him, and well, that just wasn't good for me. I hope you can understand that."

Riley swallowed a hard lump that rose up in her throat. "I think I can, Ms. Simmons," she said quietly. After all, it was the same reason she herself had fled from San Antonio—to escape the memories.

An odd light suddenly filled Leona's eyes. "Can you understand?" she pressed, a hint of bitterness lacing her words. "Can you *really?*"

Without meaning to, Riley took an instinctive step backward. "I should probably go. My grandmother—"

"There's so much you can't begin to understand,"

Leona murmured wearily, closing her eyes and pinching the bridge of her nose. "If you only knew what I've been through these past three years. A mother should never have to bury her own child. Especially when that child—" She broke off abruptly with a mournful shake of her head.

Riley waited, not daring to breathe, willing the woman to finish what she'd started to say.

But when those green eyes met hers they were clear once again, if not slightly embarrassed. "Don't mind me, hon. The doctor's got me on these new antidepressants. They mess with my concentration at times. Either that, or I'm finally getting old," she joked lamely.

Riley smiled, but it fell as flat as Leona's failed attempt at humor.

Leona wagged a reproachful finger at her. "Don't you go worrying about me, Riley Kane. I can see the concern in your eyes, but it's not necessary. I told you I'm fine." She glanced at her slim gold wristwatch. "Listen, I'd better run. Tell your family I said hello, and if you happen to see Noah, tell him hey for me."

"I will," Riley promised softly.

But as she stood there watching Trevor's mother climb into a cherry-red Mustang convertible—a car that some would argue was inappropriate for a sixty-year-old woman—a chill ran through her, twisting and coiling in the bottom of her stomach.

Because Riley knew with unerring certainty that

Leona Simmons was *not* fine. And what ailed the woman went deeper than grief.

What ailed Trevor's mother was the burden of a terrible secret.

With a Cuban cigar clamped firmly between his teeth, Noah leaned over the pool table, positioned the tip of his cue stick, and took aim at his next target. In a matter of a few effortless strokes, he ran the table, the final ball rolling into the pocket with a satisfying *clack*.

He straightened slowly and reached for the Heineken sweating on a corner of the table next to two other empty bottles. He removed the unlit cigar from his mouth to take a swig of beer. He had just enough of a buzz to ensure he'd sleep soundly and dreamlessly through the night—the dreamless part being the most important.

Since Riley's return to San Antonio, he'd dreamed about her every damn night. When he awakened that morning reaching for her in his bed, he knew something had to be done. The only problem was, he didn't know what. He couldn't exactly force her to go back to Washington, D.C. This was her hometown; she had as much right to be here as he did. And because she'd been doing such a great job at the office, he couldn't fire her, not without providing a rational explanation to Kenneth and Janie.

The only way he could get rid of Riley was to give her what she wanted. A private investigation into Trevor's shooting.

And that wasn't going to happen.

Some way, somehow, he had to make the dreams stop and get the woman out of his system once and for all—without losing his soul in the process.

From the big-screen television behind him, highlights from the NBA finals blared on ESPN, competing with the bluesy strains of John Coltrane pouring from an elaborate stereo system. Noah knew it was wrong to taint Trane's masterpieces with sports news, but he found a certain amount of comfort in the cacophony of sounds. It drowned out the noise in his own head.

As he racked the balls on the table to play another game, the doorbell rang.

Removing the cigar from his mouth, Noah glanced at the clock on the wall. It was after ten o'clock. He wasn't expecting any visitors, so who could be ringing his doorbell at this time of night?

Beer in hand, he left the game room and went to answer the door. When he saw Riley standing on the other side, he wondered if she was a figment of his tortured imagination. Had he finally gone over the deep end?

She didn't speak for a prolonged moment, half-confirming his suspicion that she was an illusion, as beautiful as the real thing in a black tank top and a white skirt, one of those long, flouncy skirts that made her look like an exotic Gypsy. She wore a pair of ankle-wrap wedge sandals he wouldn't have cared for on any other woman's feet but Riley's. Even her toes were beautiful, the nails painted a deep, sexy shade of red.

He leaned on the doorjamb and deliberately allowed his eyes to slide down her body before easing back up to her face like a long, languid caress. When she shifted uncomfortably from one foot to another, he felt a twinge of wicked satisfaction.

Let her suffer a little discomfort, he thought. It was nothing compared to the hell he'd been going through for the past five years.

"To what do I owe the pleasure of this visit?" he drawled sardonically.

She moistened her lips with the tip of her tongue, and he forced himself not to follow the gesture with hungry eyes. "I need to talk to you."

"It's after ten o'clock," he said flatly.

"I know. It couldn't wait." She paused. "May I come in?"

He took a lazy swig of beer, looking at her from underneath his lashes. Without releasing her gaze, he slowly lowered the bottle and wiped moisture from his bottom lip. "It's after ten o'clock."

Those fallen-angel eyes turned imploring. "Please, Noah?"

He hesitated, then reluctantly stepped aside to let her enter, leaving just enough room that she had to squeeze past him. Big mistake. As her bare shoulder brushed against his chest, the warmth of her skin penetrated the thin cotton layer of his T-shirt to sear his flesh.

He stifled a groan. He'd always been a glutton for punishment where she was concerned.

Glancing back at him, she said, "I hope I didn't catch you at a bad time?"

"That's never stopped you before," he muttered under his breath, his back to her as he closed the door and threw the dead bolt.

She didn't hear him, or pretended not to. "Where's Eskimo?" she asked, glancing around expectantly.

"Spending the week at my mother's while she keeps the twins. They always ask for Eskimo."

Her lips quirked in a smile. "And you're kind enough to share him. What a wonderful uncle you are."

He shrugged. "I'm going to be out late doing surveillance most of this week, anyway. Would you like something to drink?"

"Sure." She nodded toward the half-empty bottle in his hand. "I'll have what you're having."

"Coming right up," he said.

She trailed him to the kitchen, murmuring her thanks as he opened a cold bottle of Heineken and passed it to her. "Can we sit in the living room and talk?"

He didn't want to talk. He had a fairly good idea what was on her mind, and he didn't want to discuss it. "Actually," he said, heading out of the kitchen and down the hall, "I was in the middle of playing pool."

She had no choice but to follow him to the game room, where he walked over to the pool table and picked up his cue stick, fully intending to resume his game.

Stepping further into the large room, Riley swept a casual glance around, taking in the oversize black leather sofa, electronic dartboard on the wall, autographed posters and other sports memorabilia. Every woman who'd ever stepped foot in the game room declared that it was a bachelor's domain through and through. Depending on who the female in question was, he either took the remark as a compliment or complaint.

He watched Riley out of the corner of his eye, trying to gauge her reaction. The last time she'd been to his house—before the previous Saturday—was for Trevor's surprise birthday party four years ago. Noah had been in the process of transitioning from an apartment and hadn't furnished the game room yet.

After lingering over an autographed San Antonio Spurs basketball in a glass cabinet, Riley wandered over to the pool table, idly running her hand along the rails as she approached.

"I always wanted to learn how to play," she murmured, watching as he skillfully sank the two-ball into the corner pocket.

"Why didn't you?" he asked, rounding the table to take the next shot.

She shrugged, sipping her beer. "Trevor was going to teach me, but…he never got around to it."

Hearing the melancholy in her voice, Noah glanced up. Before he could respond, she walked over to the television, picked up the remote control and punched it off.

He scowled at her. "I was watching that."

"No you weren't," she said matter-of-factly. "Besides, I couldn't hear Coltrane."

"You like Coltrane?"

She shot him a do-you-even-have-to-ask look. "Of course. Who doesn't?"

"Plenty of people. Trevor didn't."

"Yeah, well, his taste in music was…different." She paused, considering for a moment. "He had excellent taste in movies though."

Noah met her gaze, his mouth twitching. "Which one?"

"Um…well…"

Noah pretended to look thoughtful. "Never heard of that one before. What was it about?"

Riley laughed, then clapped a hand to her mouth, like a child who'd been caught giggling while the teacher's back was turned.

Noah chuckled softly. "It's all right. Trevor and I didn't share the same taste in music or movies, either." *Too bad the same didn't apply to our taste in women.*

Dark eyes glittering with mirth, Riley walked back over to the pool table. "He used to make me watch these awful B-movies with him, movies I'd never even heard of before. With titles like—"

"Terror in Toyland?"

"Yes!" Riley cried, grinning. "We watched that movie so many times I could recite all the cheesy lines after a while. And what made it even worse was that I found myself remembering certain lines at the most inopportune moments. Like sitting in the middle of an important meeting—"

"Or interrogating a suspect," Noah wryly admitted.

"Oh my God!" Riley burst into laughter, and it was such a warm, infectious sound that Noah couldn't help but laugh as well.

Minutes later they were still chuckling quietly, calmly, their eyes lingering over each other as they were transported back in time, each reliving their own special moments with Trevor.

"I miss him," Riley said softly.

"Yeah," Noah murmured, "me, too."

They gazed at each other for another moment before Noah looked away, returning his attention to the pool table. As he leaned over to take the next shot, Riley said casually, "Maybe you could teach me how to play pool."

He hit the cue ball hard, sending it flying off the table and thudding across the floor.

Riley laughed. "Or maybe not."

Noah went to retrieve the ball, grumbling, "You're messing with my concentration, woman."

"You?" Riley snorted in disbelief. "I didn't think that was possible. Trevor used to brag about what a pool shark you were. He said all the other cops called you a hustler, the kingpin of the Sunday Night Pool Sharks."

"I don't know about all that," Noah muttered.

She laughed. "Oh, don't be so modest, Noah. Come on, show me that move Trevor used to talk about. What was it called? The mace…mass…"

"Massé," Noah supplied.

Riley snapped her fingers. "That's it. The massé. Some sort of complicated technique where you make the cue ball follow a curved path. He told me it takes a lot of skill and concentration, and you were one of the few players he'd ever known who could do it on a consistent basis. So let me see it, Noah. Come on. Please?"

He chuckled, shaking his head. "I'm not in the mood for showing off."

"You're not showing off if someone asks you to do it. And I'm not just asking—I'm *begging*. Come on, Noah."

He shook his head again. "If you wanna see it done," he said, arranging balls on the table, "you can watch it on the Internet. There are dozens of Web sites that show clips of the massé and other pool moves."

Riley folded her arms across her chest, arching a brow at him. "What's wrong, Noah?" she taunted. "Afraid you've lost your touch?"

His mouth twitched with humor. "Reverse psychology? You can do better than that, Riley."

She gave a dismissive shrug. "It's okay if you can't do the move anymore. I mean, you *are* getting a little old. What are you now? Thirty-six? Just a few years away from the big four-oh." She shook her head, fighting the tug of a grin. "Oh, yeah. Won't be long now before you'll be bouncing your grandkids on your lap and telling them stories about what a pool shark you used to be, back in the day when you were so good you could—"

"Do this?" With one deft stroke of his cue stick—and without taking his eyes off hers—Noah sent the white cue ball spinning into a curve, then sliding in a tight turn around two other balls before knocking the intended target, the nine-ball, cleanly into the pocket.

She gaped first at the table, then at him. "H-how did you—"

He lifted one shoulder in a lazy shrug. "Practice." Then, because he wasn't entirely immune to the age-old male tendency to want to impress a beautiful woman, he added, "Come back and see me in forty years, and I'll still be able to do 'em."

Riley grinned at his cocksure promise. "Can you teach me how to do a massé?"

He arched a brow. "Shouldn't you learn how to play pool first?"

"All right, then. Teach me how to play pool."

He shook his head as he began racking the scattered balls. "I'm not touching that with a twenty-foot pole."

"Why not?"

He stared at her, and saw with some surprise that her expression was perfectly innocent. "Are you serious? It's a cliché, Riley. A cliché that's been done a thousand times over in books and movies—"

She looked genuinely baffled. "What are you talking about?"

"This whole setup. You asking me to teach you how to play pool. It…it…" Didn't she know? Hadn't she read books or watched movies where the man teaching a woman how to play pool invariably wound up "teaching" her a hell of a lot more? Did she have no clue where this little encounter could lead?

And that's when it came to him. The solution to his problem.

In order to get rid of Riley Kane once and for all, he had to do something horrible. Overworking her hadn't done the trick. Kissing her hadn't worked either-though, admittedly, driving her away had been the last thing on his mind when he'd kissed her.

It was time to up the ante, raise the stakes so high she'd have no choice but to flee.

He had to seduce her.

Oh, he knew he wouldn't get very far. Riley would stop him before anything serious happened. But once she realized what he was capable of, how low he was willing to stoop by hitting on his best friend's fiancée, she'd hate him, maybe even for the rest of her life.

He'd worry about that part later.

His eyes narrowed on her face, searching for any signs that she was trying to con him by feigning naiveté. After all, she'd shown up at his house that evening to get something from him. What if she was desperate enough to try and seduce him in order to get what she wanted?

Riley pointed a finger at him. "You're just afraid that if you teach me how to play, one day I'll be better than you." Her dark eyes glinted with laughter and a challenge he simply couldn't resist, though he knew he should.

"All right, Miss Kane," he murmured, watching her carefully. "You're on."

Grinning with triumph, she took a swig of beer, then set down the bottle and sidled over to him. "Where do we start?"

"Let's begin," he said, picking up his cue stick from the table, "with an anatomy lesson."

She raised a brow. "Anatomy?"

"The anatomy of the cue stick," he drawled. "In order to understand pool, you have to familiarize yourself with the equipment. Proper handling of the cue stick is essential to becoming a good player."

"All right. I'm listening."

"A cue stick has three parts. The tip," he explained, rubbing his thumb back and forth against the pointy end of the stick, "is what you use to hit the cue ball. And then the shaft—"

"The shaft?"

He nodded, hiding a smile as he watched her bite her lower lip. She was either playing him for a fool, or she was genuinely amused. "The shaft is the smooth, narrow length between the tip and the middle of the stick. And the last part is the butt. No, I'm not making that up," he added when her eyes narrowed suspiciously. "The butt is the thicker portion of the stick that falls between the middle and the end, with a rubber bumper on the bottom."

She snickered when he'd finished speaking. "I guess I don't have to wonder whether it was a man who made up the game of pool."

His lips curved. "That obvious, huh?"

"Oh, most definitely." Her eyes danced with mirth. God, she was beautiful. "Okay, master, now that I've learned the 'anatomy' of the exalted cue stick, teach me how to use it."

He chuckled softly. "Impatient, aren't we?"

"What can I say? I'm a fast learner."

"Mmm, we'll see about that." Indeed. "Now, normally, before I start a game of pool, I prep my hands with chalk so they won't be slippery while I'm holding the cue stick. But in the interest of time, we'll skip the chalk."

She held up her slender hands for his inspection. "I'm good, anyway."

Noah passed her the cue stick, then stood behind her as she raised it to a wobbly ninety-degree angle. "The first thing you want to do is stand close to the table with your legs lined up to the edge." As she shifted her body accordingly, he struggled not to stare at the smooth, shapely calves peeking out from beneath her long skirt. "Keep your feet slightly braced apart," he continued with forced normalcy, "and balance your weight equally between both feet."

"Like this?" she asked, glancing over her shoulder at him.

He nodded. "Bend your knee closer to the table while keeping your back knee straight, then lean toward the table. No, like this," he murmured, bending to apply light pressure to her legs as he positioned her. The skirt was soft and crinkly, her skin warm and supple underneath. Heat sizzled through his veins, and for a moment he imagined himself lifting her skirt up her legs, past the delicious curve of her thighs—

"Better?" Riley asked, a husky catch to her voice. If she'd been looking back at him, she would have seen him close his eyes and take a deep, steadying breath before rising to his feet again.

"Better," he said softly. "Now, grip the butt of the cue stick with your dominant hand."

"Which hand?"

"This one," he murmured, placing his right hand over hers. He felt a little tremor run through her at the contact, and it gave him a wicked twinge of satisfaction. If she was attempting to seduce him, it was only fair that he score a few points first.

Stepping closer behind her, and deliberately keeping his right hand over hers, he said, "Put your other hand palm down on the rail of the table." He guided her, allowing his fingers to slide through hers for a moment. She trembled again and he smiled to himself.

Oh, yeah, he could definitely do this.

"When you're taking a shot, you'll lay the shaft in the crease between your thumb and the side of your hand. Like this," he demonstrated, slowly sliding the stick back and forth in the crease of her palm. "See how it glides smoothly and evenly?" he murmured next to her ear.

She nodded jerkily.

"Now you try," he instructed, keeping his voice a low, silky caress.

Riley awkwardly imitated his movements.

"A little smoother," he corrected. "Not so hard. Your hands are a little damp. Do you want some chalk?"

She shook her head. "I'm fine. It's just a little warm in here." Her voice was tight, as if she were having trouble breathing.

He knew the feeling. Pressed close to her warm body, with her light, exotic scent filling his nostrils, he felt intoxicated. But he had to remain focused.

Riley looked back, and with their faces only inches apart, their eyes met and held. "Like this?" she whispered. As she slid the cue stick back and forth in the crease of her hand, he could no longer keep at bay an image of her stroking his penis in the same manner, slow and sensual. He went hard and fully erect just thinking about it.

When Riley's eyes flared slightly and her breath hitched, he realized he'd been standing too close to her to conceal the sudden straining at his fly.

She made a sound in her throat, soft and unintelligible. It wasn't the purr of a scheming seductress basking in victory over her prey. It was the honest-to-goodness sound of an aroused woman.

It set him on fire.

They both released the cue stick at the same time, and before it clattered to the floor, Noah had cupped her face in his hands and was kissing her. She met him eagerly, wrapping her arms around his neck and parting those sweet, lush lips beneath his. Her warm, fruity taste filled his mouth, and at the first touch of her tongue to the tip of his, a jolt of pure need sped through his veins, racing to his groin and throbbing heavily there.

His hands fell to her waist and slid around the firm, curvy swell of her bottom. She gasped, then moaned as he gently kneaded her, holding her tightly against his rigid arousal.

As the kiss deepened, grew hotter and wilder, a voice in the back of his mind reminded him that he wasn't supposed to go all the way. Someone—anyone—was supposed to douse the flame before it blazed out of control.

Any minute now.

But he couldn't bring himself to do it, not when her soft, full breasts were flush against his chest, her belly pressed to his throbbing erection. He lifted his head, thinking for a split second that he might have the strength to end the madness. Instead his mouth sought the fragrant skin of her neck, the silky warmth of it against his tongue, the thrum of her pulse beating against him.

She moaned his name, clutching a handful of his T-shirt in her fist and pulling him closer as his lips returned to hers. His tongue traced the soft fullness, licking the inner seam before dipping sensually inside. Their tongues tangled in an erotic mating dance, as ancient as time. He wanted her, wanted her with a ferocity that would've shocked him if he weren't already used to the feeling.

With a rough, guttural sound, he lifted her into his arms, and her legs locked around his waist. He held her in the air for a moment, sliding his hands under her skirt to squeeze her thighs and palm her bottom through the flimsy layer of her lace panties. They groaned in mutual pleasure and anticipation.

As he set her down on the pool table, she parted her legs and he stepped between them. Leaning down, he crushed his mouth to hers while he lifted her skirt past her thighs, until it settled in a rumpled pool above her knees. As he stepped back, she gazed at him, her lids at half-mast, her plump lips moist from his kisses. The look of smoky desire in her eyes was enough to tempt him into taking her right then and there. But, no, he couldn't rush this. Not when it was all he'd fantasized about for the past five years.

He held her close, his hands roaming up and down her back. Seeing that she wore no bra, he tugged down her tank top, and what sprang free were the most beautiful breasts he'd ever seen. Firm, round, the dusky areolas dipped in smooth chocolate.

She trembled beneath his hungry gaze and instinctively moved to cover herself, but he captured her wrists in his hands and gently drew her arms around his neck.

"Don't hide from me, Riley," he said huskily. "I've waited too long for this moment."

Thankfully, Riley seemed too far gone to register

the meaning of his words, her eyes hazy and heavy-lidded with desire as she watched him cup her breasts in his hands. They spilled from his palms—warm, soft, and fragrant. Need stabbed through him, tightening in his groin.

"You are so damn beautiful," he uttered, rasping his thumbs against her nipples.

She blushed with pleasure, biting her bottom lip.

Keeping his gaze on hers, he bent to draw one erect nipple into his mouth. At the first touch of his tongue, her breath caught sharply, and she closed her eyes on a helpless moan.

Spurred by her reaction, as well as his own raging lust, he sucked her hard into his mouth. She moaned in ecstasy and he closed his eyes, too, giving himself up to the exquisite taste of her, pouring years of pent-up desire onto that one breast.

"Noah," she whimpered brokenly, arching backward as her arms tightened around the back of his neck. *"Noah..."*

The sound of his name on her lips sent another wave of desire coursing through his body. His tongue circled her nipple while he played with the other one, teasing and stroking it into a tight bead.

Switching his mouth to her other breast, he pressed himself deeper within the cradle of her legs, his hips rolling in the same slow, subtle rhythm that he used on her nipple.

She moaned fitfully, her hips undulating in response, nearly making him come.

He dragged his mouth from her breast and kissed her—a long, carnal kiss that left them both panting.

Voracious now, Noah reached beneath her skirt and tugged at her panties, unbearably aroused to find the crotch already damp. He slid the black lace down her legs and over her wedge sandals, pocketing the underwear like a souvenir. He then knelt between her thighs, his mouth homing in on the hot, wet gift that awaited him.

Riley cried out at the erotically intimate kiss, her fingernails digging into his shoulders through his shirt. Lust raged through his body, throbbing relentlessly in his groin. Grabbing her hips, he rasped his tongue over her slippery feminine lips, murmuring huskily, "You're so sweet, so damned sweet."

"Noah…" She moaned his name over and over as he licked, nibbled and suckled her, filling his mouth with her essence. He tortured her until he thought she might shatter apart, her hips lifting off the table to press into him, her breath loud and gasping.

He had to have her. He'd wanted this for so long, wanted to make her scream his name and shudder in his arms. But when it happened for the first time, he wanted to be buried deep inside her. He wanted to feel her wet heat surrounding him, contracting, pulling, driving him toward the exquisite end.

He surged to his feet, intending to pick her up and carry her to his bedroom. Of all the times he'd fantasized about making love to Riley, he'd never imagined taking her on a pool table, as if they were acting out some scene from a book or movie.

But when she unbuttoned the snap of his jeans and impatiently unzipped them, then reached inside his boxers, he knew they wouldn't make it to the bedroom.

He sucked in a harsh breath as her warm fingers encircled his penis, then began stroking up and down the swollen length until he thought he'd explode in her hand.

Placing his hand over hers, as he'd done during the pool lesson, he guided the tip of his shaft between the wet, inviting folds of her body. The first touch of her blazed through him, scorching his nerve endings and setting him on fire. The urgency he felt made him thrust deep with a single stroke, penetrating her as far as he could. Riley cried out sharply, arching tautly against him and throwing back her head. He swore under his breath, closing his eyes as if he were in agony. The tight, silken clasp of her body was like nothing he'd ever imagined, and for a prolonged moment he remained perfectly still, afraid the slightest movement would push him over the edge. He wanted to take his time with her, savor every moment of this incredible experience like it would be his last. Because it probably would.

Opening his eyes slowly, he began moving inside her, pacing himself, willing himself to go slow and not ravage her. But then she tilted her hips to take him deeper and did something with her inner muscles that snapped his resolve.

With his heart pounding violently, he began pumping harder, faster, deeper inside her. She spread her thighs wide to accommodate him, her arms braced on the table to support herself as he withdrew, then thrust again and again in a heavy, pounding rhythm that made their breath come in ragged spurts.

Noah couldn't take his eyes off her exquisite face, at the ripeness of her beautiful breasts, at their urgent coupling. How many times had he imagined this moment, making love to the woman of his dreams? And as vividly erotic as his dreams had been, nothing could compare to the mind-blowing reality of this night.

He grasped her bottom and lifted her off the table, driving into her until she arched against him with a loud cry. He felt the rapid contractions of her climax as he kept thrusting, plunging into her until he reached his own powerful release. He shuddered and groaned loudly, his entire body growing taut with the force of the spasms that gripped him in the most intense orgasm he'd ever had. Fitting that it should be with Riley, the first and only woman he'd ever loved.

For a long while they remained locked in that position, Riley's legs wrapped around him, neither willing to end the embrace. Slowly he eased her back down onto the table and kissed her closed eyelids, then her lips.

As her lashes fluttered open, he gazed deep into her eyes, searching for any signs of regret. When he found none, he cradled the back of her head and drew her close for a stirring, openmouthed kiss.

"Okay?" he murmured, when they at last pulled apart again.

She nodded, her mouth curved in a dreamy, tantalizing smile. "I don't think I've ever been better."

His heart soared. Even as he told himself she couldn't possibly know what she was saying, he lifted her into his arms and strode purposefully from the game room, in search of a bed for round two.

Chapter 12

In hindsight, Riley realized she probably shouldn't have insisted on learning how to play pool. But she'd been in trouble long before Noah picked up that cue stick and began his lesson on "anatomy."

She'd been in trouble the moment she hopped into her car and drove all the way across town to his house.

As he carried her from the game room and down the hallway to his bedroom, she clung to his neck and pressed her face against his chest. She felt vulnerable and wonderfully protected at the same time.

Inside his bedroom, he switched on the bedside lamp and lowered her gently onto the king-size bed, his body following hers. She reached up to pull off his shirt and toss it aside, then his lips covered hers again, hot and coaxing. She opened her mouth to welcome his probing tongue as they shared a long, deep, provocative kiss.

They stripped off the remainder of each other's clothes, hands tangling in their haste. A simultaneous ripple shook them as their naked bodies joined on the bed, skin to skin, hard against soft.

Desperate to touch him, Riley found the flat brown button of his nipple and caught it between her teeth. She rubbed the tip of her tongue back and forth against the tiny bud, then opened her mouth and suckled, drawing a low, agonized groan from him. Her hands stroked down the corded muscles of his back and over the taut firmness of his buttocks while he watched her through heavy-lidded eyes.

She gasped as his hand moved between her spread thighs and found her wet, pulsing center. He parted the delicate folds of her flesh with his fingertips and slipped one thick finger inside. She moaned and arched against him, her head rocking back and forth against the bed, her fingers clenching a handful of the sheets as she felt herself building toward another orgasm.

She whimpered in protest as Noah pulled back, reaching into the nightstand and removing a condom from the top drawer. Dimly it occurred to her that they hadn't used protection the first time. But she'd been too far gone to notice or care, and now all she wanted was to feel him buried inside her again.

He sheathed himself quickly and mounted her, cupping her bottom and fitting her to his length. Holding her gaze, he entered her with one hard, steady thrust, burying himself to the hilt. She cried out, wrapping her legs tightly around him.

He withdrew a little and thrust again, his eyes intent on her face. And she felt, in that moment, a powerful sense of connection that went beyond the joining of their bodies. This was more than sex. This was lovemaking—life-affirming, earth-shattering lovemaking that brought a rush of hot tears to her eyes.

Seeing her tears, Noah paused mid-stroke, looking concerned. "Am I hurting you?"

Riley shook her head. "No," she whispered quickly. "Don't stop. Please don't stop."

"I won't," he vowed, looking at her with an intensity that made her shiver. "Ever."

As he began thrusting deep inside her, she clung to him with desperate hands, her nails digging into his back as each demanding stroke drove her closer to the edge. He wasn't gentle, nor did she want him to be. All she wanted was him, the fierce possession of his body locked into hers, the wondrous sensation of belonging to him.

Bracing himself on both arms, his hands on either side of her head, Noah increased the force and tempo of their lovemaking, plunging in and out of her, reaching deeper with every stroke until Riley began climaxing. She cried out at the strength of it, holding him tight as her body convulsed around his penis, milking an orgasm out of him. She felt him come, felt the sudden rigidity in the muscles of his back as he thrust one final time, then called her name hoarsely, almost reverently.

Then stillness…the only sound their ragged breathing. Neither of them moved.

Riley waited for the recriminations to rush to the surface of her mind. But all she felt was warm and deliciously satiated. And something else.

She felt an overwhelming sense of…completion.

After another moment, Noah rolled off her and drew her into the protective strength of his arms. Closing his eyes, he brushed his lips across her temple and stroked her damp hair. "Stay with me," he said huskily.

And she did, obeying without question. Because she knew, in that moment, there was no place else she'd rather be.

For the first time in weeks, she slept long and hard, and awakened at some point during the night to find her and Noah spooned together in the large bed, the covers drawn up to their waists, his arm resting lightly on her hip. She didn't move for several moments, marveling at how perfectly their bodies fit—a thought that was scary enough to galvanize her into action.

Slowly, so she wouldn't wake him, she eased toward the edge of the bed and sat up. As she scanned the moonlit darkness, trying to remember where her clothes had been discarded earlier, he stirred. She froze.

"Don't go," he murmured, low and gruff.

Without turning around, she closed her eyes. "I have to."

"No, you don't." She felt the mattress dip slightly as he moved toward her, placing a warm, gentle hand on her shoulder. She trembled at his touch, already feeling herself weakening.

"Riley," he said in a voice that reached deep into her soul. "Stay."

She was lost, helpless to refuse him as he drew her back onto the bed and into his arms. He leaned down and kissed her, a deep, drugging kiss that burned away the last of her resistance. She moaned softly as he slid between her legs and filled her with one long, possessive stroke. She closed her eyes and surrendered to him, allowing herself to be swept away.

In the morning, when daylight brought clarity, she would deal with the guilt and recriminations she knew would be waiting.

The guilt hit hard.

So hard that the moment Noah stepped into the bathroom to take a shower, she bolted from the bed where she'd been feigning sleep and scrambled around the room throwing on her discarded clothes. It was only as she peeled away from the house that she remembered Noah still had her panties, which he'd tucked into his pocket before they made love.

No way in hell was she going back for them.

In fact, if she never saw Noah Roarke's house again, it would be too soon.

What had she been thinking? She'd made love with Noah, breaking Rule Number One in the book of what *not* to do with your fiancé's best friend. She'd not only slept with Noah; she'd enjoyed every earth-shattering moment of it. And that *had* to be Rule Number Two in the book—don't enjoy the act of betrayal.

Because there was no other word to describe what she'd done. She'd betrayed Trevor by making love with his best friend, a man who'd been like a brother to him. As if it weren't bad enough that she'd returned to San Antonio to launch a private investigation into Trevor's murder, an investigation that could prove his involvement in illegal activities. Wasn't that betrayal enough? Did she have to add sex with his best friend to her rap sheet of crimes?

Riley groaned as she got off at the next exit. Her first mistake of the night had been showing up at his house at ten o'clock. She'd gone there to tell him about her encounter with Trevor's mother and to gauge his reaction to Leona Simmons's strange remarks about her son. She'd been prepared to plead her case for why Noah should help her investigate Trevor's shooting. Instead she'd found herself receiving a lesson on how to play pool. Never could she have imagined how arousing such an innocent thing could be, starting from the "anatomy" lesson laced with innuendo, to the sexually charged demonstration on how to use the cue stick. *A little smoother,* he'd murmured in her ear, sliding the long pole between her hand. *Not so hard.* The memory of it made a shiver of warmth puddle in her groin. She'd never look at another pool table the same way again.

Still, even if she could excuse the first encounter between them, what about the second, third and fourth time they'd made love? What about the fact that she'd had unprotected sex with him, something she'd done with no man but Trevor? She hadn't been on the pill in three years. What if, God forbid, she got pregnant?

She didn't even want to think about accidentally conceiving a child with Noah.

Yet she couldn't stop thinking about how explosive their lovemaking had been. After losing Trevor, she'd never expected to find sexual compatibility with any other man. But what she and Noah had shared went beyond sexual compatibility. The moment their bodies joined, she'd felt a powerful connection that transcended the physical act of sex. She'd felt a sense of…rightness.

But how could that be? How could she feel right about something that was so inherently wrong?

Minutes later, she pulled into the driveway of her parents' home and cut off the ignition. The house was silent when she crept through the door, like a teenager sneaking in after curfew. She tiptoed through the living room and had made it halfway upstairs when she was halted by her grandmother's distinctly amused voice.

"Must've been quite a long talk you and Noah had.

You left at nine-thirty last night. It's now six-thirty in the morning."

Busted. Damn.

Without turning around, Riley said casually, "Yeah, well, we had a lot to discuss. Important stuff."

"I'm sure it was." There was an unmistakable smile in Florinda's voice.

Riley flushed. "I, uh, need to take a shower and get ready for work."

"Of course. Would you like some breakfast before you leave? You and Noah probably worked up quite an appetite…talking."

Riley's face grew hotter. "Gotta run, Grandma," she said in a rush, taking the rest of the stairs two at a time. "I'll grab something on the way to the office."

"All right, baby," Florinda called after her. "Be sure to give Noah my best."

"I will," Riley promised, then smothered a groan at the thought of seeing him again in a couple of hours. With any luck, he'd spend another day out of the office, saving her the trouble of having to avoid him.

Too bad she'd never put much stock in luck.

When Noah emerged from the bathroom and found Riley gone, he wasn't surprised. He'd fully expected her to bolt at the first opportunity. And maybe it was for the best. He needed to be alone to sort through what had happened between them last night, and he couldn't think clearly with her around.

He'd made love to Riley, his best friend's fiancée,

a woman he'd sworn he could never have. He'd made love to her not once, but several times during the night. He'd whispered erotic things to her, had pressed his mouth to the feminine heart of her and ridden her through one mind-numbing orgasm after another. He'd exulted in her cries of ecstasy and had taken satisfaction in the way she'd screamed his name and clawed his back.

He should be hanging his head in shame, racked with guilt and regret over what he'd done.

But how could he regret what had been the most incredible night of his life? Nothing he'd ever experienced could compare to the indescribable pleasure of making love to Riley. He'd dreamed about it so many times, had tortured himself with fantasies that now paled in comparison to the reality.

He'd made love to her, and although he knew deep down inside that Trevor wouldn't have approved, Noah couldn't summon an ounce of regret.

What kind of man did that make him?

A grim smile curved his mouth. *A man who's in love. Deeply, hopelessly, in love with the wrong woman.*

Chapter 13

Noah was already at the office when Riley arrived a few minutes after eight o'clock.

To her immense relief, he was in a closed-door meeting with his brother and a client—which worked out perfectly for her.

She hung around the office long enough to return a few phone calls and finish some paperwork before making her escape, telling Janie she had a lot of errands to run and wouldn't be back until later that afternoon.

She spent half the day delivering documents to clients, conducting research at a local law school library, and sitting in on a civil court case that had an impact on one of their prospective clients. For lunch, she hooked up with an old friend and colleague from the *San Antonio Express-News*.

"What's this I hear about you working at Roarke Investigations?" Leticia Barnett demanded as soon as they were served their meals at an outdoor table nestled along the Riverwalk. Lety was a petite, brown-skinned woman with beautifully dreadlocked hair that hung halfway to her waist and eyes the color of bittersweet chocolate. An award-winning investigative reporter for the *Express-News*, the two women had met when Riley left Houston and returned home to work for the local newspaper. On Riley's second day, Lety had taken her out to eat at the same restaurant they were now seated outside. Over lunch, they'd talked about being one of only a handful of black women in their college journalism classes, and had traded horror stories about tyrannical managing editors. They'd been friends ever since.

"Word spreads fast around this town," Riley murmured, buttering a hot, crusty roll.

Lety snorted. "What did you expect? You're Riley Kane—beloved daughter of the San Antonio Police Department, hometown girl gone AWOL for three years. Of course it's gonna cause a minor commotion when you return home. Besides," Lety added accusingly, "it's not as if *you* were going to tell me you were working at Roarke Investigations. Look how long it took you to give me a call to let me know you were back in town."

Riley felt a sharp pang of guilt. "Girl, I'm sorry

about that. I've been trying to get settled in and take care of some last-minute details for my grandmother's birthday party. Which reminds me, did you receive your invitation in the mail?"

"I sure did. And you know I wouldn't miss Florinda's seventy-fifth birthday bash even if the president himself was granting me an exclusive interview."

Riley laughed. "Well, considering how you feel about the current President…"

Lety grinned and cut into her blackened salmon. "Stop avoiding my question. Why are you working at Roarke Investigations? I thought you were on sabbatical."

"I am," Riley said, absently twirling fettuccine around her fork. "But you know me. I can't just sit around the house for the next two months doing nothing. I'd go stir-crazy. When Janie Roarke offered me the job at the detective agency, I thought it was a great way to keep myself occupied and learn about the inner workings of the P.I. business, which I've always been curious about, anyway." *A half-truth is better than nothing at all,* she mentally reasoned, suffering another stab of guilt when Lety nodded, seeming to accept her explanation.

"Have you done anything exciting yet?" she asked. "Staked out a motel room to catch a cheating spouse in the act? Gone on a high-speed chase to track down a deadbeat dad?"

Riley shook her head. "Nothing that exciting, I'm afraid. I've mostly been doing background checks on new employees and making a lot of trips to the court-house."

"Waste of your talent," Lety pronounced indignantly.

Riley laughed. "No, it's not. The work I've been doing is just as essential to the business as anything else they do. And I'm learning a lot."

"If you say so." Lety speared another forkful of salmon and chewed for a moment, her eyes narrowed thoughtfully on Riley's face. "Another reason I was surprised by the news is that I couldn't see you voluntarily deciding to work with Noah."

Riley kept her expression neutral. "Why not?"

Lety frowned. "You know why. Because you've never particularly cared for him."

"That's not true," Riley said, pausing with her fork halfway to her mouth. "I never said I didn't like Noah. He was Trevor's best friend."

That seemed to be the refrain of the day. *He was Trevor's best friend, Trevor's best friend.*

And she'd slept with him.

"Maybe it's not so much what you did or didn't say about Noah," Lety elaborated. "It was the way you were around him. Slightly uncomfortable. A little on edge. For example, I remember being at Trevor's birthday party and watching you go out of your way not to walk past Noah and the woman he'd brought as his date."

Riley gave a dispassionate shrug. "So maybe I was trying to avoid *her.* I seem to recall most of us thinking she was a bit of an airhead. Whatever happened to her, anyway?" she asked offhandedly. "Did she and Noah date for very long after I left town?"

Lety snorted. "Of course not. You know that bimbo couldn't hold the interest of a man like Noah Roarke. Neither could most of the women he's dated since then. Although," Lety said thoughtfully, tapping a manicured finger against her upper lip, "there *was* that one woman he stayed with for a long time."

Riley was surprised by how hard her heart was pounding. "How long?"

"Several months—at least five, I think. Her name was Kimberly and she worked in the District Attorney's Office. Smart, really pretty. From what I heard, she was absolutely crazy about Noah and was just waiting for him to pop the question."

Riley's throat felt inexplicably tight. "So what happened?"

Lety shrugged. "They broke up. According to what Kimberly told other people, Noah had 'serious commitment issues' and seemed to be holding out for a 'perfect woman that doesn't exist.' As you can tell, she was pretty bitter about the whole thing. And who could blame her? Noah Roarke's quite a catch. He's caring, intelligent, has a great sense of humor, runs his own successful business. Not to mention that he's fine as hell." She chuckled, shaking her head at Riley. "You're the only woman I know who seems to be immune to what a total package he is."

Little do you know, Riley thought, taking a sip of

her white Zinfandel. She wondered what Lety would say if she knew Riley had spent the night making love to Noah, sobbing his name and doing unspeakable things with him.

"Anyway," Lety said with a mischievous grin that made Riley wonder for a panicked moment if she'd read her mind, "I figure now that you're back in town, you can help a sista out."

"Sure. With what?"

"Now that you're working closely with Noah, you can put in a good word for me."

Riley stared at her in confusion. "You want to work at the agency?"

Lety laughed. "No, silly! Girl, you've been out of the game for too long. I wasn't talking about getting a *job* with Noah. I want you to hook me up with him."

"What?"

"You heard me. I want you to get him to ask me out on a date."

Riley shook her head quickly, maybe too quickly. "I can't do that."

Lety scowled. "Why not?"

"Because I'm terrible at matchmaking. Just ask any of my old friends from college. Every time I tried to play matchmaker for them—which I'll admit wasn't often—it turned out to be a disaster."

Lety grinned. "Well, we're not in college anymore, and I'm sure your matchmaking skills have improved since then."

"Don't count on it."

"Come on, Riley. You've known Noah for years, longer than you've known me. And even though you say you've never been close to him, you could definitely tell me what his likes and dislikes are, what he looks for in a woman and what turns him off."

"Says who?" Riley sputtered.

Lety gave her a look. "He was your fiancé's best friend. Between what Trevor must have told you about Noah, and what you observed yourself, I think it's safe to assume you know him pretty well."

"I wouldn't be too sure about that." Noah Roarke was an enigma, a man she'd never understood or pretended to understand. Before kissing her senseless last week, he'd scarcely ever touched her. And now that they'd become lovers, she had a feeling he would remain a mystery to her. He, like her, probably regretted what they had done last night. He was too noble, too devoted to Trevor's memory, to make light of the transgression they'd committed. To cope with his own guilt, she could see him pushing her even further away.

That, she realized, was an incredibly depressing thought.

Lety was watching her carefully over the rim of her wineglass. "If you don't think Noah would be interested in me—"

"No, it's not that. It's just—" *The thought of him with another woman, any woman, makes me feel slightly ill. I know that sounds crazy, but it's the truth.* "Tell you what," she said aloud. "I'll bring up your name to Noah. If he seems receptive, I'll start talking you up. *Subtly,* of course."

"Of course," Lety agreed with a sly grin. "But not so subtly that he doesn't get the message that I'm available."

Riley chuckled, glancing at her watch. "Of course. Anyway, I've gotta head back to the office. It's getting late."

"Yeah, me too," Lety said, signaling for the waiter. She shook her head as Riley pulled out her credit card. "Don't worry about it. Lunch is on me."

"Oh, girl, you don't have to—"

"I know, but I want to. Consider it a small homecoming gift. Besides, it's the least I can do for the woman who may be hooking me up with my future husband."

Riley could only muster a weak smile.

Ten minutes later, as she drove back to Roarke Investigations, she realized that it had never occurred to Lety that Riley might be interested in Noah.

Which is as it should be.

When Riley arrived at the office, she was unprepared for the sight of Janie, Kenneth and Noah huddled around Janie's computer in the reception area. All three glanced up in unison as she approached the large desk.

"Hey Riley," Janie and Kenneth greeted her cheerfully.

"Hey y'all." Her eyes met and held Noah's for a prolonged moment before sliding away. Striving for a normal tone that would mask the sudden quaking in her knees, she asked, "What're you guys watching on the computer?"

"Daniela e-mailed some photos from Italy," Janie answered.

"Looks like she and Caleb are really having a nice time on their honeymoon," Kenneth added.

"*Nice?* Try incredibly, unbelievably romantic. They're taking moonlit gondola rides in Venice, exploring lush, beautiful vineyards in Tuscany, touring ancient cathedrals and museums in Florence. Oh, look, here's a photo of Michelangelo's *David!*" Janie sat back in her chair and heaved a long, plaintive sigh. "All right, I admit it. I'm jealous."

Chuckling, Noah clapped his brother on the back. "Looks like you'd better start calling travel agents."

Janie tilted back her head and batted her long eyelashes at her husband. "Well, now that I think about it, our anniversary *is* coming up in August…."

Kenneth scowled good-naturedly. "Damn that Caleb Thorne."

Smiling at the couple, Riley left the reception area and headed down the corridor to her office. She'd barely sat down behind the desk when Noah materialized. Dressed entirely in black—his surveillance attire, as she'd learned—he struck a negligent pose in the doorway, propping a shoulder against the door frame and folding his arms across his wide, muscular chest.

He didn't speak for several moments, his dark, hooded eyes roaming across her face as if he were trying to reconcile the coolly aloof woman before him with the passionate lover who'd writhed in his arms the night before. If Riley had anything to say about it, he would never see that side of her—the wanton side—again.

"Did you have a productive day?" he murmured.

She nodded briskly. "I took plenty of notes from the court hearing I attended this morning. I'll go over everything with you and Kenneth whenever you're available. Also, I typed up the minutes from Friday's meeting with Delilah Stanton and left it on your desk while you were out yesterday. Did you see it?"

"I did," he said softly. "Thank you, Riley."

She faltered for a moment, at a loss for words. Seeing her reaction, his lips curved in an ironic smile. "Contrary to what you might think of me as a boss, I *do* know how to show my appreciation when it's deserved."

"Good to know." Clearing her throat, she pointedly shuffled papers on her desk. "Was there anything else you wanted? If not, I have a lot of work to do before I leave at five."

"Actually," Noah murmured, "I do want something from you."

The way he said it, in that low, silky baritone, made Riley's pulse accelerate. As carnal images rolled through her mind, she strove to maintain her composure. "What is it?"

"I want you to go out on surveillance with me this afternoon."

"What? Why?"

He chuckled softly at her stricken expression. "Because my brother thinks it's time for you to be shown the ropes."

"But...*today?*"

He lifted one shoulder in a lazy shrug. "Today's as good a day as any."

"Not really. Like I said, I have a ton of work to do and—"

"Riley."

"What?"

There was a hint of steel beneath the smile he gave her. "It wasn't a request."

Riley opened her mouth to protest, then snapped it shut, opting to glare at him instead.

Unfazed, he chuckled again and slowly straightened from the doorway. "Be ready to go in half an hour."

With that, he turned and sauntered from the room.

When Riley climbed into the nondescript sedan parked outside the office building thirty minutes later, she was still seething with indignation. She didn't appreciate being manhandled by Noah, boss or not. It was a rather bad habit of his that would have to be nipped in the bud.

He was speaking quietly on the cell phone and barely glanced at her as she slid into the passenger seat and fastened her seat belt. He started the car and backed out of the parking space, and within minutes they were headed north on I-35.

"Sorry about that," Noah said as he got off the phone. "Anxious client."

Riley nodded shortly. "Where, exactly, are we going?"

"To Joseph Stanton's workplace. He's supposed to get off at four. We're gonna tail him to see if he goes straight home."

Despite her annoyance with Noah, Riley couldn't help feeling a twinge of excitement at the idea of being on her first surveillance assignment. It was the same rush she felt when chasing a hot lead for one of her stories.

Noah's mouth twitched as he watched her out of the corner of his eye. "Yeah, I figured you might change your tune about accompanying me once we were out on the road," he drawled.

Riley scowled. "That doesn't excuse your high-handedness, Noah. Just for the record, you don't have to order me around to get what you want."

He inclined his head slightly. "You're right." Before Riley could gloat over the concession, he added, "Next time I'll just pick you up, throw you over my shoulder and carry you out to the car."

Riley gasped. Without thinking, she reached over and punched him on the arm.

"Ouch! Hey, you can't hit me. I'm your boss."

"So fire me!" she hissed.

Noah looked at her, took in the ferocious expression on her face, then threw back his head and roared with laughter.

Huffing out a sigh of disgust, Riley crossed her arms and leaned back in the seat. But she wasn't entirely immune to the rumble of his deep, husky laughter, and it wasn't long before she found herself fighting the tug of a grin.

When Noah's mirth had subsided, he shook his head and smiled at her. "You're priceless, Riley Kane. I never knew you had such a temper."

"Yeah, well, there's a lot about me you don't know," she grumbled.

"True enough." Their eyes met briefly, then slid away.

Silence stretched between them until Noah reached over and turned up the volume on the CD player. As John Coltrane's "I Want to Talk About You" filled the interior of the car, Riley was flooded with vivid memories of coupling frantically with Noah on the pool table with the seductive wail of the sax in the background. As heat pooled in her belly, she clamped her thighs together and turned her face to the window.

Soon Noah exited onto a busy downtown street and parked two blocks down from a small glass office building.

"Stanton is a maintenance worker for the property-management company located inside that building," Noah explained as he threw the car in Park, cut the engine and buzzed down the windows to let in a cool summer breeze. "He drives a beige Chrysler three hundred with tags that read NO AVG JOE, so he shouldn't be hard to spot. He gets off at four, so we've got another twenty-five minutes to wait for him to pull out from the rear parking lot."

Riley nodded, peering through the windshield. "Should we get closer?" At Noah's vaguely amused look, she clarified, "To the building, I mean."

"I know what you meant, and no, we shouldn't get any closer. We don't wanna risk detection."

"Do you think Joseph Stanton knows his wife has hired a private investigator?"

"It's possible," Noah said, leaning back in his seat. "I always advise my clients not to do anything to alert their spouses to the fact that they're being investigated. Don't change your habits, don't ask too many questions about their activities, and never, ever, threaten to hire an investigator."

"Shouldn't that last one be obvious?"

"You'd be amazed how many people, especially women, blurt out threats like that in the middle of a heated argument. It makes it that much harder for us to monitor a cheating spouse who already suspects he—or she—is being watched."

"No kidding," Riley murmured. Absently she reached inside her purse and dug out a box of Hot Tamales, which she held out to Noah. "Want some?"

"No, thanks." He grinned as she began munching on the cinnamon-flavored candy. "You look like you're sitting courtside at a Spurs game. Are you enjoying this, Riley?"

"Not really. Are you?"

"About as much as I'd enjoy a root canal." At her

surprised look, he said grimly, "Believe it or not, domestic surveillance cases are my least favorite. I hate having to break the news to my client that their spouse is indeed cheating, especially when you throw children into the equation. It's a lose-lose situation for everyone involved."

Riley observed his stony profile. "So why do you take domestic surveillance cases if you hate them so much?"

A shadow of cynicism touched his mouth. "It's part of the services we offer. And, yes, it helps pay the damn bills."

"Hey, I'm not judging you." She smiled ruefully. "There were times, back when I was at the *Houston Chronicle,* that I hated being an investigative reporter. I had to be pushy and obnoxious just to get the scoop, which meant I often crossed the line and intruded on people's lives at a time when they needed their privacy the most, like after they'd suffered a devastating tragedy." Idly she ran a finger down the pleat of her cream-colored slacks. "I've never told anyone this, and I'll kill you if you breathe a word to anyone, but there were days I used to go home and cry myself to sleep because I felt so horrible about the kind of work I did."

Noah had stopped staring through the windshield and was now watching her quietly.

"It's true," Riley said with a shaky little laugh. "I was a barracuda reporter by day and a weeping willow by night. And then one day I received a letter from this sixteen-year-old girl whose parents had been murdered a year earlier. She told me that my articles on the murders had helped the police solve the case and find the real killer. She actually thanked me for being such a good reporter. Can you believe it?"

"I can," Noah said softly. "You are a good reporter."

She gave him a grateful smile. "I keep that letter in a special place in my office. Every time I begin to question the integrity of what I do, I pull out the letter and read it over and over again until I feel better." Her smile softened. "And wouldn't you know it? That sixteen-year-old girl is now a prelaw major at Howard University in Washington, D.C. We get together once a month for lunch or a trip to a museum or to see a play. She's like the little sister I never had."

When she'd finished speaking, Noah said huskily, "That's an incredible story, Riley."

"I think so, too." She laughed, waving a hand beneath her eyes. "Okay, you have to stop looking at me like that, Noah, or I'm going to embarrass myself by blubbering like an idiot. And then you'd never take me on another surveillance assignment."

He chuckled softly, but glanced away as she'd asked.

After a few moments, Riley said, "What percentage of your clients' spouses are actually proved to be cheaters?"

"Hmm. About eighty-five percent of the men, less than forty-percent of the women. But we don't get a lot of husbands wanting to investigate their wives, so those numbers are skewed."

Riley nodded, leaning her head back on the headrest and studying him from beneath her eyelashes. "But I'm sure it still holds true that men are more likely to cheat than women."

"That's probably an accurate assessment."

"Why do you think that is, Noah? Why do men cheat?"

His mouth twitched. "I can't speak on behalf of all men, Riley."

"All right, then. Speak on your own behalf. Have you ever cheated on a woman?"

He scowled. "Can we please concentrate on keeping an eye out for Stanton?"

She chuckled. "We have fifteen more minutes. And you're avoiding my question. Have you ever cheated on a woman, Noah?"

He turned his head slowly to meet her curious gaze. "Not intentionally."

"What's that supposed to mean?"

"It means," he said softly, "you can cheat on your girlfriend without ever touching another woman. You can cheat in your heart by wanting something else— someone else—and not being fully committed to the person you're with."

As Riley stared at him, she wondered if he was thinking about Kimberly, the woman he'd dated for five months, according to Lety. Had he had an affair of the heart that led to his breakup with Kimberly?

Was that what she'd meant when she told others Noah was holding out for a perfect woman that didn't exist?

Before she could probe further, Noah turned away. As she watched, his lips curved in a sardonic half smile. "So what about you, Riley? Have you ever cheated?"

She shook her head, feeling inexplicably off balance. "No, I never have."

"Not even in your heart?"

"Not even there."

"Good for you," he murmured, but there was something beneath his words, a subtle edge she couldn't begin to define.

Turning her head, she looked out the window. After another moment, she said quietly, "Did Trevor ever tell you about the time he almost cheated on me?"

When Noah said nothing, she glanced over at him. The muscle ticking in his jaw gave her the answer she needed.

"Of course you knew," she said mildly. "He was your best friend. The two of you must have shared everything with each other. So he told you about the night he got mad at me after I'd turned down his marriage proposal the first time? He told you how he was so devastated he went to a nightclub and picked up the hottest girl he could find, then took her back to his apartment intending to get back at me by sleeping with her?"

When Noah remained silent, Riley chuckled humorlessly. "I'll never forget being awakened at three o' clock in the morning by a loud pounding on the front door. It was Trevor, and he was bawling his eyes out and rambling about what a stupid fool he'd been. At first I thought he was drunk. But then he took my hand and led me over to the sofa, and proceeded to tell me how he'd taken a beautiful woman home to punish me for turning down his proposal. But he couldn't go through with it, because every time he went to touch her, all he wanted was me. He got down on his knees that night, tears and all, and *begged* me to forgive him for almost destroying the best thing that had ever happened to him. I honestly didn't know whether to send him packing or put him on a suicide watch." Shaking her head, she slanted Noah a teasing, albeit wobbly grin. "Do you know you're the main reason I stayed with Trevor?"

Noah whirled around to stare at her. "*What* did you just say?"

A little taken aback by his reaction, Riley forced a laugh that sounded strangled to her own ears. "Well, I always figured that if Trevor was really un-stable, you probably wouldn't have remained his best friend all those years. Because you always seemed so…normal."

"Normal," Noah echoed flatly.

"Yes. Don't make it sound like a bad thing, Noah. Believe me, it was good. Your friendship with Trevor was my litmus test, of sorts. In that moment, when he was on his knees sobbing hysterically and begging my forgiveness for a transgression he supposedly hadn't committed, I told myself, 'Okay, he can't be dangerous or psychotic because his best friend is the sanest, most levelheaded guy I know, and if something were seriously off about Trevor, Noah would've told me a long time ago."

Noah was watching her with an unreadable expression. "And that's how you reached the decision to trust him?"

"Nope. That's how I reached the decision not to call for help. I made the decision to trust him because I felt it in here," she said, pointing to her heart. "I knew he was telling me the truth and was genuinely sorry for what he'd planned to do, which I let him know was the dumbest thing he could've ever done. We sat and talked for a very long time after that and came to a tentative understanding of my reasons for not being ready for marriage, which were too long and complicated to get into right now."

"I agree," Noah murmured.

Riley stuffed the box of Hot Tamales back inside her purse, then, unable to resist, asked, "What did you tell him when he came to you about what he'd done that night?"

Noah's expression hardened as he stared straight ahead. "It's not important."

"It is to me."

"It shouldn't be."

She softened her voice. "Come on, Noah. Humor me."

When he answered, his voice was low and chillingly succinct. "I told him if he ever *thought* about cheating on you again, he wouldn't have to worry about you killing him. I'd kill him myself."

For several moments Riley could only stare at Noah, an unnamed emotion clogging her throat. Finally she whispered, "Thank you, Noah."

He said absolutely nothing.

At that moment, Joseph Stanton's car pulled out onto the street and headed east, away from where they were parked.

"That's him!" Riley blurted, sitting forward in her seat. "Let's go! Hurry, or we're going to lose him!"

But Noah seemed in no hurry as he started the ignition and slowly eased into the flow of traffic with that smooth, one-handed style of his. He maneuvered through the congested downtown streets with the skilled ease of a professional, and in just a few minutes brought them to within three car lengths of the beige Chrysler.

When he slanted her a lazy glance, Riley sat back with a sheepish grin. "Guess I shouldn't have doubted you. You were a cop—of course you know how to tail someone."

And he was really good. As the Chrysler sped down the busy interstate, frequently changing lanes, Noah managed to keep pace while maintaining a safe, discreet distance. He even took a phone call and switched the Coltrane CD for another, all without ever missing a beat.

Riley sent him an admiring look. "You could probably do this in your sleep."

He shrugged. "Stanton's easy. I've followed other subjects who presented more of a challenge."

"How so?"

"By being super aggressive drivers. Or, if they already suspected they were under surveillance, they repeatedly checked their rearview mirrors and were very aware of their surroundings. In those cases, I'm usually accompanied by Kenneth or Daniela in another vehicle."

They soon exited and headed down a long stretch of highway where the trees grew lush and full. Because there were less cars on the road, Noah had to hang back a little more to avoid the risk of detection.

"He's going home," he murmured.

"It appears so," Riley agreed.

Stanton hung a right at the next light and turned down a quiet residential street lined by gated entrances. The Chrysler pulled up to the first gate that guarded a community of large stone-and-stucco houses surrounded by impeccably manicured green lawns. Noah drove past without turning down the street.

Two minutes later, his cell phone rang. He spoke briefly to the caller before disconnecting.

"Mrs. Stanton?" Riley inquired.

Noah nodded. "She had a doctor's appointment this afternoon, so she was already home from work. She said her husband just pulled into the driveway."

Riley glanced out the window at the passing scenery. It came as no surprise to her that Delilah Stanton, with her designer pumps, Hermès handbag and six-figure VP salary, lived in one of the wealthiest sections of town.

"Do you think Joseph Stanton is really cheating on her," Riley wondered aloud, "or do you think she's just looking for an out?"

"Well, if she's just looking for an out, shelling out money for a private investigator probably isn't the best way to do it. I can't create infidelity that doesn't exist. If she honestly doesn't believe her husband is cheating on her, she'd be a damned fool to pay us to prove otherwise."

"So you think her suspicions could be legitimate?"

"I wouldn't have taken the case if I didn't." Noah looked amused. "Don't let your personal feelings about Delilah Stanton cloud your ability to be objective."

Remembering the way the woman had sunk her red talons into Noah, Riley scowled. "I'll try to remember that."

Noah chuckled softly. "Let's head back to the office."

Chapter 14

When they returned to Roarke Investigations, the building was empty. Janie and Kenneth had already left for the day.

"I'm just going to tie up some loose ends before I go," Riley said.

"Me, too," Noah murmured, and they headed to their separate offices.

An hour later, Riley appeared in his doorway to let him know she was leaving. Noah, kneeling before two cardboard boxes crammed with old files, muttered distractedly, "Have a nice evening."

Riley hesitated. "Do you need help finding something?"

"No, I'm fine. You go on ahead."

She paused for another moment, then with a small sigh of resignation, she set down her attaché case by the door and walked over to him. Unbuttoning and rolling up the sleeves of her paisley silk blouse, she dropped to a crouch beside him and reached for the other box. "What're we looking for?"

"An old case file. Folder should be labeled Mulroney. He was one of our first clients when we launched the agency four years ago."

Riley's pretty little eyebrows furrowed together. "You don't have your archives stored on the computer?"

He shot her a look. "We didn't have Janie then. Cut us some slack."

"All right, all right," she said, grinning as she held up her hands in surrender.

As they worked together in companionable silence for several minutes, Noah's concentration was divided between the task at hand and the light, exotic scent of the woman beside him. He'd been trying since that morning to push thoughts of her out of his mind, but it was a lost cause. Even while she'd been out of the office for most of the day, he'd daydreamed about her, torturing himself with vividly erotic memories of their lovemaking. He couldn't stop himself from wanting her any more than he could've stopped himself from going into her office that afternoon and compelling her to accompany him on the surveillance assignment. Contrary to what he'd told Riley, Kenneth had nothing to do with the directive. It had been strictly Noah's doing. He'd asked her along for purely selfish reasons—because he wanted to be alone with her. And if that made him a pathetic fool…well, what else was new?

"Found it," Riley sang triumphantly, pulling a folder out of the box.

Noah didn't know whether to be relieved or disappointed by how quickly she'd located the file he was looking for. He'd wanted more time with her.

He *needed* more time.

As she handed him the faded manila folder bound by a thick rubber band, their fingers brushed. Heat shot through his veins, and their eyes met as an undercurrent of awareness passed between them.

"Thanks," Noah murmured, setting aside the folder. "I owe you one."

"No problem." After another moment, Riley rose to her feet. Noah followed more slowly.

Nervously she moistened her lips, and he envied the hell out of her tongue. "Thanks for letting me tag along this afternoon," she said with a breathless little catch to her voice. "Now I can say I've been on my very first surveillance assignment."

"Nothing like those firsts," he said, low and husky. "I always remember mine."

The look in her sultry dark eyes told him she'd caught his veiled meaning. Beneath the silk blouse she wore, her chest rose and fell more rapidly as she struggled to regulate her breathing. It gave him a dark thrill of pleasure to know he could affect her even half as much as she affected him.

When her gaze drifted to his mouth, it took every ounce of self-control he possessed not to haul her into his arms and lower her quickly to the floor.

"Noah…" She closed her eyes for a moment and drew a deep, calming breath. "What happened between us last night was a mistake."

He'd been waiting all day for her to say that. And he still wasn't prepared for the dagger her words sent through his heart. "A mistake," he repeated slowly, as if testing the word on his tongue.

Riley looked him square in the eye. "Yes, a mistake. We both know it was. Neither of us meant to hurt Trevor that way."

Anger flared in his chest. "Trevor's gone."

She flinched, enough to make him regret his harsh tone—if he were feeling a little less reckless. A little less desperate.

Riley edged toward the door. "I—I should go," she mumbled. "I'm having dinner with my grandmother and she'll worry if I'm late."

"You can run as far as you want," Noah said in a soft, silky voice that belied the savage beating of his heart, "but you'll never outrun the truth. And the truth is that you want me, Riley. I tasted it in your kiss, saw it in the way you looked at me when I entered your body for the first time." Hearing her breath catch in her throat, he shook his head slowly. "What happened last night wasn't about mistakes, or guilt, or the past. It was about us. About you and me, about this unexpected, incredible, amazing connection we have. And if you stand there and tell me you don't feel it, Riley, I'll have to call you a liar."

The expression on her beautiful face was one of such naked terror Noah would have chuckled if there'd been anything remotely amusing about the situation.

He took a step toward her. "Riley."

She shook her head quickly. "I—I can't do this, Noah. I have to go."

He caught her wrist to halt her retreat. When she turned around, he cupped the back of her head and pulled her against him. As his mouth descended upon hers, she stiffened in protest, her arms lifting to shove him away. He was on fire for her, need and desire whipping through his body like flames, but he'd never forced himself on any woman, and he wasn't about to start now with the woman he loved.

But as Riley's hands flattened against his chest, a wonderful little thing happened. Instead of pushing him away, her fingers curled around a fistful of his shirt and drew him closer. Noah groaned his relief and satisfaction into her mouth, then proceeded to devour her. There was no other word to describe the way he seized her lips and tongue in a kiss of such fierce, searing possession that she moaned into his mouth.

The sound snapped what little self-control he'd had left.

Reaching down, he cupped her sweet, curvy bottom in both hands and backed her against the door, too impatient for the floor. Tearing his mouth away from hers, he knelt in front of her and unsnapped the button of her slacks. She quickly stepped out of her heels and kicked them aside, then stood trembling as he slid the pants off her body. She gasped as he reached for her panties and practically ripped the scrap of black lace in half in his haste to tug it over her hips and down her legs.

He nudged her thighs apart, parted the soft, springy curls there, and pressed his mouth to her hot, moist center. She moaned deep in her throat, her hips arching off the door, her hands scrambling for purchase and settling on his shoulders. Cradling the back of her legs, he tilted her pelvis closer, stroking and tasting her honeyed flesh with his tongue while she made helpless little mewling sounds. In and out, back and forth, his tongue flicked over the smooth, wet folds, feasting on her sweetness. When her thighs began to quiver uncontrollably beneath his hands, he plunged deep inside her one last time, making her sob his name as her body convulsed in the grip of an orgasm that nearly buckled her knees.

He banded his arms around her waist and held her steady for a moment, his heart slamming against his rib cage, his penis throbbing painfully inside his pants.

He couldn't wait any longer. He had to have her.

He reared back from her and stood, taking out a condom from his pocket and tossing the wallet aside. With impatient fingers, he unzipped the fly of his jeans and reached inside his boxers. He quickly sheathed himself, then lifted Riley into his arms again, groaning as she wrapped her luscious legs around his waist and curved her arms around his neck.

She cried out sharply as he drove into her with one long, demanding stroke. Her back arched and he thrust into her a second time, burying himself deeper in her tight, exquisite heat. Fighting to control the orgasm already threatening to erupt, he moved slowly within her, his gaze locked fiercely onto hers.

"This isn't a mistake, Riley," he whispered. "Does this feel like a mistake?"

She whimpered and shook her head. He increased the sensual tempo, grasping her buttocks as he stroked deep inside her. "What about now?" he murmured, bending his head to nuzzle her arched throat. "Does it feel like a mistake now?"

"No," she breathed, closing her eyes and licking her lips.

He'd intended to go slow, to prolong their lovemaking for as long as he could. But when she began rocking against him, her hips undulating erotically, his restraint broke.

Seizing her lips in a plundering kiss, he thrust into her, forcing her harder and faster to the peak, driving her to it as her inner muscles began to clench around him.

"Noah...I'm coming!" Her fingernails bit into his shoulders and her back arched as another climax tore through her.

He exploded inside her with a force that wrenched a hoarse groan from him. And still he kept thrusting, grasping her thighs and holding her tightly against him as he continued pumping furiously into her. His second orgasm erupted in a jolt of sensation that shook his entire body.

His loud cry joined hers as they clung tightly to each other. Riley burrowed her face against his neck and he held her in place for several moments, his chest heaving against hers as he whispered her name over and over again.

He wanted to stay like that forever, buried deep inside her. Heaven couldn't get any better than this.

And then heaven spoke. "Take me home, Noah," she whispered.

Drawing back, he searched her flushed face to see if he'd heard right. "You want me to drive you home?"

She shook her head. "Take me home with you. I want to spend the night with you."

He stared at her. His throat worked, but no sound came forth. How many times had he dreamed about Riley uttering those very words to him?

Mistaking his silence for reluctance, she looped her arms around his neck and leaned close, kissing him. Softly at first, then with increasing hunger. "Please, Noah? Please?"

"You don't even have to ask," he growled. He crushed his mouth to hers, and as shirts went flying, they slid to the floor.

Hours later, they lay spent in each other's arms, listening to the lazy drone of nocturnal insects outside Noah's open bedroom window. A soft, balmy breeze stirred the sheer curtains and wafted inside the room to wash over their damp, heated flesh.

"My grandmother knows about us," Riley said, snuggled against the solid warmth of Noah's body with her head tucked beneath his chin, their legs tangled together beneath the covers. For the first time in much too long, she felt completely relaxed, body and mind.

"Yeah?" There was a hint of amusement in the deep timbre of his voice. "What tipped her off? The fact that you didn't come home last night, or the fact that you called to tell her you wouldn't be home tonight, either?"

"It's not funny," Riley protested, trying to pinch him somewhere on his chest. Her efforts were futile; the man didn't have an ounce of body fat. She settled for poking him in the ribs instead.

He laughed, capturing her hand and bringing it to his soft, warm lips. "Why does it bother you that your grandmother knows about us? Are you worried that she won't approve?"

"Not at all. In fact—" She broke off abruptly and bit her lip.

Noah waited a beat. "In fact what?"

"Nothing. It's not important."

"Riley."

She hesitated. "I was going to say that she'd probably start planning our wedding." A wry smile curved her mouth. "I don't know what kind of spell you cast over my grandmother, Noah Roarke, but she positively worships you and the ground you walk on."

He chuckled, a low, husky rumble against her ear. "Implying that someone has to be under the influence of a spell in order to like me."

"You know that's not what I meant."

"I know." He nibbled on her fingertips, sending shivers of warmth down her spine. "It's the same way with my mother. She thinks the world of you."

Riley smiled. "The feeling's mutual." She paused thoughtfully. "Ironic, isn't it?"

"What?"

"My grandmother and your mother—two of the most important people in our lives—thinking so highly of us, when you and I spent the last five years as virtual strangers."

"Hmm," he responded noncommittally.

After another moment, she said, "Noah?"

"Yeah?"

"What was your first impression of me?"

He stopped toying with her fingers and splayed them across his chest. She could feel the strong, steady beat of his heart beneath her hand. "My first impression was formed before I even laid eyes on you," he reminded her.

Riley chuckled ruefully. "Of course. I rear-ended you. Not exactly the best first impression to make."

"Not exactly," he agreed with a smile in his voice. "I used a few choice adjectives to describe you even before I got out of the car."

"I'll bet."

"But it got better once I actually saw you."

She traced lazy patterns on his flat, muscled abdomen. "Better in what way?"

"For starters," he said huskily, "I thought you were the most beautiful woman I'd ever seen."

Riley's heart thumped. It was the last answer she'd expected to hear. Slowly she lifted her head and searched his face in the moonlit darkness. "You really thought that?"

He nodded. "I still do."

She shook her head, her throat suddenly tight. "You can't say things like that to me, Noah," she whispered.

"Why not?"

"Because…because…" *Because you've already gotten inside my head. Don't get in my heart too!*

He laughed softly, letting her off the hook as he drew her back into his arms. He kissed the top of her head, then murmured, "Don't ask questions you're not ready to hear the answer to, baby girl."

He was right, of course.

"So now it's your turn. What was your first impression of me?"

She grinned. "Really want to know?"

"I asked."

"Well, the first thing I thought was that you looked mean, which, under the circumstances, was perfectly understandable. I was terrified of you. You looked so mad."

He chuckled. "It wasn't all directed at you. I'd already been having a bad morning."

She nodded. "Once you got closer, your expression softened. Probably because you saw the sheer terror on my face and took pity on me," she added with a grin. "Anyway, once I realized you weren't going to arrest or strangle me, I relaxed enough to see how good-looking you were."

"Good-looking, huh?"

She smiled against his chest, grateful he couldn't see her face, because suddenly she found herself blushing. "Better than good-looking. Fine as hell. I remember marveling at how incredibly broad your shoulders were and thinking you had the most amazing, penetrating eyes I'd ever seen." She paused, deep in thought for a moment. It was funny how the mind played tricks on you. She'd buried those memories deep into her subconsciousness, ashamed to admit, even to herself, that she'd found Trevor's best friend so damned appealing. "You know, before I met Trevor, I'd only been attracted to brown- and dark-skinned men. There's just something irresistible about smooth, rich mahogany skin," she murmured, running her hand up and down Noah's chest, feeling the muscles bunch and quiver beneath her touch. "I love your skin, Noah. Every beautiful inch of it."

"That goes both ways." His voice was tight, rough.

"It's entirely possible," Riley continued philosophically, "that if I'd met you and Trevor at the same time, say, like, at a nightclub, based on physical appearance alone, I might have danced with you first."

"Just once?"

She grinned. "Okay. Maybe a second and third time."

He chuckled, tipping her chin up so that he could see her face. He brushed a kiss over her forehead, then across her mouth. She opened for him, seeking his tongue, and they kissed deeply and provocatively.

Noah's eyes were glittering with desire when they at last drew apart. "You know what I think?" he said softly as he pulled her on top of him. "I think we would've danced all night."

"You think so?" Riley's heart was pounding violently against her ribs as she straddled him. "All night?"

He groaned as she lowered her body onto his long, thick shaft. "And into the morning."

"Mmm. Like this?" He groaned softly as she began to gyrate on him, slowly and seductively, closing her eyes as she gave herself over to the exquisite sensations. He reached up and fondled her breasts, teasing and caressing her nipples until they hardened to aching points.

Heat poured through her limbs, drawing her backward like a bow. With her head thrown back, she braced her hands on his upper thighs and rode him while he thrust hard, fast, deeper with every stroke.

As their bodies slapped noisily together, she could feel another climax building, just as powerful as the others had been. *"Noah,"* she moaned.

"Dance for me, sweetheart."

Her back arched tautly as her body began to contract around his throbbing penis, wringing an orgasm out of him at the same time she came with an exultant cry.

When her spasms tapered off, she collapsed against him in boneless exhaustion, and he gave a low, husky laugh. As she snuggled against him, he stroked lazy hands down her back and over the curve of her bottom. Lulled by his gentle caresses, she soon drifted off to sleep, not knowing that Noah remained awake long afterward, whispering words of love to her.

Chapter 15

Early the next morning, Riley sat on a bar stool at the center island in Noah's kitchen sipping a cup of fresh-brewed coffee. As she read the newspaper, her foot swung from side to side, matching her buoyant mood.

She'd gotten very little sleep the night before, she still had to drive home and get grilled by her grandmother, and she was probably going to be late for work on her second week on the job.

But none of that mattered.

For the first time in years, Riley felt at peace. And she knew it had everything to do with the gorgeous man who sauntered into the kitchen just then, buttoning the cuffs of the gray-and-white-striped broadcloth shirt he wore.

Riley's pulse quickened as he walked over and leaned down to kiss her softly, sweetly, their lips clinging before he drew away to nuzzle her throat.

"Something smells wonderful," he murmured.

"I made coffee."

He lifted his head and winked at her. "That's not what I was talking about, but that smells good, too."

He walked over to the counter and poured coffee into the ceramic mug she'd set out for him. "Great brew," he said after taking a sip.

"Thanks." She smiled. "I have my talents."

"Believe me, Riley Kane, you're a woman of *many* talents," he said in that low, velvety tone that had a dangerous effect on her heart rate.

She eyed him warily. "Don't look at me like that. You've already made me late by insisting we take a shower together."

"Hey, I was helping you out. This way, all you have to do when you get home is throw on some clothes. I saved you time by having you take a shower with me."

"Yes, but a *thirty-minute* shower, Noah?"

His grin was downright wicked. "I wanted to make sure we didn't, uh, miss a spot."

She laughed. "Yeah, right."

He chuckled. "Besides, it doesn't matter if you're late to the office. I already called Janie and told her you're accompanying me on an errand this morning."

"I am?"

"Sort of. Before we head into the office, I thought we could have breakfast somewhere, and I'm not talking about IHOP. Somewhere with linen-covered tables and fresh-cut flowers as centerpieces. How does that sound?"

Riley warmed with pleasure. "It sounds wonderful, Noah." She hesitated, biting her lower lip. "But I don't want to start getting preferential treatment just because I'm sleeping with the boss."

He grinned. "Hell, that's one of the perks of the job. Just ask Janie."

Riley laughed, rising and walking over to the sink to wash out her empty cup.

"By the way," Noah said, leaning back against the counter, "what did you want to discuss with me on Monday night?"

"Monday night?" she echoed blankly.

"Yeah. You came here to talk to me about something. We got…sidetracked."

"Oh!" Riley was shocked, and more than a little dismayed, to realize she'd completely forgotten about her encounter with Trevor's mother. How could something urgent enough to send her racing to Noah's house in the middle of the night have been forgotten so easily?

You knew this would happen. Getting involved with Noah is already interfering with your mission.

She jumped as Noah took the coffee mug from her hands, which she'd been scrubbing vigorously, and set it down in the empty sink. Taking her hand, he led her over to the small breakfast table and made her sit, then pulled out another chair and nimbly straddled it.

"Talk to me," he murmured. "Tell me what happened."

Riley hesitated. "I ran into Trevor's mother on Monday."

Noah's expression softened. "I'm sorry. That must have been very difficult for you."

"Not as difficult as it was for her."

As she relayed her entire conversation with Leona Simmons, Noah listened in impassive silence. Even when she told him about the woman's odd, distracted behavior and her remark about Trevor, Noah said nothing.

"Well?" Riley prompted when she'd finished her account. "What do you think?"

"I don't know what to think."

Riley frowned. "'A mother should never have to bury her own child. Especially when that child—' She didn't complete the sentence. Especially when that child what? What did she stop herself from saying?"

"Especially when that child had such a hard life," Noah suggested. "'Especially when that child was all I had left in the world.' I don't know, Riley. The woman is still grieving. Nothing she said was out of character for a mother mourning the loss of her only child."

"I know that. But it was the way she said everything, and the strange way she behaved. I'm telling you, Noah, Trevor's mother is hiding something."

Noah frowned. "Because she lied about not getting your letters or phone messages? Her reason made perfect sense. I know it was painful for her to see you again after all these years. Hell, Riley, when *I* saw you for the first time a couple of weeks ago, it was painful. You brought back so many memories of Trevor—"

"I'm sorry," she said softly. "I'm sorry the sight of me causes you so much pain."

Noah closed his eyes for a moment. "That's not what I meant and you know it."

"You're right. I'm sorry." She drew a deep, weary breath and slowly exhaled. "I think Ms. Simmons is hiding something, and I want to know what it is. That's what I came here to talk to you about on Monday night. I know it may not seem like it because I forgot to tell you, but until I get some answers, that conversation with Trevor's mother is gonna bug the hell out of me."

In silence Noah studied her face for several moments. Finally, in a resigned tone, he said, "I'm going to call one of my contacts in the police department. Maybe it's time to get you in front of a sketch artist to give your description of the man you saw at Trevor's funeral."

Riley's throat constricted as she gazed at him. Words couldn't begin to describe the depth of gratitude she felt. "Thank you, Noah," she whispered.

And somehow, she knew that was enough.

"We missed you at Fast Eddie's on Sunday," Paulo Sanchez said to Noah that evening when they met for drinks at a local bar. Noah had chosen somewhere off the beaten path, where they could talk in private without being observed by other cops.

"Sorry about that," he said, signaling the bartender for two beers. "Something came up."

"Something," Paulo countered with a sly grin, "or someone?"

"None of your damned business," Noah said good-naturedly.

Paulo gave a shout of laughter. "I knew it!"

"Knew what?" As the bartender set down two bottles of beer in front of them, Noah reached for one and took a healthy swig.

"As soon as I heard Riley was working for you," Paulo said, "I knew it was only a matter of time before something would happen between the two of you." His grin widened as he lifted his beer to his mouth. "Didn't waste any time, did you?"

"I don't know what you're talking about."

"Aw, come on, Roarke! You're gonna hold out on *me,* the guy you poured your heart out to?"

"While I was in a drunken stupor," Noah reminded him.

Paulo laughed. "Don't blame the alcohol. You wanted to unburden yourself. I could tell."

"Whatever you say, Sanchez. But just for the record, the reason I didn't make it on Sunday is that I took Riley to get new tires. By the time they finished working on her car, it would've been too late for me to run home and change my clothes and make it to Fast Eddie's on time."

Paulo gave him a knowing look. "So you *haven't* slept with Riley? Is that what you're telling me?"

"I'm not telling you anything," Noah grumbled.

Paulo wagged his head at him. "You're a man of many secrets, my friend."

"Hard to keep any in this damned town. Who told you about Riley working at the agency, anyway?"

"Lety, who heard it from a friend of hers who works at the courthouse. Apparently Riley's been making a lot of trips there on behalf of Roarke Investigations. Lety was mad she had to hear the news from someone other than Riley."

"Maybe that's because Lety's always been a little loose lipped."

Paulo grinned, taking a gulp of beer. "Don't let her hear you say that. It'd break her heart. You know she's got a thing for you."

Noah grimaced. "God, I hope not."

"Of course," Paulo said with mock sobriety. "Doesn't she know that as far as you're concerned, all other women pale in comparison to the lovely Miss Kane?"

Noah grinned, not even bothering to deny the allegation.

"Seriously though, Roarke. What's it like working with her? Everything you ever thought it would be?"

"I never actually fantasized about *working* with Riley." Noah's mouth twitched. "My fantasies were of a…different variety."

"Yeah, I'll bet." Both men shared a low chuckle.

"So what've you got her doing?" Paulo asked. "The company newsletter?"

"We don't have a company newsletter."

"Too bad. It'd be a great place to announce your engagement."

Noah choked on a swallow of beer. Paulo reached over and pounded him hard on the back, his face all innocence. "Was it something I said?"

Wiping beer from his mouth, Noah glared at the other man. "We're not engaged."

"Not yet. Give it time." Paulo's knowing smile held the wisdom of a sage.

Noah shook his head, absently rubbing his thumb back and forth against the frosty condensation lining his bottle. "I haven't even told her how I feel about her."

"Well, you've got until the end of August. But I wouldn't wait that long if I were you."

Noah remembered the way Riley had reacted when he told her she was the most beautiful woman he'd ever seen. How would she react to the news that he'd been in love with her for the past five years? Would it send her fleeing back to Washington, D.C. on the first thing smoking?

He didn't even want to imagine. Which was why he hadn't bared his soul yet.

Coward, an inner voice taunted.

On the nineteen-inch color television mounted above the bar, the Spurs were trying to avoid elimination in the NBA finals. Noah watched the game in silence for a few moments, then said, "I need a favor."

Paulo grinned. "I'd be honored to be your best man—as long as your brother doesn't mind."

"That's not the favor I need," Noah muttered, reaching for the large yellow envelope he'd placed on the counter beside him, "but, yes, Kenneth *would* mind."

"Figured as much. What's this?"

"A composite sketch of a person I'm investigating for one of my clients. Could you run it through the system to see if you get a positive ID?"

Paulo opened the envelope and partially withdrew the charcoal illustration of the German man Riley had described for the freelance sketch artist that afternoon. "Doesn't look familiar. One of your cases, you say?"

Noah nodded.

Paulo folded the envelope and tucked it inside the front pocket of his black sport coat. "I'll see what I come up with."

"Thanks, Sanchez. I owe you one."

Paulo flashed a crooked grin. "Just make me your best man and we'll call it even."

Noah laughed. "Hell, if I ever work up the courage to ask Riley Kane to marry me, I'll name our first-born after you."

Sitting cross-legged on the floor of her parents' musty attic, Riley lifted a faded black-and-white photograph out of a box and smiled at the image of her grandparents posing outside their first home, a small clapboard house located on the east side of town. In the photo, Florinda and Elgin Kane were beaming at the camera, their smiles bright and full of hope for the future. After twenty-five blissful years of marriage, Elgin had died of esophageal cancer. Riley, who'd only been a toddler at the time, had grown up with no memories of her grandfather other than the tales she'd heard from her grandmother. Florinda, who'd moved in with her son and his family shortly after burying her husband, had never remarried. In that moment, it occurred to Riley that she'd never asked her grandmother why.

With her lips pursed in thought, Riley added the photograph to a box of memorabilia she planned to showcase at Florinda's seventy-fifth birthday party. As she was securing the lid on the box, her attention landed on an old wooden trunk pushed into a corner of the attic.

She got up and walked toward the trunk, already knowing what was inside as she unhooked the latches and raised the heavy lid. There, carefully wrapped in layers of muslin, was her grandmother's wedding gown.

As a child, Riley had been utterly fascinated by the vintage silk chiffon creation that resembled gowns worn by brides in old black-and-white movies. But while she'd been permitted to *look* at the dress, her mother forbade her from ever touching or removing it from its safe confines in the trunk.

Wagging her finger at Riley, Barbara Kane would lecture, "Your great-grandfather spent his life savings on that dress just to make sure his daughter would look absolutely beautiful on her wedding day. If I catch you messing with it, Riley, your behind is mine."

Riley remembered creeping upstairs to the attic to sneak peeks at the gown and run her hand over the silk ivory fabric, knowing she risked life and limb. Even now, as she stood before the trunk, her mother's stern warning echoed through her mind.

Biting her lower lip, Riley glanced over her shoulder toward the stairwell, half-expecting to find her mother charging toward her with teeth bared. But Barbara Kane was vacationing in Hawaii until next week, and Florinda was out for the evening.

Chuckling at her own paranoia—she was a grown woman, for God's sake—Riley reached inside the trunk, unwrapped the gown and lifted it out as gingerly as if it were made of tissue. As she held it up to the light, a soft gasp escaped her lips. Though she'd just finished poring through her grandmother's wedding photos, she'd forgotten how lovely the actual dress was. With a fitted bosom, a nipped waist, and a skirt so wide and full it demanded attention, it was, quite simply, the most beautiful wedding gown Riley had ever seen.

Grace Kelly, eat your heart out.

Glancing around the attic, Riley located an old floor-length mirror with a tiny crack running vertically down the center. She crossed to the mirror and held up the gown to her body. Almost at once, she was flooded with memories of trying on wedding dresses at a local bridal boutique while her mother and grandmother looked on. The one she'd finally settled on had been simple and contemporary, a strapless, straight-fitting number with an open back. She'd always thought that was the style

she wanted, but now, looking at her grandmother's exquisitely classic...

Riley was shocked by the train of her thoughts.
Why on earth was she thinking about wedding gowns?
Since Trevor's death, she'd never even allowed herself
to consider the possibility of finding love again, let
alone getting married.

"Something you want to tell me?"

Riley whirled around. Florinda stood at the top
of the stairs watching her with an amused expression on her face.

"You scared the living daylight out of me,
Grandma!" Riley exclaimed.

Florinda chuckled. "Sorry. I just got back home
and didn't know where you'd gone off to." She
climbed the last step and made her way across the
cluttered room, a soft smile on her face as she beheld
her old wedding gown held up to Riley's body.

"I was just, uh, looking at it," Riley said quickly.
"I hope you don't mind?"

"Of course not, baby. That was your mother's
hang-up, not mine."

Riley gaped at her. "You mean all this time...you
didn't care if I touched your dress?"

"Goodness, no," Florinda said with a dismissive
wave of her hand. "But every time I tried to take it out
of the trunk and show it to you, you ran off terrified."

Riley chuckled grimly as she turned back to the
mirror. "I was terrified of my mother."

"I know." Florinda's reflection joined hers in the

cracked glass. She wore a quiet, reminiscent smile. "It's quite a dress, isn't it? I still remember how awe-struck I was when my father bought it for me. It was far too expensive, more than we could afford, but he didn't care. Only the best would do for his little girl, he said. When I wore the gown on my wedding day, I felt like royalty."

Riley grinned. "You *looked* like it, too."

"Why, thank you, baby." Florinda's gaze softened as she studied Riley's reflection in the mirror. "You know, if you ever decide again to get married, I'd be honored if you wore my dress."

Riley's throat constricted with emotion. "That's very sweet of you, Grandma," she whispered. "But—"

"But what? You don't think you're ever going to find another man worth marrying?"

"Well…yeah."

Florinda shook her head slowly. "You don't believe that any more than I do."

Dropping her gaze from the mirror, Riley walked back over to the trunk and began to fold up the voluminous gown. "If you're implying that Noah—"

"I didn't imply anything, Riley. *You* brought up his name, not me."

"But you were thinking it."

"And so were you."

Riley pushed out a heavy sigh. "There's nothing going on between me and Noah."

"You've spent the last two nights with him. I'd say that's more than nothing."

Florinda was right, of course. But how could Riley explain to her grandmother what she herself didn't fully understand? Last night she'd asked—practically begged—Noah to take her home with him. She'd wanted to be with him, wanted it in a way she'd never imagined was possible. What was happening to her?

"There's nothing wrong with finding yourself attracted to another man," Florinda said gently.

Riley groaned. "But we're not just talking about *any* man. We're talking about Noah."

"All the more reason it's perfectly normal."

Riley shot her grandmother a look. "He was Trevor's best friend."

Florinda met her gaze steadily. "I know, baby. And as hard as it may be for you to accept, Trevor's not coming back. The sooner you move on with your life, the better."

Riley turned away, busying herself with wrapping the gown in muslin the way she'd found it in the trunk.

"I've upset you," Florinda murmured.

Riley shook her head. "I'm not upset, Grandma. I'm just…confused."

"About your feelings?"

"Yes." Riley swallowed a hard lump in her throat. "He's not the man I'd always thought he was. He's different. He's…incredible," she finished with a quiet note of wonder.

Florinda appeared at her side to help her with the gown. "I always knew if you got to know him better, you'd reach that conclusion."

"Well, you were right." Riley smiled at her grandmother. "As usual."

"So what're you going to do about it?"

"I don't know. I can't think that far ahead. I'm just getting used to the idea of us being friends." *More than friends,* an inner voice reminded her. *Lovers.*

Together she and her grandmother closed and latched the trunk. As they started toward the stairwell, Florinda draped a companionable arm around Riley's shoulders.

"Can I ask you a question, Grandma?"

"Of course, dear."

"Why didn't you ever remarry?"

Florinda stopped walking and turned to Riley with a surprised expression. "Do you realize this is the first time you've ever asked me that question?"

"I know," Riley murmured, a little embarrassed. "I've always wondered, but it just never occurred to me to come right out and ask you. Probably because you came to live with us when I was barely two, and as I got older, I not only took your presence for granted, I became used to having you all to myself." Her lips curved in a rueful smile. "Sorry. I guess that was pretty selfish of me."

Florinda laughed. "Not at all. You were—*are*—what brought me the most joy. After my Elgin died, I needed a new purpose in life. Looking after you gave me that purpose. And as you got older, I did date every now and then."

Riley nodded, recalling a string of polite, handsome gentlemen who'd shown up at the house to take Florinda out on a date, only to be subjected to intense scrutiny by her overprotective son.

"But you never wanted to remarry?" Riley prodded.

Florinda was silent for several moments before she answered. "I can't say that I did. The men I met after your grandfather died were nice enough, but none of them ever came close to being the wonderful person my Elgin was." She gave her granddaughter a quiet, intuitive smile. "Of course, if a man like Noah Roarke had ever come along in *my* life, there's no chance on earth I would've let him get away." Her tone gentled to match the stroke of her hand down the side of Riley's mussed hair. "Everything happens for a reason, sweetheart. Even tragedy."

Chapter 16

The next afternoon, Noah sat across the desk from Delilah Stanton, who'd shown up unannounced at the office for a "follow-up meeting" they'd never scheduled. Wearing a formfitting designer skirt suit and stiletto heels, she sat with her long, shapely legs crossed and a coquettish smile flirting about her red-painted lips.

She didn't look like a woman who was concerned about a cheating husband.

She looked like a woman on the prowl for a new one.

"Have you had an opportunity to check the credit card bills for any large or unusual purchases, Mrs. Stanton?" Noah inquired, trying to steer the conversation back to business after she'd casually asked him about his family.

She nodded. "There was nothing suspicious on the bills, nor on any of the debit card receipts I found in his wallet." She frowned. "He's covering his tracks very well."

Or he doesn't have any tracks to cover at all, Noah thought sardonically. Aloud he said, "As you know, I've been tailing your husband for several days now. To and from the office, during his lunch breaks, last night when you called to say he'd just left the house. He drove to a sports bar to have drinks with friends and watch the game." Leaning back in the chair, Noah steepled his fingers together and thoughtfully regarded Delilah Stanton. "It's too early in the investigation for me to say your husband's not cheating, but I think we have to consider that possibility."

Her mouth tightened with displeasure. "That man is definitely up to something, Noah. You have to take my word for it."

"Unfortunately," Noah countered mildly, "unless I can conclusively establish Mr. Stanton's infidelity, it's going to be your word against his in a court of law."

"He's been spending a lot of time on the Internet lately," Delilah blurted. "And he waits until late at night, after I've gone to bed."

"That's why I provided you with the software to monitor his e-mail, chat room discussions, and other Internet activity."

"I'm having difficulty installing the program. I

know you said it was easy, but I'm not the most technically savvy person." The smile she gave him was full of innocence. "I was hoping you might be able to come over and install it for me—when Joseph's not home, of course."

Noah frowned. "I think you know that wouldn't be a good idea, Mrs. Stanton. For all you know, your husband may have hired a private investigator to monitor *you*. Which is why you really should stop coming to the office. Anything we need to discuss can be handled over the phone."

"You're right. You're absolutely right." She heaved a sigh. "I guess it never occurred to me that Joseph might actually hire someone to follow me. He knows I would never cheat on him."

Noah wasn't so sure about that, but he kept the thought to himself. "If you'd like, Mrs. Stanton, I can give you a demonstration of how to install the surveillance software on your computer at home."

She was already out of her chair and rounding the desk before he'd finished speaking. Suppressing a wry chuckle, Noah accessed the software demo site on his computer. "I'm going to install a test version on my machine so you can see how easy it is."

"All right." As she leaned close for a better view of the monitor, Noah's nostrils were filled with the heavy, expensive scent of Opium.

"As I told you before," he explained, "the surveillance software records all e-mails sent and received, all chat and Instant Message conversations, all keystrokes typed, all Web sites visited, all log-on/log-off activity, and all applications run. You will automatically be forwarded a copy of every e-mail, chat and Instant Message the moment it is sent or received."

"Very impressive," Delilah purred, leaning closer to him. "And you're absolutely sure Joseph will never know what I'm doing?"

"Correct. The program doesn't show up as an icon on the computer, doesn't appear in the Windows system tray or task list, and it can't be uninstalled without the password you specify."

"Hmm. So it's virtually secret-proof, then."

"That's right." By now, her breasts were pressed so firmly against Noah's back he could feel her nipples protruding through the thin silk of her blouse.

Clearing his throat, he discreetly edged away, only to have her follow. Frowning, he looked up to say something to her and got an eyeful of cleavage. When the hell had she unbuttoned her shirt?

"Mrs. Stanton—"

There was a brisk knock at the door just then. Before Noah could open his mouth, the door opened and Riley stepped quickly into the office. "I need you to sign this notary pub—" When she saw Delilah standing behind the desk, her eyes flew wide. "I'm sorry. I didn't realize you were with a client." A second later, her gaze narrowed as she watched Delilah unhurriedly step away from Noah's chair and fasten the top button of her blouse.

When Riley looked at Noah, he mentally groaned

at the fury reflected in her dark eyes. Fury and something suspiciously akin to betrayal.

He stood. "Riley—"

"I've obviously caught you at a bad time," she said evenly. "I'll come back when you're less...preoccupied." Without another word, she spun on her heel and left the office, yanking the door closed behind her.

Delilah watched the entire exchange with a look of amused speculation. "*Tsk-tsk,* Noah. That's why it's never a good idea to get involved with the hired help."

"Nor is it a good idea to get involved with clients," Noah growled. "I think it's time for you to leave, Mrs. Stanton."

She frowned. "But you haven't finished—"

"Oh, yes, I have. You're a smart woman—I have every confidence in your ability to install the surveillance software on your own. And if you need help, call technical support." He strode to the door and held it open for her. When she'd taken two steps into the hallway, he said, "One more thing, Mrs. Stanton."

She glanced back hopefully.

Noah said tersely, "I don't know what kind of game you're playing, but I'm not interested. The next time you decide to show up here unannounced, I'm canceling our contract and refunding your money. Are we clear?"

She hesitated, then gave a short nod before continuing down the hall with her head held high.

Noah's cell phone rang as he was about to make

his way to Riley's office. He swore under his breath and dug it out of his pocket, glancing at the caller-ID screen.

He answered quickly when he saw that it was Paulo. "Whatcha got for me?"

"Got a positive ID on your man," Paulo said. "Name's Karl Ludwig. When I didn't get any matches through the system, I showed the composite sketch to my cousin Rafe. It turns out this guy was a person of interest in an FBI investigation a few years ago."

"For what?"

"Suspected money laundering. Ludwig was the head of a large family of German immigrants who ran an antiques business in Fredericksburg. Three years ago, the FBI received an anonymous tip that the family was using the business as a front for a money-laundering operation. But the Bureau's investigation turned up nothing. Nada. The books were clean as a whistle."

Noah felt the muscles in the back of his neck tighten. He remembered Riley telling him about the time she'd stumbled upon Trevor conversing with a German man outside an antiques shop in Fredericksburg. Could it have been Karl Ludwig? If so, what the hell was Trevor's connection to the suspected leader of a criminal enterprise?

"Anyway, it doesn't really matter now," Paulo said.

"Why not?"

"Karl Ludwig's dead. He had a massive heart attack a couple of years ago. After that, apparently, many members of the family got deported for unrelated violations. The only one who's still here is Ludwig's grandson, Jonas. He runs the antiques shop with his wife and three teenage children. From all accounts, he's operating a legitimate business." Paulo's voice was muffled as he spoke to someone in the background, then came back on the line. "Listen, I gotta head to a task force meeting. Let me know if there's anything else you need, and I'll see you on Sunday."

Noah thanked Paulo for the information and hung up the phone, then went in search of Riley.

She was seated behind her desk tapping furiously at the computer. She didn't so much as blink as he stepped into the office and closed the door behind him.

"Why are you mad?" he demanded, propping a shoulder against the wall.

She lifted incredulous eyes to his face. "Are you serious? After what I just walked in on?"

"You didn't 'walk in on' anything."

"Give me a break, Noah! That woman was draped all over you. And her blouse was unbuttoned!"

"I'll admit she was trying to come on to me, but she didn't get very far."

Riley snorted derisively. "Only because I interrupted. Again, please accept my humblest apologies for barging into your office in the middle of your afternoon tryst with poor Mrs. Stanton, whose husband is supposedly cheating on *her!*"

Noah's temper flared. "Damn it, Riley! You think I'd be dumb enough to fool around with a client? For the last time, nothing happened. She tried to come on to me, and I set her straight. End of story."

"Whatever, Noah," Riley muttered, resuming her typing.

He scowled. "'Whatever, Noah'? What's that supposed to mean?" When she ignored him, he pushed off the wall and quickly rounded the desk. A startled gasp escaped from Riley as he swiveled her chair around to face him, planting his hands on either side of her to prevent her from getting up.

"Again I ask," he said, low and controlled, "why are you mad?"

She swallowed convulsively. "I'm not mad."

"The hell you aren't."

"Noah—"

"You can't even look me in the eye."

"Fine!" she exploded, her magnificent eyes flashing with fire. "You're right. I *am* mad! I'm mad because I thought there was something going on between you and Delilah Stanton, and when I saw her practically sitting in your lap, I was jealous. So jealous I could hardly see straight! I'm mad because ever since we made love, I can't stop thinking about you, daydreaming about you. I'm mad because you made me feel things I've never felt with any other man before—not even the man I was going to marry! I'm mad because I keep hearing this ugly little voice in my head that tells me I almost spent the rest of my life with the wrong man. I'm mad because I think I'm falling—" She broke off abruptly, a stricken look on her face as she stared at him.

Noah had stopped breathing. His heart was knocking so hard against his rib cage it hurt like hell. His throat was as dry as sandpaper.

"Say it, Riley," he half pleaded, his voice husky with choked emotion. "Damn you, don't leave me hanging like this. If you knew how long I've waited for this moment, you'd put me out of my misery right now."

Tears shimmered in her dark eyes. "I don't understand," she whispered.

Slowly he sank to his knees in front of her. The day of reckoning had arrived. "I'm in love with you, Riley. I have been for the past five years." Hearing her soft intake of breath, he smiled. "It happened the very first time we met, when you rear-ended me because you were in such a damned hurry to meet with the police chief. One look at you and I didn't stand a chance. By the time Trevor came outside and I found out who you were, it was too late. I was already a goner. The funny thing is, before meeting you, I'd always laughed at people who talked about love at first sight. Guess the joke was on me that day."

Riley was gazing at him in wide-eyed wonder. "All this time…I never knew."

"You weren't supposed to," Noah said ruefully. "It became my mission in life to make sure you never knew, even if it meant I had to keep my distance. Even if it meant we couldn't be friends, and I had to let you think I didn't like you. Believe me, Riley, it was pure torture. There were so many times I was tempted to tell you how I felt, if for no other reason than to wipe the hurt look off your face every time you thought I was being rude or indifferent toward you. I didn't know how else to handle my feelings but to keep you at arm's length. And I couldn't betray Trevor by letting him know I was in love with you. I couldn't do that to him."

Riley traced his features with her eyes. "And after he died…"

Noah shook his head. "After he died I felt even guiltier. I still wanted you with a vengeance, and I hated myself for that. I hated the fact that a small part of me wondered if I'd subconsciously willed Trevor out of the way so I could finally have a chance with you."

Riley's expression softened. "You had no control over what happened. You were just as devastated by his death as I was."

His mouth twisted sardonically. "How would you know? I never opened up to you, or gave you the friendship and support you so desperately needed." His voice deepened with regret. "I'm truly sorry for that, Riley. I hope you can forgive me for not being there for you."

Tenderly she reached up and laid a hand against his cheek. "I forgive you," she said in an achingly soft voice, "if you can forgive me for foolishly trying to outrun my feelings for you." She drew a deep, shaky breath and slowly exhaled. "I love you, Noah. God help me, I've never loved another man as much as I love you. Does a part of me feel like I'm betraying

Trevor? Maybe. But does it change the way I feel for you? Not a chance."

Noah didn't think his heart could contain the amount of joy swelling inside his chest. He closed his eyes, lowered his head and tried to draw as many lungfuls of air as he could.

Riley moved to the edge of her seat and cradled his face in both hands. "I love you," she whispered, brushing her lips gently against his. "For as long as I live, I'll never stop loving you, Noah."

With a muffled groan of surrender, he opened his mouth to hers, hungrily and fiercely, pouring all the love he'd suppressed for five years into that one kiss. As Riley moaned and wrapped her arms around his neck, desire, yearning and need swept through him. And then he was sweeping Riley into his arms and striding purposefully from the room.

As he yanked open the door, Kenneth and Janie sprang back in surprise. They exchanged sheepish glances with each other, then grinned at Noah and Riley.

Janie said, "We were just, uh, on our way to the—"

"Supply closet," Kenneth finished. "I ran out of, uh, black ballpoint pens, and Janie was going to help me look for more."

"Because we all know Kenneth can't find his way around the supply closet."

"Uh-huh, likely story," Noah grumbled as Riley buried her face in his neck to smother her giggles. He kissed the top of her head, then started down the corridor, tossing over his shoulder, "We're leaving early for the day. Hold down the fort for us."

"No problem," his brother called after them. "You crazy kids enjoy the rest of the afternoon."

"Oh, we will," Noah promised, his heated gaze locked on Riley's. For her ears only, he added huskily, "We're going to enjoy every last minute of it."

Chapter 17

"Are you nervous?" Noah asked two days later, glancing over at Riley in the passenger seat of his Yukon.

Riley shook her head, gazing out the window at the quaint little shops and restaurants that made the small town of Fredericksburg one of the most popular tourist destinations in Texas. Located an hour and a half away from San Antonio and nestled in the heart of Texas Hill Country, the town was mostly populated by Germans and boasted a charming array of wineries and vineyards and some of the most romantic bed-and-breakfasts for miles around.

The last time Riley had been to Fredericksburg was over three years ago with Trevor.

A lifetime ago, it seemed.

And now she was back, to get the answers she'd so desperately sought since his death.

Noah turned down a bustling street lined with boutiques and bakeries bearing German names. He found parking behind a tiny nineteenth-century chapel shaded by large, leafy trees, lush with the bloom of summer.

As he and Riley started up the brick path back toward Main Street, he reached out, capturing her hand in his, infusing her with his warm, comforting strength. Riley smiled at him, and knew that no matter what happened, everything was going to be all right.

The man who greeted them inside Our Haus Antiques was in his early forties with a sturdy build, a broad, craggy face and pale green eyes that crinkled at the corners when he welcomed them with a warm, albeit tentative smile.

"You must be Noah Roarke and Riley Kane," he said, stepping from behind a rustic wood counter to shake their hands. "Jonas Ludwig."

"Thank you for agreeing to see us, Mr. Ludwig," Noah said.

"Please, call me Jonas." He walked over to the front entrance and flipped the sign on the door to read Closed For Lunch—Will Return At Two P.M. "My wife and children have gone peach picking, otherwise I'd have one of them attend to customers while the three of us talk in private. Can I offer either of you something to drink? My wife made some fresh apple cider this morning before she left."

"That sounds lovely," Riley answered with an easy smile.

"I'll be right back. Feel free to browse around. The prices on everything are negotiable."

The store was exactly as Riley remembered it from her previous visit. Filled with the warm, inviting scent of candles, the large shop offered a wide selection of antique tables, lamps, porcelain, glassware, linens, furniture, and other vintage knickknacks.

"You like antiques?" Noah asked as she paused in an aisle to admire a rosewood étagère circa 1883. At Riley's nod, he chuckled softly. "No wonder Daniela likes you so much. Her favorite pastime is going antiquing with my mother. Someday she'd like to open her own antiques store."

Riley smiled. "Maybe she'd let me become her business partner."

Noah grinned. "Sounds like a plan."

Jonas Ludwig emerged from the back carrying two glass mugs of cider, which he passed to them. "I'll admit that when you called yesterday," he said ruefully to Noah, "I had my reservations about speaking to you. It's not easy for me to talk about my grandfather's legacy of crime and violence, which afflicted the rest of the family like an aggressive tumor."

"I understand," Noah said.

"We're just trying to get to the bottom of Trevor's connection to your grandfather," Riley added.

A cloud passed over Jonas's face. "Well, then, we'd better have a seat," he said grimly, gesturing them into a European settee before claiming a straight-backed chair for himself. He looked from Riley to Noah. "I don't know where to start."

"Start from the beginning," Noah said quietly.

"All right. I first met Trevor Simmons about four years ago. He came into the shop looking for my grandfather." Jonas paused, his focus on Riley, silently communicating to her that she should brace herself for what was coming next. "Trevor's mother had finally told him the truth about her side of the family. My grandfather, Karl Ludwig, was Leona Simmons's estranged father."

Riley's fingers tightened around the glass mug she held. Her heart pounded. So she'd been right. Trevor's mother *had* been harboring a secret.

"So that means Leona Simmons is your aunt," she said in a faint voice, "and Trevor is—was—your cousin."

Jonas nodded, watching her with a sympathetic expression. "I was as shocked as you are when I found out. Before Trevor showed up here that day, I never even knew he, or his mother, existed. My grandfather had had an affair with Leona's mother a very long time ago. When she got pregnant, he washed his hands of her and the unborn child. Leona grew up not knowing who her real father was until her mother finally broke down and told her, shortly before she died. Leona was devastated. She decided that since Karl Ludwig had wanted nothing to do with her, she would have nothing to do with him."

"So she continued the legacy of silence with Trevor," Riley murmured.

Jonas nodded. "She refused to tell him about his grandfather or the German side of her family. To this day, I still don't know what finally changed her mind about that. Trevor never told me."

Noah said quietly, "She felt guilty. She'd always felt guilty about Trevor's father running out on them when Trevor was just a baby. She blamed herself for that, and for not creating a more stable home for him."

Riley gazed at him. "She told you that?"

"Yes. When Trevor and I graduated from college." Noah's expression was remote, reflective, as he stared into the amber contents of his glass, seeing nothing but his memories. "She told me I was probably the best thing that had ever happened to Trevor. She said if it weren't for me, he may never have attended college. He would've fallen in with the wrong crowd and squandered his potential. She thanked me for being such a good influence on him, and said she'd be forever indebted to my family for taking him in the way we had."

Jonas nodded, smiling softly. "He spoke very fondly of you, Noah. Of both of you."

Riley looked at Jonas. "So what happened to him?" she asked, half-afraid to hear the answer. But she'd come this far. She had to know. Once and for all, she had to know the truth, no matter how much it hurt.

"Trevor wanted to meet his grandfather and get to know him better. In the end," Jonas said somberly, "that was probably his downfall. The need to fit in, to belong. It kept him around, even after he'd learned the truth about who and what our grandfather was— a cunning, ruthless, cold-blooded criminal who'd sell out members of his own family to protect his own interests."

Noah leaned forward on the settee. "Was your grandfather using this store as a front for his money-laundering operation?" he asked point-blank.

"No," Jonas said with such conviction Riley believed him. His mouth twisted cynically. "Karl Ludwig was too clever for that. He knew a family-owned business was the first place the government would look. So he didn't tamper with the shop. He used other, less obvious venues to move his dirty money. He was so skilled at covering his tracks, in fact, that he even fooled the FBI. My grandfather took a lot of secrets to his grave."

So, apparently, had Trevor.

Riley swallowed past the tightness in her throat. "When did Trevor get involved in the money laundering operation?"

Jonas hesitated, shooting a wary glance at Noah, as if to ask him whether Riley could handle the truth. Riley bristled, even as Noah gave a subtle nod.

Jonas took a deep breath and slowly exhaled. "He became involved about a month after meeting our grandfather and other members of the family who were part of the enterprise." Jonas hesitated. "He asked to be cut into the deal."

Riley's heart plummeted sickeningly. Although she'd had three years to get used to the idea that Trevor may have been involved in criminal activity, nothing could have prepared her for the gut-wrenching reality of this moment. Tears stung her eyes, and nausea churned in her stomach.

Noah reached over, taking the untouched glass of cider from her trembling fingers and placing it on the floor. She looked at his face, saw his tightly clenched jaw and realized he was holding his emotions in check for her sake. He was as devastated by Trevor's duplicity as she was. How could they both have been so wrong about him? How had they missed the signs that he was in deep trouble?

"At first Trevor became involved because he wanted to impress our grandfather. He wanted to prove he had what it took to be a Ludwig. And for a while it worked. Karl embraced him, the biracial grandchild he'd previously rejected. But there's something you have to understand about Karl Ludwig. His loyalty was conditional, and it was often short-lived. Cross him once, and you'd live to regret it." Jonas's mouth thinned to a grim line. "Trevor learned that the hard way."

"What happened?" Riley whispered shakily. "Why was Trevor killed?"

"Because he got greedy, and as a result, he fell out of favor with our grandfather. Once he found himself on the outside, Trevor became vindictive. And then he committed the unpardonable sin. He threatened to expose the money-laundering enterprise."

"He called the FBI to provide an anonymous tip," Noah said.

Jonas nodded. "That pretty much sealed his fate. Karl started having him followed after that. On the morning of the shooting, Karl knew Trevor would be in the vicinity of that convenience store. He sent one of his associates there, an ex-convict named Conrad Weiss. Although Weiss was wearing a stocking mask, Trevor still recognized him. When he walked into that convenience store and saw Conrad, he must have known it was a setup."

"So when Weiss took off and Trevor gave chase," Riley said, piecing it all together, "he probably didn't call for backup because he didn't want to risk Weiss identifying him in front of other police officers. Trevor pursued Weiss down that alley fully intending to kill him." Just as she'd always suspected.

"Why didn't you come forward sooner about your family's criminal activities?" Noah's voice vibrated with suppressed fury. "You could have prevented what happened to Trevor."

"Maybe. Or maybe I would have ended up in the same morgue as him, along with my wife and three children." Jonas frowned. "Look, the truth is I didn't know what my grandfather was planning for Trevor. I found out about everything much later. Not being part of the criminal enterprise meant I wasn't privy to a lot of things, including assassination plots. I'm sorry," he said, seeing Riley flinch. "I didn't mean to—"

She lifted a trembling hand. "It's all right. You

don't have to sugarcoat anything for me. I've spent the last three years torturing myself, imagining the very worst. But there's something else I'm curious about, Jonas."

"What's that?"

"How…how did you stay out of it?"

"The money-laundering operation, you mean?" At Riley's nod, he smiled ruefully. "Even if I'd ever wanted that life, I wouldn't have survived. I don't have that kind of ice in my veins, and the others would have taken it for weakness and eaten me alive. At the risk of sounding trite, all I've ever wanted is a quiet, simple life. I went away to college because my parents, God rest their beloved souls, worked hard to make it possible. When I returned home to Fredericksburg, I met my beautiful wife, Annaliese, a farmer's daughter. If there'd ever been any doubt in my mind before, meeting Annaliese solidified for me the kind of life I wanted to lead. Once I made it clear to my grandfather that I wanted nothing to do with the money-laundering operation, he more or less disowned me. But he also made it clear to me that if I ever breathed a word to the authorities, he wouldn't hesitate to retaliate against me and my family." Jonas shook his head slowly. "I knew what Karl Ludwig was capable of. I wasn't willing to risk the lives of my wife and children. I know that may be difficult for both of you to accept, considering what happened to Trevor, but I make no apologies for doing whatever was necessary to protect my family."

Riley was silent. How could she judge Jonas Ludwig for the difficult decision he'd made? Would she have done anything differently?

"Your grandfather came to Trevor's funeral," she said softly. "How could he have shown his face there, knowing he'd orchestrated Trevor's murder?"

Jonas's mouth curved in a humorless smile. "Karl Ludwig always believed in paying his last respects, even to his enemies." He hesitated. "I believe part of the reason Trevor never told either of you about his grandfather is that he wanted to protect you. If Karl had suspected you knew about the operation, your lives would've been in danger. Trevor understood that, and he made sure our grandfather knew he'd never told you about the business. Now, I'm not saying Trevor didn't have ulterior motives for concealing the truth from you. We can assume he did, for the simple reason that he didn't want to lose his relationship with his best friend and fiancée. But I just want you both to know that he cared about keeping you safe."

Riley nodded, swallowing convulsively. "Do you think…did Trevor ever tell you he regretted becoming involved with the operation?"

Jonas was silent for so long she wondered if he intended to ignore her question. Finally he said quietly, "I know you're looking for the silver lining in all this, a reason to forgive Trevor for the way he betrayed your love and your trust. But speaking from experience, I can tell you that knowing whether or not he regretted the choices he made won't change the outcome. The challenge for you is to try and find a way to come to terms with what he did, and then, somehow, to pick up the pieces of your life and move on from there. Sometimes, Miss Kane, there are no silver linings."

Riley nodded, her throat clogged with emotion. Reaching over, Noah took her hand and gently squeezed. Their eyes met and held in a moment of shared pain and sorrow. It was more than they'd ever shared in the aftermath of Trevor's death.

Without releasing her hand, Noah turned back to Jonas, who had been watching them with gentle, discerning eyes. "Thank you for taking the time to talk to us, Mr. Ludwig," he said quietly. "As difficult as it's been to hear these things about Trevor, it was important for us to finally learn the truth about what happened."

Jonas inclined his head. "I hope, in time, you'll both find closure." He looked at their joined hands and smiled softly. "Perhaps I was wrong. Perhaps there's a silver lining after all."

Noah and Riley exchanged meaningful glances.

As they prepared to leave the antiques shop a few minutes later, Noah said to Jonas, "Just out of curiosity, how is it that so many of your family members managed to be deported back to Germany? From what I understand, no charges were ever brought against anyone for the money-laundering operation."

"That's true," Jonas calmly acknowledged. "You

know, when you consider the recent political debates surrounding illegal immigration in this country, it's not surprising to discover just how many people have educated themselves on deportation laws. What you may find surprising, and perhaps a little alarming, is how simple it is to get someone deported. In some rare cases, all it takes is one discreet phone call to a high-ranking friend in INS to get the ball rolling." His expression was all innocence. "Not that I'd know anything about that, of course."

Noah and Riley stared at him, then looked at each other and laughed.

A warm, fine mist began to fall from the sky as they walked back to the church parking lot in silence. Even after they'd climbed inside the truck, they sat without moving or speaking for several minutes, the only sound between them the soft patter of rain against the windshield.

It was Noah who finally broke the silence. "I'm sorry," he said thickly.

Riley's gaze flew to his face. "Why are you sorry?"

"For not believing you when you first came to me about your suspicions. For ridiculing your instincts."

"You don't have to apologize for anything, Noah," she said gently. "Who could blame you for your re-action? It was a lot to digest at once. I'd had three years to grapple with my fears and suspicions, and what I brought to you wasn't exactly a slam-dunk case. Talk of dreams, gut feelings, faceless men with

German accents. Anyone in your shoes would've had a hard time believing my story. *I* had a hard time believing it."

Noah shook his head. "But there were signs all along, things I purposely chose to ignore. Not glaringly obvious things, like a new Porsche on a cop's salary or hidden wads of cash in his kitchen drawer. What I'm talking about was the way he'd disappear for days at a time, and come back with stories about visiting you in Houston, which he later contradicted in other conversations. Or the way he behaved whenever his mother came around—antsy and irritable, as if he was afraid she'd slip up and say something she wasn't supposed to. At the most, I wondered if he was cheating on you."

"In a way he was," Riley murmured, staring through the windshield. "Cheating on both of us by lying and deceiving us about who he'd become. He was leading a double life that we never knew about. When I think about the hypocrisy of him getting on his soapbox and criticizing corrupt cops…" She shook her head angrily. "If he were here right now, I'd kill him."

"You'd have to get in line behind me," Noah growled.

Riley's lips twisted bitterly. "I honestly don't know what hurts me more. The fact that Trevor kept such a terrible secret from me, or the fact that he got involved with criminals. Why didn't he confide in me? We were going to spend the rest of our lives together. Is that how he planned to start off our marriage? With lies?"

She thought about her dreams, in which Trevor slammed the door in her face to prevent her from overhearing a conversation between him and Conrad Weiss. She now realized that Trevor closing the door on her was metaphorical for the way he'd shut her out of his life by keeping secrets from her. Her subconscious had made the connection, even if her heart hadn't been ready.

Gloomily she said, "I always knew that deep down inside, he was just a scared little boy trying to find his place in the world, trying to figure out where he belonged. I wish he'd realized his place was among those who loved and accepted him for who he was, even if the same blood didn't run through our veins."

"Yeah," Noah said quietly, "me, too." He turned his head, glancing out the window for a moment, giving her a view of his stony profile. "I'm angry with him, damned angry. He was like a brother to me, and the fact that he didn't trust me enough to confide what he was going through is tearing me apart. I'm mad as hell, Riley, and I honestly don't know how long it's going to take me to get over that."

Her heart clutched in her chest. Reaching across the console, she placed her hand over Noah's tightly clenched fist. After a few moments, the muscles began to relax, enough for her to lace her fingers through his.

"This won't be like before," she told him, her

voice breaking with emotion. "We're going to get through this, Noah. And this time, we're going to get through it together."

When he turned his head to look at her, the moisture glistening in his dark eyes matched the tears blurring her own. He raised her hand to his lips and tenderly kissed the center of her palm, pouring heat through her veins.

"Do you promise?" he asked huskily.

"I do," Riley whispered.

"Let's go home," Noah said softly.

Riley nodded, settling comfortably into the seat for the ninety-minute drive back to San Antonio.

The thought of returning home had never sounded better.

Chapter 18

"Everything looks wonderful, Riley."

Riley turned to smile as her mother appeared at her side and draped an arm around her shoulders. Barbara Kane had dark, almond-shaped eyes and smooth mahogany skin that defied her fifty-seven years. Thick shoulder-length braids marched back neatly from her face and accentuated her exotic features. She was effortlessly chic in a white sheath dress that flared out gracefully from gently rounded hips she wryly referred to as the "love handles I ain't lovin'."

Smiling now, Barbara stroked a hand down the cropped, silky layers of Riley's hair. "You really outdid yourself this time, baby."

"Thanks, Mom," Riley said. "But I can't take all

the credit. The caterers did a fabulous job with everything, from the menu to the amazing decorations. Look at this place. I feel like I'm back in Washington, D.C. in the middle of January."

"It is rather amazing, isn't it?" Barbara agreed.

Riley nodded as she and her mother surveyed the festive scene before them. The oversized backyard had been transformed into a breathtaking winter wonderland to commemorate the fact that Florinda Kane had been born during a rare snowstorm in San Antonio—the largest snowstorm in the city's recorded history. Fake snow powdered the large oak trees and was sprinkled liberally across the lawn. Linen-covered tables arranged under a tent were adorned with silver candles and vases filled with fresh-cut white flowers. The band was playing a golden oldie that had lured many partygoers to the dance floor, which had been decorated to look like an ice rink.

Invitations had been sent to one-hundred-fifty people, and if the number of entries in the guest registry was accurate, all had shown up to celebrate the seventy-fifth birthday of one very remarkable woman.

"Your father and I felt so guilty about going to Hawaii and leaving all the party planning to you," Barbara confessed.

"Don't feel guilty," Riley said with a dismissive wave of her hand. "I told you guys to go, remember? Between your patients at the practice and Dad's classes, June was the only month you could coordinate your busy schedules. Believe me, I know you both needed to get away for a while and recharge your batteries. Besides, I had a lot of fun organizing the party. It gave me something to do."

Her mother sent her a knowing smile. "From what your grandmother tells me, you found plenty to do."

Riley couldn't stop the smile that curved her mouth. "Maybe."

"Uh-huh, that's what I thought." Barbara chuckled. "Don't think I'm letting you off the hook that easy, young lady. I know we haven't spoken often over the past few weeks—"

"Which is as it should be. You were supposed to be enjoying your vacation, not worrying about what was happening at home."

"Don't change the subject. Not once during any of our phone conversations did you mention that you and—"

"Great party, Miss Riley!" said a passing guest, an elderly man from the community center where Florinda volunteered.

"Thank you, Mr. Taylor!" Riley called back, watching as he made his way to the dance floor to cut in on Crandall Thorne, who'd snagged Florinda the moment the band struck up again after a short break. Florinda, understated elegance in a white pant-suit, laughed as Crandall scowled at Mr. Taylor and grudgingly relinquished her. He then proceeded to cut in on Caleb and Daniela Thorne, who'd just returned from their honeymoon two days ago. As Daniela stepped into her father-in-law's arms, she sent her husband a conciliatory grin. But Caleb wasn't without a partner for very long. He was quickly snatched up by Riley's great-aunt, who saved him from the clutches of one of the matchmaking mamas who'd been scouring the crowd for young, handsome prospects for their granddaughters. Although they knew Caleb Thorne was off the market, that didn't stop them from seeking him out in the hopes that he'd drop the names of a few close, unattached friends. They'd already flocked to Noah—which was probably the reason he'd conveniently disappeared from the party.

"The last time I saw him," her mother said with a knowing little smile, "he was talking to your father."

"Oh." Heat crawled up Riley's neck. "Was it that obvious I was looking for him just now?"

Barbara's smile widened. "Sweetheart, you haven't stopped looking for Noah since he arrived."

It was probably true. In the two weeks since they'd learned the truth about the circumstances surrounding Trevor's death, she and Noah hadn't spent as much time together as Riley would have expected. Although they'd agreed to keep Trevor's secret to themselves and help each other through the painful aftermath, an awkward tension had worked its way between them. Confronted with the horrible revelation that Trevor wasn't the man they'd both loved and trusted, they'd suddenly found themselves at odds with each other, unsure how to proceed in their new-found relationship. After all, if they were so wrong about Trevor, could they also be wrong about their feelings for each other?

As if by mutual consensus, Noah had retreated into his work, and Riley quietly left her job at the agency and threw herself into last-minute preparations for the party.

And then, just yesterday morning, she'd received an unexpected phone call from her editor at the *Washington Post*. He'd indicated, without actually coming right out and saying it, that if she wanted to keep her position at the paper, she should seriously consider cutting her sabbatical short and returning to D.C.

The conversation had haunted her for the rest of the day.

She'd come home to San Antonio to uncover the truth about Trevor's death and finally exorcise the demons that had plagued her for the past three years. Now that she'd gotten the answers she wanted, she could, in all reality, go back to D.C. and the new life she'd started. She had a great apartment in Foggy Bottom and a great job at one of the most prestigious newspapers in the world. Her editor liked her well enough and believed she could have a solid future with the *Post*. Who in their right mind sacrificed an opportunity like that?

When Riley left D.C. and embarked on her truth-seeking mission, she'd had every intention of going back at the end of two months, no matter what the outcome of her efforts to investigate Trevor's death.

But she hadn't anticipated what would happen between her and Noah.

She hadn't anticipated falling in love with him.

"For what it's worth," her mother said, breaking into Riley's reverie, "your father and I think Noah is a wonderful young man. I still remember how good he was with Florinda at your engagement party four years ago, so patient and easygoing as she took him around, introducing him to different young ladies. He really made an impression on all of us that day."

"I remember," Riley murmured with a soft, reminiscent smile.

"Of course you do." Barbara gave her shoulder a gentle squeeze, then sighed. "I'm going to go mingle with Pamela and Lionel Hubbard. I haven't seen them since their wedding. Don't spend the entire night running around playing hostess," she warned her daughter as she started away. "You've done more than enough tonight and over the past several weeks. Let the caterers do what you hired them for."

Riley grinned. "Yes, ma'am," she said with a mock salute. "Who am I to argue with the woman who's footing the bill for this shindig?"

As she watched Barbara wend her way through the crowd toward the tent, plucking a glass of champagne from a passing waiter's tray, Riley decided her mother was right. She deserved a break. The food and music were great, drinks were flowing freely, and the guests seemed to be having the time of their lives.

She glanced at her watch. Everything was right on

schedule. In less than one hour, wedges of rum cake iced with butter cream would be served, and then Riley would unveil the special birthday presentation she'd prepared with the help of Janie and Lety. She couldn't wait to see her grandmother's face when she saw what they'd done with all her old memorabilia. She hoped Florinda would light up like the fireworks that were also on tap for the evening.

Deciding to steal a few minutes to herself, Riley headed across the sprawling yard and started up a winding footpath that led away from the festivities. Night had fallen, and the moon shone bright and full in the starlit sky.

"Not so fast, young lady. Wait up for me."

Riley turned and smiled as Florinda joined her on the path and linked a companionable arm through hers. "What do you think you're doing?" Riley teased. "You're not supposed to leave the party. You're the guest of honor."

Florinda chuckled. "It's my party," she quipped good-naturedly. "I can leave if I want to. Besides, I'm not leaving. I'm taking a short break to spend time with my granddaughter, who refuses to let down her hair and enjoy the fruit of her labor."

Riley laughed, slowing down a little to accommodate her grandmother's leisurely stride. "I am enjoying myself. I've danced a couple of times, had a glass of champagne, and conversed with many of the guests, all of whom adore you and have nothing but glowing things to say about you."

"Oh, hush," Florinda said, but Riley could tell she was pleased.

They soon reached a gazebo that was painted white and draped with a twinkling canopy of fairy lights. As they stepped inside and sat down on the wraparound bench, Florinda remarked, "You look beautiful, baby."

"Thanks, Grandma." Riley, like her mother, wore a white sheath dress that featured a fitted bodice, scooped neckline, and a full skirt that billowed out Marilyn Monroe style. She'd talked herself into a pair of white strappy high-heeled sandals that were already making her long for the flip-flops on standby near her bedroom door.

She slipped out of the heels and reached down to massage one aching foot.

"So how are you doing tonight, baby?" Florinda asked. "You've seemed very distracted since yesterday—and not just because of the party. What's on your mind?"

Riley hesitated, then answered truthfully, "My editor at the *Post* called yesterday. He wanted to know when I was planning to return."

Florinda frowned. "I thought he approved your leave time."

"He did." Riley smiled ruefully. "I don't think he believed I would actually take the whole two months off. He knows what a workaholic I am."

"Were," Florinda corrected. "You're not the same person who left D.C. several weeks ago."

"No," Riley agreed softly. "I'm not."

Apart from Riley and Noah, Florinda was the only one who knew about Trevor's involvement with his family's money laundering operation. She'd reacted to the news with sorrow and disappointment, but not with shock, as Riley had expected. It was as if she'd already prepared herself for the worst. In a way, so had Riley.

Florinda asked, "So what did you tell him? Your editor?"

Riley shrugged. "I told him I was busy with last-minute preparations for your party and would call him back on Monday."

"What are you going to tell him?"

"I don't know. I haven't decided yet." She hesitated, glancing sideways at her grandmother. "Now that I've learned the truth about Trevor's murder, I can say that I've accomplished what I set out to accomplish."

"You could." Florinda gave her a long, measuring look. "I think this journey home was less about Trevor, and more about you finding yourself."

Riley stared at her. "What do you mean?"

"Do you remember when I told you the confusion you'd been feeling about everything in your life would someday make sense?" At Riley's nod, Florinda explained, "I think part of the confusion you'd been experiencing had to do with Noah and your unresolved feelings about him. It's always bothered you that he kept you at arm's length for so many years. Haven't you ever wondered why it troubled you so much?"

Suddenly, Riley's mouth felt like it was stuffed with cotton. She could only stare mutely at her grandmother and wait for her to continue.

"I think, as important as it was to you to find out the truth about Trevor's death, it was even more important for you to learn the truth about yourself and Noah." Florinda paused, smiling gently. "He was the first person you sought out the day you arrived back in town."

"That's because he was the only person who could help me."

"Maybe. Or maybe not."

"Grandma—"

"I think it's possible that when you ran away from here three years ago, you weren't just outrunning memories of Trevor. You were trying to escape your feelings for his best friend."

"But that's ridiculous, Grandma," Riley protested. "I never even looked at Noah that way."

"That's because you didn't allow yourself to. Your conscience wouldn't let you entertain thoughts of him or the possibility that you may have chosen the wrong man."

Janie's question whispered through Riley's mind. Do you think you would have made the same choice?

Would she?

Would she have chosen Trevor over Noah if she'd met them at the same time at that conference?

"I believe, darling granddaughter, that you took after me in a lot of ways."

"How's that?" Riley mumbled. "I don't have your special gift, Grandma."

"Ah, but I think you do. It's called intuition." Florinda took her gently by the shoulders and gazed at her. "Even before you got into that car and drove 1,600 miles across the country, I think you already knew, deep down inside, that your instincts about Trevor were right. I'm not suggesting you didn't come here genuinely seeking answers about what happened three years ago. I would never suggest that. What I'm saying is that once you were here, getting to know Noah became just as important to you as finding closure about Trevor's death. Because in finding that closure, you'd finally unlock that part of your heart that had always belonged to Noah anyway."

Riley couldn't move, couldn't speak. A fine sheen of tears filled her eyes, blurring her grandmother's image.

"Oh, baby." Florinda gathered her gently in her arms. "I didn't mean to upset you. This is supposed to be a joyous occasion."

"I'm not upset," Riley said gruffly, resting her head on her grandmother's shoulder, keeping her tears in check so she wouldn't smudge Florinda's white pantsuit.

Florinda chuckled softly. "Maybe I'm wrong about everything I just said. What do I know, anyway? I'm just an old woman. A seventy-five-year-old woman, at that."

Riley laughed through her tears. "Yeah, right."

Florinda sighed. "Well, even if I was right about your feelings for Noah, maybe you weren't ready to hear those things yet." She paused meaningfully. "Just as you weren't ready to hear five years ago that he was in love with you."

Riley shook her head in disbelief. "You knew all that time. And you never said a word."

"It wasn't my place, darling."

"When? When did you find out how he felt about me?"

"When I met him for the first time at your engagement party. Oh, it wasn't anything he said or did. He's too smart, too self-possessed, to play his hand like that. But there was a hint of something in his eyes when he thought no one else was watching. Tenderness, longing, misery." Florinda shook her head with a sympathetic chuckle. "Poor dear. He probably never even saw it coming."

Riley knew the feeling. Whether or not she'd fallen in love with Noah five years ago, or within the past month, remained to be seen.

"Anyway," Florinda said, lightly patting her knee, "I just wanted to give you some food for thought, in case you were getting any crazy ideas in your head about going back to D.C."

Riley lifted her head from her grandmother's shoulder to look at her. "Would that be so crazy?"

Florinda gave her a gentle smile. "Only you can answer that question, baby. But you said it yourself not too long ago. Mr. Right only comes around once in a lifetime. You missed him the first time, but Providence has smiled down on you and blessed you with a rare second chance. Think long and hard before you walk away from what may be your final chance."

That said, Florinda rose from the bench, then leaned down to plant a kiss on Riley's forehead. "I'm heading back to the party. Wouldn't do to have the guest of honor missing out on her own celebration."

Riley smiled. "I'll be there in a minute. My dance card is full—I owe Daddy, Kenneth, Uncle Chesteen, and Mr. Taylor a dance."

"Don't forget to save a dance for Noah," Florinda advised. "And when you see him, tell him he owes me one, too."

"I will. Oh, and Grandma?"

Florinda glanced back inquiringly. "Yes, baby?"

"Happy birthday."

Florinda smiled warmly. "Thank you, Riley."

After her grandmother left, Riley sat and thought about the life that awaited her in Washington, D.C. Sixty-hour work weeks at the *Post,* a next to nonexistent social calendar, lonely nights that would be filled with bittersweet memories—not of Trevor this time, but Noah. She'd fall asleep imagining his arms around her and wake up feeling bereft without him.

Riley had never believed in long-distance relationships. That was the main reason she'd agreed to quit her job at the *Houston Chronicle* and move back home to San Antonio to be closer to Trevor.

She'd loved him, and in her own way she always

would. What they'd shared had been special, and she wouldn't diminish it by drawing comparisons to her newfound relationship with Noah. She couldn't predict the future any more than she could undo the past. She wished with all her heart that Trevor had made different choices in life. If he hadn't gotten involved with dangerous criminals, he and Riley would have celebrated their third wedding anniversary this year. And she and Noah…

Riley's heart squeezed in her chest. She loved Noah. She loved him more than she'd ever believed was possible. She couldn't even imagine what her life would be like without him. As devastating as Trevor's death had been, losing Noah now, after having a taste of bliss, was inconceivable. Were they destined for each other, as her grandmother seemed to believe? If Trevor had lived, would she ever have found her way to Noah? Would he have moved on eventually and forgotten about her?

She didn't know. All she knew was that she didn't want to spend another day apart from him, much less another three years. She wanted to be with him, and no job on earth was worth forfeiting her second chance at love.

They could work through the awkwardness that had settled between them over the past two weeks. For five years they'd been virtual strangers. It would take time for them to learn how to completely trust and lean on each other. Rome wasn't built in a day, and neither was true love.

Not even for soul mates.

Riley reached down and hurriedly began sliding her feet into her shoes.

"There you are. I've been looking all over for you."

Riley's head snapped up at the deep, husky timbre of Noah's voice. He stood in the entrance to the gazebo, devastatingly handsome in a black tuxedo with an unfastened tie and a crisp white shirt he'd already unbuttoned at the collar in deference to the warm weather.

"Noah hates wearing tuxes," his sister, Daniela, had laughingly confided to Riley earlier in the evening. "But he hasn't complained once about having to wear one tonight. Girl, he must really love you."

He loves me, Riley thought now with a quiet sense of wonder. *Noah Roarke loves me. I must be the luckiest woman on the face of the planet.*

"You're missing one helluva party," he murmured, stepping into the gazebo. "Which is a shame, considering all the hard work you put into making this the most spectacular night of your grandmother's life."

A shy smile curved Riley's mouth. "That's very sweet of you to say that."

"Thanks, but those weren't my words. I just saw your grandmother, and she told me herself that this was the most spectacular night of her life." Noah's expression softened as he reached out, taking Riley's chin between his thumb and forefinger and tipping her head up to meet his gaze. "You've made her very happy, Riley."

She swallowed a knot of emotion in her throat. "It's the least I can do for the woman who practically raised me, and who's always been there for me."

Noah smiled. "She wasn't just talking about tonight with the party. She said you make her happy every day, and you're the best thing that ever happened to her."

"Oh, Grandma," Riley murmured, blinking back tears.

"And do you know what I told her?"

Riley shook her head.

"I told her we had something in common," Noah said quietly. "Because you're definitely the best thing that ever happened to me, Riley."

Her heart swelled. "I love you, Noah," she whispered, turning her face into his palm and kissing him. "I love you so much."

"I love you too, baby," he said tenderly. "In fact, your grandmother and I were talking, and we agreed that there's one more thing you can do that would make us both very happy."

Riley looked up at him. "What's that?"

Noah lowered himself to one knee. "Say you'll be my wife."

Riley clapped a trembling hand to her mouth. "Oh my God…"

Gazing deep into her eyes, Noah said huskily, "Riley Kane, will you marry me?"

She could no longer hold back the tears. They spilled from her eyes and rolled down her cheeks. An inexpressible joy flooded her from head to toe. "Yes," she whispered.

Noah smiled softly. "You're gonna have to speak up, baby. I've waited too long for this moment to have you go quiet on me."

Her shoulders shaking with sobs, Riley launched herself into his arms with such force that they toppled backward to the ground. "Yes!" she answered breathlessly. "Oh my God, Noah. Yes, I'll marry you!"

Laughing, and a little winded, Noah cupped her face in his hands and drew her mouth down to his for a deep, intoxicating kiss. "I love you," he said against her lips. "I always have, and I always will."

"Good," Riley whispered. "Because you're stuck with me for life."

"Sounds like a plan." Drawing back slightly, he searched her face. "These past two weeks…I wasn't pushing you away, baby. We both needed time to ourselves. I needed time to sort through everything, wrap my mind around what Trevor had done. He was like a brother to me, Riley. I never would've imagined…" He trailed off, shaking his head as he gazed at her. "I had to do some serious soul-searching. And I had to come to terms with all the guilt I'd been carrying around for the last five years. Guilt for loving you, for wanting you even when I thought I could never have you. Guilt for allowing myself to wonder if Trevor's death had happened for a reason…to bring us together."

"And now?" Riley whispered, her eyes hungrily tracing his features. "Do you still feel guilty?"

He shook his head slowly. "Not anymore," he said huskily. "I'm too damned selfish to let anything come between us ever again, Riley."

Her smile was wobbly. "Then that makes two of us."

She bent her head, kissing him softly. Their tongues mated, slid, stroked, and with each slippery-sweet caress inside their joined mouths, Riley felt heat coiling deep within her. When Noah reached up and curved his hands around her waist to settle her more fully against the hard length of his body, her breath snagged.

"We should probably...get back to the party soon," she suggested without much conviction.

"In a minute," Noah murmured, nibbling on the beating pulse at the hollow of her throat. "I haven't given you your ring yet."

"Oooh," Riley purred. "You bought me a ring? Where is it?"

"In my pocket. But you have to move so I can get it."

"Do I have to?" she protested, using the tip of her tongue to trace the soft shell of his ear. "I was just getting comfortable."

He chuckled, a low, rough sound that curled her toes. "I always knew there was something different about you, Riley. Most women would be ripping off my tux right now to get to that ring."

"Oh, I'm going to rip off your tux," Riley promised, unbuttoning his shirt to get to his warm, naked skin. She could feel his heart pounding beneath her hands, fast and strong. She smiled. "While I'm still in the party-planning mode, I'm thinking about a wedding at the historic San Fernando Cathedral downtown. Somewhere big enough to accommodate our family and friends, not to mention all the cops in this city who'd be offended if they weren't invited to our wedding. Say, in three weeks?"

"Works for me," Noah said, his eyes smoldering with desire as he reached under her dress to cup her bottom. "I didn't want a long engagement, anyway. I've waited long enough."

"Well, you know what they say about good things coming to those who wait," Riley murmured, marveling at the feel of strong, rippling muscles beneath her exploring hands. "And speaking of waiting, where did you disappear to for such a long time? I was looking for you."

"I was talking to your father. You know, getting his blessing and all that. 'Course, if he'd known I planned to debauch you in the gazebo less than an hour later," Noah drawled, making her moan as his fingers slipped beneath her silk panties to stroke her intimately, "he might have reconsidered giving his blessing."

"Mmm. Probably. At any rate," Riley breathed, already on the verge of release, "you owe me a dance, Mr. Roarke."

"It'd be my pleasure." His voice deepened with promise. "If you want, we can dance all night."

"Oh, I want. I…want," Riley cried out hoarsely, arching against him as waves of pleasure shimmered through her.

Noah held her tightly in his arms, brushing his mouth across her forehead and whispering tender endearments. After several moments, he gently rolled her over so that he was on top. As she wrapped her legs around his hips, he gazed down at her. The look in his eyes was powerfully seductive, fiercely possessive, and full of such reverence it stole her breath.

"I love you, Riley," he said fervently. "I love you so damn much."

"Don't ever stop," she whispered.

"I won't," Noah vowed, bending his head to capture her lips as surely as he'd captured her heart. "Ever."

Every smart woman needs a plan!

DOWN AND OUT IN
FLAMINGO
Beach

National bestselling author
MARCIA KING-GAMBLE

Joya Hamilton-Abrahams's plan was simple: make a short visit to Flamingo Beach to give her ailing granny's failing quilt shop a makeover—then hightail it back to L.A. and civilization. Settling down in the small town was never on her agenda...but neither was falling for hunky construction worker Derek Morse.

Available the first week of May wherever books are sold.

KIMANI™
ROMANCE

www.kimanipress.com

KPMKG0160507

He loved a challenge...and she danced
to the beat of a different drum.

Enchanting
MELODY

National bestselling author
ROBYN AMOS

Escaping poverty had driven Will Coleman to succeed on
Wall Street, but in his spare time he taught ballroom dancing.
Then into his dance studio walked Melody Rush, a feisty
society beauty who enjoyed the freedom of slumming.
And the enchanting dance of love began....

Available the first week of May wherever books are sold.

KIMANI™
ROMANCE

www.kimanipress.com

KPRA0180507

Sinfully delicious and hard to resist...

Can't Stop LOVING *You*

Favorite author

LISA HARRISON JACKSON

Kaycee Jordan's new neighbor, pro athlete turned café owner Kendrick Thompson, was as irresistible as the mouthwatering desserts she created. When he agreed to help build her bakery business, days of work gave way to nights of luscious pleasure...until their relationship caused a rift between their families.

Available the first week of May wherever books are sold.

KIMANI™
ROMANCE

www.kimanipress.com   KPLHJ0190507

"The prolific Griffin's latest story pulls at the emotional strings..."
—*Romantic Times BOOKreviews* on
Where There's Smoke

BETTYE GRIFFIN

A LOVE

for All Seasons

Alicia Timberlake was the woman of Jack Devlin's
dreams, but Alicia had always kept people at a distance,
unwilling to let anyone close. Still, Jack isn't about to give
up without a fight. But when a family tragedy reveals a secret
that makes Alicia question everything she's ever known,
she's suddenly determined to reassess her life and learn,
finally, how to open herself to love.

Available the first week of May
wherever books are sold.

ARABESQUE®

www.kimanipress.com   KPBG0100507

A soul-stirring, compelling
journey of self-discovery...

journey
into My Brother's Soul

Maria D. Dowd

Bestselling author of
Journey to Empowerment

A memorable collection of essays, prose and poetry,
reflecting the varied experiences that men of color face
throughout life. Touching on every facet of living—love,
marriage, fatherhood, family—these candid personal
contributions explore the essence of what it means to
be a man today.

**"*Journey to Empowerment* will lead you on a
healing journey and will lead to a great love of self,
and a deeper understanding of the many roles we
all must play in life."—*Rawsistaz Reviewers***

Coming the first week of May
wherever books are sold.

www.kimanipress.com   KPMDD0290507

tangled
ROOTS

A Kendra Clayton Novel

ANGELA
HENRY

Nothing's going right these days for part-time
English teacher and reluctant sleuth Kendra Clayton.
Now her favorite student is the number one suspect in a local
murder. When he begs Kendra for help, she's soon on the road
to trouble again—trying to find the real killer, stepping into
danger...and getting tangled in the deadly roots of desire.

"This debut mystery features an exciting new
African-American heroine.... Highly recommended."
—*Library Journal* on *The Company You Keep*

*Available the first week of May
wherever books are sold.*

KIMANI PRESS™

www.kimanipress.com   KPAH0680507

Celebrating life every step of the way.

YOU ONLY GET *Better*

New York Times bestselling author
CONNIE BRISCOE
and
Essence bestselling authors
LOLITA FILES
ANITA BUNKLEY

Three fortysomething women discover that life, men and
everything else get better with age in this entertaining
three-in-one anthology from three award-winning authors!

Available the first week of March wherever books are sold.

KIMANI PRESS™
www.kimanipress.com   KPYOGB0590307